Summer Rush

KACIE KENT

DEDICATION

This story is for everyone who thought they'd let "The One" get away.

CONTENTS

PROLOGUE
Present Day

Katie

The bright, brilliant sun was reaching its zenith over Florida's gulf coast, but Katie Carter's hopes of an equally illustrious honeymoon weren't following suit. She leaned over the dock's railing, heaved up the rest of her lunch, and watched it float away on the choppy river waves. As she straightened, her unchecked tears mixed with the brackish water below. She sat back down on the bench overlooking the inlet that broke off from the Suwannee River and ran right behind Cypress Cove Lodge.

Tears continued to silently stream down her cheeks as she recalled the three-hour drive from Jacksonville to Cypress Cove. She reached into the pocket of her khaki shorts and pulled out a torn, crumpled tissue that was still damp from an earlier barrage of tears. She absentmindedly rubbed her stomach, still unknotting itself from the upheaval. Her usually crisp, white polo was now stained with tears and makeup.

Danny, her husband of twenty-four hours, hadn't said

more than a dozen words to her voluntarily on the trip across Florida. This excursion was supposed to be their short honeymoon, the only one they could afford with three children back home in Jacksonville waiting to become a happily blended family once their parents returned. But the drive down had been the worst three hours Katie had ever spent with her usually even-tempered partner. Their argument had begun over why Carlie, Katie's daughter from a previous relationship, wasn't staying with Katie's grandma like Danny's boys were.

No, she reasoned, *it's beyond Carlie staying with the Donahues. He always gets this way whenever he feels threatened.*

Katie had tried to make it easy on her Grammy. Watching two rambunctious toddlers was difficult enough, even with the help of Katie's little sister Shannon, who still lived at home. She'd tried to ease the workload of her seventy-two-year-old grandma by having her daughter's other grandparents watch Carlie. She didn't know Danny was going to get so bent out of shape over it.

Now she was standing on a dock, overlooking the river, crying because she had let Brian's parents keep Carlie for the weekend. Danny was angry with her for this very reason, and her honeymoon hadn't really started. If this was how they were going to spend their honeymoon, she wished that they'd stayed home. At least Danny could give her the silent treatment somewhere she could do the laundry and clean the house after their very intimate, at-home wedding.

Katie turned and walked back up the dock, wiping tears from her cheeks. One thing she refused to do was let Danny see how upset she got over stupid arguments. *If he wants to pick fights, then he can fight with himself*, she thought. "Because I'm certainly not going to do it anymore," she said out loud as she rounded the corner of the hotel they were staying at.

"You're not going to do what anymore?" Danny asked.

He was standing outside their hotel room, leaning against the rental car. He popped a piece of gum in his mouth, a habit he had taken up since he'd quit smoking. His dark blonde hair, curly from the gulf humidity, was a wrangled mess under his beat up ball cap.

"Nothing." Katie shrugged, swiping at her runny nose.

"I'm going to Newton, to see Jimmy. Do you want to come?" Danny asked. He tossed the gum wrapper in the car and tugged the cap lower over his eyes. His steely gaze flitted from Katie's face to the ground and back again.

She felt the nerve under her left eyelid twitch and blinked a couple of times to control it. *Yeah*, Katie thought, *that's exactly what I want to do on my honeymoon, go see your brother who has never even bothered to speak to me when he calls you.*

"Never mind," Danny said, "I can tell by the look on your face. Well, I'll be back in a while." Danny shuffled around to open the door of the rental car and fell in. Straightening the cap yet again, he pulled from the lot without a backwards glance.

"Great," Katie said, talking to herself again. "Maybe we can spend some time together on *our* honeymoon. Of course, that would be too much to ask, wouldn't it?" She threw her hands in the air, waving away imaginary responses and receiving suspicious looks from a couple who had just exited the hotel's diner. She lowered her voice but continued her one-sided conversation. "I mean, really, we just got *married* twelve hours ago. What was I thinking? He's never gonna grow up. Always running from his problems. Maybe Aunt Maggie can give me some words of wisdom on how to deal with this."

Katie unlocked her room and entered to change into more comfortable clothes. The humidity of the gulf coast caused her polo to cling to her damp back. She stripped her shirt from her, again unconsciously rubbing her rumbling belly, before digging a tank top out of her suitcase. She pulled the shirt on over the new bra she'd bought herself for the wedding and honeymoon and swiped her hair up into a top bun.

After pocketing extra tissue and brushing her teeth, Katie stepped back out into June's midday heat. Her aunt's river house was just a mile or so down the highway, but with the June heat she had to be careful of dehydration. She stopped by the hotel's diner and got a to-go cup of ice water.

Once she'd made her way out of the labyrinth of one-way back roads in the tiny town of Cypress Cove, she began walking down State Road 349 toward her aunt's house. The solitary road that led away from Cypress Cove was the same one she had ridden in on thirteen years earlier, when she met Danny for the first time.

Maggie Crews' small bungalow squatted among the overgrown azalea bushes that had been tiny shrubs the first day Katie had stepped foot in Cypress Springs. The shady lot buzzed with bees and the business of birds flitting among the crepe myrtle branches. Katie paused just outside the fence--another new feature in the last few years--and took a gulp of water. The liquid sloshed from the cup and left a dotted trail along the front of her tank top.

She climbed the steps to the porch and had to catch her breath. A wave of nostalgia washed over her as she reached out a hand to give the porch swing a push. The creaky chain caused her to startle, and before she could pause the swaying, the door jerked open.

"I told you kids..." Maggie cried from the opening. Her reprimand ceased as a smile stretched across her face. "Katie-did! What a surprise to see you. Lena didn't tell me you were coming this way."

"When did you last speak to her, Aunt Maggie?" Katie fell into the woman's open embrace, then followed her into the dim living room of the house. Much of the decor had changed over the last decade, but not the homeyness of the room. Though Katie had visited her aunt in Cypress Springs a few times after that first summer she'd spent here, the memory of her fifteenth summer was the one that always stuck out.

"Must have been about two weeks ago. Come on in. I was just heating up some lunch." Maggie flipped a cushion on a ladder-back chair that sat against the wall and motioned for Katie to sit. "Want some?"

Katie shook her head, then perched on the edge of the chair, her hands wringing the wadded tissue she'd pulled from her pocket. "Then, you didn't hear that I got married," she said. She shoved her left hand out in front of her, wiggling her ring finger. As simple as the rings were, she was proud of the tiny solitaire diamond set in the unadorned, ten caret gold engagement ring and accompanying band.

"Married? When--? Who--?" The older woman stumbled through her questions at the surprise of such news. "Is it Carlie's daddy? Did he finally come around and do the right thing by you?"

"No, Grammy must not really talk about me that much," Katie said, a flitter of sadness passing over her otherwise serene face. "Brian died in Iraq. Killed in a roadside bombing a few months ago."

"Oh, honey, I'm sorry." The woman reached over from her seat to pat Katie's knee.

"Yeah, well it'd been over for us a long time before this happened. He never met Carlie, then I get the news that he died...." She let the story trail off as she dug another tissue from her pocket. "I'm just sad for Carlie, that she won't know her daddy."

"But you're married!" Maggie changed the subject. "Tell me about him." Her eyes lit up with interest.

"You already know him," Katie said. "You were the one who introduced us, in a way."

Maggie's face went from interest to surprise. "You don't mean that boy who used to come over that summer you stayed with me?"

"Yep." Katie smiled at the memory. Things were simpler then. Her sneaking out, the reason for her banishment to Cypress Springs, as it was called back then, seemed inconsequential now, compared to so many other events in her life. "I'm Mrs. Danny Carter now. As of yesterday."

"You don't say that with much joy, honey." The woman rose from her chair and retrieved a water bottle from the refrigerator. She offered it to Katie, and as the younger woman took it, the tears began to flow again.

She poured out her heart to her aunt, all the struggles the couple went through to be together, the years they barely kept in touch, all the way up to the most recent incident this morning.

"I just don't know what to do," Katie concluded. "It seems every time we face any kind of difficulty, his first instinct is to run or avoid it."

"You know that's the way he's always been," Maggie said. "It's his coping strategy. When things got tough at home, I remember that boy coming over to the Morrises and staying for more than a week. He'd always go back home, but that's how he handled it when life got too tough. Run to a safer place."

"But I should be his safe place," Katie cried, the tears welling in her eyes again. "I've stood by him, even though we were miles apart, for nearly a decade. Shouldn't he want to work it out with me?"

"What is it that you two are fighting over? You've only been married a day."

"Something not even that important." Katie looked at her aunt, who sat waiting patiently for her response. Finally, she sighed and pulled another tissue from the box her aunt offered. "Fine. It was about who Carlie would stay with while we came on this short honeymoon." She glanced up to see Maggie leaning forward, elbows on her knees, waiting for more of the story. Katie continued, "I called Brian's parents to see if they could keep Carlie for the weekend while we were gone. I did it because Grammy and Shannon are watching Danny's boys, and I didn't want them to be overburdened with three young children. Grammy's not as young as she once was."

"That sounds reasonable."

"That's what I thought, but Danny flipped out, got all territorial."

"Doesn't he understand that you both had a whole life apart before this? You're both going to have some baggage."

"I think he thinks I should just cut Carlie's other family completely out of her life."

"That's not good for the baby."

"That's what I said."

"And how did he respond?"

"He said, it was good enough for his boys." Katie saw the confusion creep across Maggie's face, so she explained. "Crystal, Danny's ex-wife has nothing to do with the boys. Neither does her family. It's like they just forgot all about them after Danny got custody in the divorce. And he's fine with that."

"Could it have something to do with him being in control?" Maggie said. The microwave dinged and she rose to rotate her lunch. "You know most of his childhood was chaotic. His parents were always scheming to swindle people. Never did an honest day's work."

"Yeah, he told me, but he's taking this too far. It's affecting our family."

"Maybe that's it, honey." Maggie pulled the steaming dish from the microwave and carried it to the table. "You're his family now and he wants to keep a tight rein on it so it doesn't become chaotic like his childhood was."

"Maybe." The smell of greens and ham turned Katie's stomach. She jumped from the chair and ran down the hall to the tiny bathroom. After rinsing her mouth and returning to the kitchen, she was met with a quizzical look. "I think I'm not feeling well from the tension and the drive," she said.

Her excuse seemed to suffice, but Maggie covered the food and hunted for some crackers in the pantry. Setting the sleeve on the table, she settled back down in front of her lunch. "Why don't you take a few of these and your water out to the dock while I eat my lunch." She pushed the package toward her niece. "It'll give you a chance to think. To clear your head. I put a covered area over part of it, so you won't be in the sun much."

"Thanks, Aunt Maggie." Katie hugged the woman. Grabbing the water and the crackers, Katie made her way out to the dock that held so many memories of that first summer she met her husband.

BEGINNING WITH YOU

ELEVEN YEARS AGO

CHAPTER 1
Sent Away

ELEVEN YEARS AGO

Katie

The noonday sun streamed into the cramped living room of the small three-bedroom river house. Katie had fallen asleep in the papasan chair the night before watching a late episode of *Star Trek: The Next Generation.* She squinted at the brightness of the room, felt the warm, summer sun on her bare legs, and realized where she was. The summer was just beginning, and for Katie it promised to be the most uneventful summer of her young fifteen years. *How exciting could it be to spend ten whole weeks in a runty little town that didn't even have a McDonald's or a Jiffy Mart?* she wondered. It was her grandmother's idea for Katie to get away from Jacksonville before her problems at school got any worse.

Just three days ago she arrived by Greyhound in Newton. She left Jacksonville on the 12:20 bus after a long, mostly one-sided argument with her Grammy about not growing up to be a loose woman, whatever that meant.

The older woman had thrown her hands up in frustration

during breakfast. "No child of my only daughter, God rest her soul, would ever be climbing in bedroom windows at three in the morning again," Lena Mayfield had said. "I will be dead and buried before I let my oldest grandchild become known as the town tramp!"

"Like that would happen," Katie had argued. "Jacksonville has at least half-a-million people. I don't think anybody cares about me missing curfew." Katie had stomped off to her room, slammed the door, and plotted how she would see Gina and Layla again. That evening, Lena had pronounced that Katie would be spending the summer in Cypress Springs and had twenty-four hours to pack. She would ride a Greyhound bus by herself, like the adult she thought she was.

As they stood in the bus depot waiting for the boarding call, Katie's lips pressed into a thin line as she glared at the wall in front of her.

"I know you're angry with me, sweetie," Lena said brushing a hand across Katie's arm, "but this is what's best for you. Ever since your mom died--"

Katie jerked her arm away from her grandma's gentle touch and rose from her seat. She swallowed back the bitter words she wanted to hurl at her grandma, settling on not giving Lena the satisfaction of a response. She stared through the wall of glass at the depot, her body shaking. *How can sending me away from my family and friends to stay with relatives I barely know be the best thing,* she thought as she swiped at a tear that threatened to fall.

"Attention passengers," the depot agent said, "loading for Bus 1342, with stops in Lake City and Newton, will begin at dock four in ten minutes." He continued with other instructions, but Katie blocked them out as she grabbed her bags at her sisters' feet. With ticket in hand and her back straight, she turned from her family and strode toward the sliding glass doors of the terminal.

"Aren't you even going to say goodbye?" Holly called.

Katie turned, her chin jutting forward, as she dropped her bags and opened her arms. Both of her sisters ran to her for a group hug. She embraced all of them until Shannon, the youngest, began to sob.

"Sissy, I don't want you to go," she said, her tiny voice breaking on the last word. "Can't you just tell Grammy you're sorry and you won't do it again."

Katie knelt in front of the eight-year-old. "I did already, but Grammy thinks this is best. I promise I'll call you as much as I can and when I get home, we'll ride our bikes to Gambler's pond to feed the ducks."

The younger child sniffled and wiped her eyes on the back of her hand as Katie stood. She looked at Holly, her twelve-year-old sister. "Make sure you take care of Chester. I don't want to come home and find out he died because you forgot to feed him."

"I will. I'll make sure Shannon feeds him the carrots when he chirps." Holly offered a sad smile to her sister and pulled Shannon closer to her.

Katie bent to grab her bags, cutting a glance at her grandma. Her anger still bubbled inside, but the realization that she was leaving the only family she'd known created a lump in her throat. *Don't you dare cry,* she told herself.

Lena stepped toward her granddaughter and hugged her. Katie stood stiffly in her embrace, her luggage dangling at her sides. With nothing left to say, the woman kissed Katie on the forehead. The girl said nothing, just hmphed, rolled her eyes, and climbed the bus steps to locate a seat. Holly and Shannon stood side by side, next to their grandma, the younger girl waving madly at the bus. As the door closed and the bus lurched forward, Katie glanced out the window. She lifted her hand for a quick wave at Holly, then smiled and winked at Shannon, who stood crying; but Katie frowned and turned her head when her Grammy blew her a kiss goodbye.

Later that afternoon, her aunt Maggie had picked her up

at the bus station in Newton, a larger town twenty miles northeast of Cypress Springs. Katie arrived with two suitcases full of summer clothes and cassette tapes. The bus ride had taken five hours because of its stop in Lake City and Trinity for pick-ups and drop-offs. The bus had a bathroom, for necessity, but it was disgusting. As soon as the doors opened, Katie made a mad rush to the bathroom even before identifying her luggage. When she returned to the waiting lounge, Maggie was waving to her from the door with Katie's bags at her side.

The conversation on the twenty-minute drive to Maggie's house was mostly one-sided. Her friendly banter wasn't enough to break through Katie's hostile silence. Deep down, Katie knew her aunt wasn't to blame for the events that led her here. Still, she was angry and hadn't yet found a good enough reason to talk to *anyone*. And as she slid from the passenger door that first day and got a good look at the small, older bungalow on a shaded, dusty lot, her anger shifted to desolation that only food and sleep would ease.

Now, as the sun bid her to awaken, Katie rolled slowly and stiffly out of the chair. Her back ached from being in a fetal position most of the night. It was almost noon, and she made her way to the dinky bathroom. *Okay,* she mused, *my first Monday is nearly halfway over! Only nine more to go.* Counting time by Mondays was a trick she'd learned from one of her friends at school, as a way of making time go by faster. She splashed cold water onto her face and spoke to herself in the mirror, "I just might make it if I don't die from boredom first." Katie brushed her teeth and pulled her auburn hair into a short ponytail.

The sound of rattling pots from the kitchen indicated that Aunt Maggie was up and about. Katie wandered into the kitchen in the blue striped boxers and tank top that she had slept in and found her aunt emptying baseball-sized crabs into an aluminum colander. She situated her petite frame into a dining room chair and watched as Maggie began tearing

14

the legs off of the crabs. "So, did you get a good night's sleep?" Aunt Maggie asked with her back to Katie, working with the crabs. "Things usually seem better in the morning after getting enough rest."

"I guess," Katie said. She stifled a yawn, still trying to wake up. The warm breeze blowing through the screened door made her want to curl up somewhere and go back to sleep. Her outlook hadn't improved much, she was still bitter about her Grammy sending her away. What the hell was she going to do for ten weeks without her friends, with no transportation, without her telephone? She got up, retrieved a glass and filled it with orange juice. Peeking over her aunt's shoulder into the sink, her nose wrinkled at the sight of smelly, dead crabs. She turned and reclaimed her seat at the small kitchen table.

"Well, Sis already called this morning to check on you," Maggie said. Sis was what all of Lenora Mayfield's brothers and sisters called her. Katie found it difficult to imagine that cool, independent, totally *rad* Aunt Maggie was related to her Grammy, the epitome of old-fashioned. But eighteen years age difference could do that. Lenora was the oldest of seven children and Maggie the youngest. "I told her you were still sleeping and that you'd call her when you woke up."

"Don't bet on it," Katie mumbled under her breath. She had every intention of not speaking to her grandmother ever again. She might call and talk to Holly or Shannon, but not to Lena Mayfield.

The noise at the sink stopped, causing Katie to look up. Her aunt was standing there facing Katie with a set of crab legs in her grip, wagging them at Katie. "Look here, girl. I know you're angry, and I know how my sister is, but you *will* call her and talk to her! She's been good to you girls since your mom died and your dad left."

"Yeah, well, you don't know how it's been living there since Mom died," Katie said. "Grammy has been on my ass-

_"

"Watch your mouth!" Maggie interrupted.

"On my butt this whole time." Katie couldn't bring herself to mention her mom's death. "I'm always reminded that I'm the oldest and *I'd better start acting like it because my sisters look up to me.*" She mimicked her grandma's biting tone, and continued, "I'm sick of it! I just want to be a regular teen. And not have to worry about if I'm being a *bad influence.*"

"From what I heard, you *are* behaving badly," Maggie said. She'd gone back to separating the crabs from their legs and shelling them as well. "What in God's name were you thinking, sneaking in at three a.m.?"

"It was only two," Katie said, dropping her gaze to her lap. "And if my curfew wasn't ten-thirty, I wouldn't have to sneak in so late." Katie finished her juice and set the glass on the counter.

"It doesn't matter about the hour," Maggie continued, "the fact is you stayed out, worried your Grammy, and snuck in your bedroom window."

"Yeah, and now I'm stuck here all summer paying for that mistake." Katie ran her hands up her neck and over her face, huffing loudly. *Aunt Maggie seems less and less like the cool one, and more and more like Grammy herself. God, if I have to listen to this all summer I really might just die.*

"That's the price you pay when you play," Maggie stated. "So, when you're finished with any breakfast you're going to get, the phone is on the wall by the back door. You can call Sis then."

"Whatever," Katie retorted. She put the juice glass in the sink and went down the short hall to the bedroom that Maggie had designated for her. Her suitcases were still on the tidy bed. Clothes overflowed out of the bags and onto the bed. Katie had only searched for a change of clothes the night before and hadn't unpacked her luggage. This was as good a time as any to do it, plus it kept her from making that phone call.

The unpacking took ten minutes with Katie placing all of her clothes into the chest of drawers. She set out a few pictures that she'd brought with her. Her favorite one of her, Holly, and Shannon she placed on the night stand next to the bed, along with one of her mom. She placed a couple of unframed Friendship pictures that she had of her and her best friends, Gina and Layla, on the bureau. Her stack of cassette tapes she arranged on the shelf above her nightstand.

Katie plopped on the bed once her clothes were put away and arranged her earphones over her ears. She pressed the play button and Night Ranger blared from the earpieces. Moments later, she felt the bed shift and peeked through slitted eyes to see her aunt sitting on the edge.

"God, *what*?" Katie jerked the earphones from her head and glared at Maggie.

"Don't take that tone with me," Maggie said. "I'm not as old as Sis. I can still whip your tail. Besides, I don't take people talking to me that way in my own home. And from the way Sis tells it, you've been heading for trouble for a long time. Not only climbing in your bedroom window at all hours of the night but skipping school to boot."

Katie glanced up at the last comment, her face reddening.

"Yeah, I bet you didn't think Sis knew about the cutting class. The school's called her many times."

"So, lots of kids skip." Katie shrugged and slid the headphones back over her ears.

Maggie popped the springy cushion against Katie's ear. "So, you're saying if your friends jumped off a bridge, you'd do it too?"

"That's lame, Aunt Maggie." Katie rolled her eyes. "Besides, it's not like I'm high all the time or I sleep around."

"Not yet!"

"For God's sake, I'm still a virgin!" Katie leveled a stare at her aunt.

"So, why all the destructive behavior?" Maggie sat patiently, awaiting a reply.

Katie turned away, not wanting to answer. She was not going to have this conversation now. She didn't even really know herself why she did some of the stupid stuff she did. It just seemed fun at the time. And maybe a little dangerous. It might be the only way she knew that she was alive, the feeling of adrenaline when she did something risky. But how do you explain that to your forty-year-old aunt, much less your sixty-year-old grandma?

Katie could just imagine the conversation:

So, honey why did you skip school and go to the mall knowing you'd get picked up by the mall police?

Maybe because I wanted you to know that I'm tired of trying to be perfect. I'm not, you know. And I don't want to pretend to be. I make mistakes. I'm human. And I want to mess up every once in a while and it be okay.

"I'm waiting." Maggie interrupted Katie's thoughts.

"Well, I'm not ready to tell you." Katie bounded off the bed. She fled down the hall and out the back door, leaving Maggie at the door.

The teen ran to the end of the dock and sank down next to a piling. She'd held her tears in until she was out of the house and away from her aunt, but once she was alone, they fell freely. How could she explain that the only reason she did what she did was because her reality hurt so much? Ever since her mother had died three years ago, Katie hadn't seemed to be able to get a handle on her life. It felt like she was spinning out of control all the time, like she'd fly to pieces at any moment. The only way to even try to gain control was to do something daring that she'd specifically chosen to do just to see if she could do it. Like the party she was sneaking in from when she got caught by Grammy. She really hadn't been interested in going down to Gambler's pond to swim, especially at night with snakes, snapping turtles, and an alleged alligator, but it was something to do to prove to herself that she had some control over her life.

Now, she was back to feeling out of control. She'd been

sent away for the summer, everything and everyone familiar taken away from her. Sure, Aunt Maggie was trying to be understanding and Katie supposed the woman loved her, but it wasn't the same. She missed her life back in Jacksonville. She even missed Holly and Shannon bugging her to play Monopoly or watch videos with them. Most of all, she missed her mom.

God, life was so unfair. Why did Mom have to die, just when I needed her the most? Katie thought back to that time three years ago when the family found out. It was so sudden: one day she was taking them to the beach in early March right after a nor'easter to search for sea glass and sharks' teeth; then less than a month later she was lying in a hospital bed, a scarf wrapped around her balding head. At the time Katie didn't even remember her mom ever really being sick.

But looking back on it now, she recalled her mom feeling so sick at the New Year's celebration that she missed the dropping of the ball on the Rockin' New Year's party. She'd gone to bed early and stayed there for the rest of the weekend. Then, there was Shannon's birthday. Tradition was broken when Grammy, not Mom, had made the cake. Mom had been so sick that day that the sisters weren't even allowed to see her until bedtime. They tiptoed into the room and kissed her gently on the cheek. She was weeping and apologizing to Shannon for missing the cake and ice cream and promised to make it up to her once she got better. But she never did. She ended going into the hospital a week later and a week after that she was gone.

Katie swiped at her eyes and wiped the back of her hand on her shorts. Her arms began to burn; the sun was at its zenith. This was her mom's favorite part of the year and her favorite part of the day, for that matter. The brightness, the warmth, the sweaty feeling that her mom said always made her feel purified. It all reminded her of what she was now missing. If her mom was here, she'd know how Katie felt. Her mom had been a dare devil, too. She'd seen the pictures and heard the stories. Grammy used to complain that she'd caused more trouble than any Katie could even think of. *It was so unfair!* The thought screamed out again. Katie sniffled and swiped at her runny nose. She searched for something to wipe it with, refusing to go inside yet, finally settling on the hem of her tank top.

Her thoughts returned to her current predicament. How was she going to make it the whole summer here with just her aunt and the occasional visit from her younger cousin, Ben? She glanced back at the house to see if Maggie was spying on her. When she finally decided she wasn't, Katie took off from the dock and ran across two back yards before reaching the two-lane road. Standing at the corner, she seriously debated hitchhiking and running away.

CHAPTER 2
Getting By

ELEVEN YEARS AGO

Danny

Danny Carter lugged the push lawn mower from the trunk of his car for the third time that day. As he set the mower on the ground, he glanced at the grime and cuts on his hands. Manual labor didn't bother him--he was used to working outside all day--but the lifting of the mower in and out of his trunk each time he arrived at a new yard was tearing up his hands and killing his back.

"I've got to get me a small trailer to pull this stuff." He left the weed eater in the car and pushed the mower to the edge of the lawn. Walking the short distance to the front door, he was met on the steps by a pretty woman younger than his mom but definitely older than himself. Still, there wasn't a problem in admiring a thing of beauty.

She smiled at him as her eyes ran over his tall, lean frame. "You're younger than I expected, but Cal said you do great work."

"Yes ma'am," Danny replied. Situating his cap more securely on his damp, blond curls, he pulled a small notepad from his back pocket and flipped to a page with his scribbled handwriting. "So, Miss Winchester"--he glanced at her for confirmation--"just the front yard needs cutting and edging?"

"Oh, yes, but now that I think about it," the lady said, a flirtatious smile playing on her lips, "while you're here, you could trim the back yard too. With the water so close to our back patio and the grass growing so thick back there, I wouldn't want any snakes to crawl up here unnoticed." She let her gaze travel over his body once more as her tongue darted out to lick her top lip.

"Uh, yeah, that's a definite concern living on the marsh." Danny cleared his throat and shifted his gaze to the yard. It was obvious the lady was flirting with him, but he didn't have the time or the urge to get involved with an older woman. He'd been down that path once before, and once was enough. "So, I'll get started here and let you know when I'm done. Cal told you my fees, right?"

"He did. He also said that you're very thorough." She stepped back into the shade of the small entryway, her smile broadening. "Just let me know if you need anything."

Danny turned back to the mower waiting in the corner of the yard. The lush, green lawn was small like most along the canals at the heart of Cypress Springs, but overgrown, nonetheless. *Even with the added work*, he thought, *this should still take less than two hours. And I could take the afternoon off, maybe go into Newton to check out the new tackle shop.*

Working for himself was both a blessing and a burden. He got to choose what to do, which customers to take, how much to charge, but he also had to manage his time. And at seventeen, that was a struggle for him, especially when many of his friends were still in school during the day or had family obligations at home.

He checked the oil in the mower and pulled the cord, beginning the cut path on the front yard. Forty minutes later, he pushed the mower to the back yard, which was half the width of the front, and continued cutting. After finishing with the mower, he pushed it to his car to exchange it for the weed eater. As he lifted the heavy machine into the trunk, his shirt got caught on the corner of the mower and ripped a hole down the side.

"Damn," he cursed, shoving the machine into the open trunk. He didn't have another shirt in the car and, though he could have run home and back in twenty minutes, he was too close to finishing this job. He tugged the shirt over his head and wiped the perspiration from his face and neck before grabbing the weeder to continue his work.

It took another twenty minutes to edge the front and when Danny turned the corner to the back yard, he found Miss Winchester reclined in a lounge chair on the patio. The black bikini she wore did little to cover her womanly parts, but it definitely enhanced a luscious figure and tan skin.

"You might want to go inside while I trim around the patio," Danny said, watching as the woman rose from the chair and retrieved a glass of ice water from the table next to her.

"I thought you might be thirsty." She sauntered over to him, the water outstretched before her. "It's so hot today," she said adjusting her sunglasses and fanning herself with her hand. Her chin dipped a little, and Danny got the distinct impression that she was again giving him the once over. "Take a break and sit here in the shade with me." She waved at the chair next to hers.

Danny took the glass of water and gulped down half of it before meeting her eyes. It'd be real easy to let himself get comfortable in that chair and shoot the shit with this uptown girl. Ultimately though, she'd say something that would return him to the reality of their different places on the social scale. Every month it happened like this. Out-of-towners trickled into Cypress Springs to their second homes on the Gulf Coast, and he'd be called to come cut their yards and get it presentable for parties they'd host. Or vacationers--families or groups of friends--would rent the houses for a couple of weeks and the owners hired him to keep the lawns manicured. Either way, once they realized how local he really was, they dropped the niceties. It was better to head it off from the beginning.

"That's a nice gesture ma'am, but I've got two more houses today," he lied, "and I don't have time to lose." He fished the ice cubes out of the glass and tossed them toward the canal. Leaning over, he dumped the rest of the cold water over his head. As he stood, the water trailed down his chest and he could almost feel the woman's lust rolling off her in waves. Danny shook his head hard, and droplets of water flew from the display.

Miss Winchester stepped back to avoid the spray, and Danny noticed the slight change in her body language. His little childish show had done the trick. He held out the empty glass to her and she took it, retreating to the depths of the shaded patio.

"Let me know when you're finished," she said, sliding the glass door open and entering the home.

Danny nodded, slid his shades down to cover his eyes, and commenced edging the yard, hoping he hadn't ruined his chance of getting a good tip.

Fifteen minutes later, Danny knocked on the glass door. Miss Winchester had slipped on a see-through dress over her bikini. She joined him on the back patio with her wallet in hand.

"I assume cash is good?" She pulled a number of bills from the billfold.

"Works for me." Danny ran his gritty hands down the back of his shorts and waited.

"You've done an excellent job," the woman said, sliding the money into Danny's open palm. "Could you come back in two weeks to cut again before we leave?"

"Sure, let me give you my number just in case." He tore a

page from the mini-notepad and scribbled his name and number before handing it to the lady. "I'll be back by in two weeks."

He dipped his hat at the woman, grabbed his weed eater, and ambled back to his car. Once there, he counted his payment and smiled. Nope, he hadn't lost his tip. In fact, tonight's dinner would be T-bone.

After stopping by his trailer to unload the lawn equipment and get a quick shower, Danny decided to go fishing. That was one of the joys of being your own boss--you had a say in how you spent your time. And there was nothing he loved more after a hard day's work than sitting on the knee of a cypress tree wetting a hook. Even in the June heat, he could laze around for hours in the shade waiting for fish to bite.

He packed a quick lunch and grabbed his fishing gear from the back porch. As he was heading out the door the phone rang. Releasing a frustrated sigh, he answered it. "Hello?"

His mother was on the other end. "Danny, it's Mom."

His chest tightened at the sound of her voice. Since he left home at sixteen, his family only called him in crisis or when they needed something. There was little love lost between the two of them. Danny had decided long ago that he couldn't trust most of his family. His sister Lisa was the exception. She was the one person he could count on, and the only one he ever worried about.

"Yeah," he replied.

"Your sister got herself in a pickle in Newton," the woman said. "She had our permission to leave school early for a doctor's appointment, but they won't let Mark check her out. Your dad's got the car, and I can't reach him."

"And you want me to go get her?"

"Well, just check her out of school. You're on her emergency card. Mark said he would take her to her appointment for us."

For any other reason, Danny would have told his mother no, but this involved his sister. And he couldn't say no to his sister. His mother continued to drone on about not really wanting to ask him for help, and Danny pressed the receiver to his chest as he considered how this delay would affect his fishing. The loyalty he felt for his sister won out and he reasoned with himself that if he hurried, he'd still have about an hour to angle before meeting his friends for a game of pool.

"Daniel, please." His mother's plea broke through his contemplation.

"Sure, Mom, I'll take care of it." He hung up the phone and loaded his pole and tackle box in the back seat. The twenty-minute drive to Newton gave him plenty of time to think about what he would do for work when winter came and there weren't yards to manicure.

His sister was in the office, ready to go, when he stalked through the doors. He spoke briefly to the same front office clerk who had been there when he'd dropped out two years before. Her responses were cool and patronizing, but Danny didn't care. As far as he could tell, quitting school to get his GED and a job was the best decision he ever made. It got him out of his parents' home and gave him the freedom with his days that he craved.

"Thanks for coming up here," Lisa said as she followed Danny out of the building. "Mark is waiting over there. He'll drive me to Dr. Barrows' office. Mom expects me home right after. Maybe we can come by this weekend? Go swimming at Fiddler's Point?"

"Sure, Sis." Danny gave his sister a hug and waved at Mark before climbing into his Nova. Such a short errand for the drive to town. While he was there, he might as well pick up some things from the store that he was low on. He pulled from the parking lot and turned opposite Mark Tyner's truck.

Later, as he drove back to Cypress Springs, he noticed someone standing on the side of the road tossing rocks into the flooded ditch. The person was a good half-mile outside the town limits. As he approached the figure, he realized it was a girl. Definitely not a good idea for a girl to be out on the side of the highway by herself.

Danny slowed and hollered out the passenger window. "Hey, you shouldn't be out here by yourself, you need a ride?" He admired her lean body, tan legs and narrow waist. Her hair hung in a sloppy ponytail between her shoulder blades. The girl jumped at the sound of his voice and turned to face him.

"No, I'm good," she said. "Just out for a walk."

"Shoulda walked the other way toward town, where there's more people." He glanced in his rear-view mirror for approaching traffic. "I can give you a lift. Hop in."

"No thanks," the girl said turning on her heels and walking in the direction Danny had suggested.

Danny inched his car alongside of her debating about following her to make sure she got back to wherever it was she came from.

"Seriously, I'm fine, so you can leave now." The girl picked up the pace and he thought she would take off running any minute.

"Don't be like that, darlin'," he said. "I'm just looking out for you. I promise I won't bite."

"It's fine," the girl repeated. "I just needed to blow off some steam before I went back...home."

A truck honked behind him before whizzing past and Danny flipped him the finger. "If you're sure then I guess I'll be going."

"Yeah, I've only got a little ways left." She pointed to a dark area on the highway still a good distance away. "Just to that road there."

"Okay, then. See ya around." He waved at the girl, and revved the engine as he pulled back onto the road but drove well below the speed limit. He watched in his rear-view mirror as the tiny frame in the distance turned onto Jacksaw Road, and he decided he'd have to find out who the little spitfire was.

CHAPTER 3
Meeting Danny

ELEVEN YEARS AGO

Katie

"Where'd you get off to?" Maggie asked when Katie wandered back into the kitchen.

"I just took a walk." She grabbed a soda from the fridge and plopped down in front of the TV, grateful that her aunt had a satellite dish out here on the edge of nowhere.

"Well, don't think you're off the hook from calling Sis." Maggie jabbed a knife toward the wall phone for emphasis.

The girl sighed, pushed herself up from the couch and made the call. The conversation was mostly one-sided, with Katie answering her grandma's questions with one-word answers. She just wasn't ready to let go of the anger she felt toward being sent away. When her grandma put her sisters on the phone, Katie became more animated, describing the bus ride and the canal behind the house. Her grandma took the line again and asked to speak to Maggie.

"Hey, Sis," Maggie said when Katie handed her the phone. "Yeah, she's been mostly civil, but that girl's got a mouth." Maggie cut her eyes at Katie and the girl rolled her eyes and trudged down the hall.

She didn't want to sit there and listen to her aunt and grandma describe all the ways Katie had turned out to be such a disappointment. She pulled a book from the small stack she'd brought and flipped to where she'd left off. Flopping onto her stomach she fell back into the prehistoric world of Ayla and the cave people who'd rescued her.

A few minutes later Maggie stuck her head in the room. "Are you going to stay inside all summer long?"

"Maybe." Katie flipped the page without looking up.

"When I was your age, my mother couldn't keep me inside." Maggie leaned against the door frame, her overalls stained from some recent chore. "It'd give her fits that she couldn't make a proper southern woman out of me. I'd much rather be outside fishing or swimming or tending the garden or animals."

"We don't really have those where we live in Jacksonville." Katie closed the book and sat up cross-legged on the bed. "But there's nothing like that to do here either," she grumbled.

"Who says? I've got fishing poles hanging up out there on the back porch. I can fix one up for you right now if you want me to. 'Course it is the middle of the day." She paused in thought, her hands diving into her pockets. "The fish are probably somewhere cooler than right near the surface, but this evening we could go sit out there for a while."

"No offense, but I'm not much on fishing, Aunt Maggie." Katie scrunched up her face like she'd smelled the rotting guts of said fish, and her body shook with disgust.

Besides, she thought, *who in the hell is worth meeting in this crappy little town.* An exasperated huff escaped her lips. She'd been here for five days and the furthest she'd been was a drive into town with her aunt to pick up some supplies she needed for a gumbo she cooked one time. *There was that walk I took, when that guy stopped and asked me if I needed a ride.* She hadn't told her aunt about him, afraid that she'd have to explain why she was nearly a mile down the highway in the first place.

"I'm just making suggestions. You need to get out of the house." Maggie turned from the room and shuffled back toward the living area.

Katie rose from the bed and followed her. "I've been outside," Katie replied. "I've gone to the dock to lay out and nearly died of heat stroke." She sat on the small sofa next to her aunt's recliner.

"Why don't you ride into town and take a look around." Maggie bent to straighten the magazines on a side table. "There are some local swimming holes up in the middle of town. And we've got a billiards room beside the restaurant at the end of 349 down there. But I don't want you going there after dark or if there are many grown men in there playing. Might not be safe then."

"I can take care of myself," Katie said, an edge to her voice. With a gentle look from Maggie, she softened. "I mean, I know what dangers to look for. That was something Grammy didn't have to worry about."

"Speaking of my sister." Maggie grasped at the obvious heated topic. "When are you going to forgive her for this invalidated trespass against you? She's trying to protect you."

Katie bristled at the turn in their talk. "Aunt Maggie, can we just not turn every conversation into my argument with Grammy. Please. I need time. Her sending me here really hurt me. She didn't even give me a chance to try to do better."

Maggie's mouth opened, as if to counter Katie's argument, but she must have thought better of it. She clamped her lips shut and turned into the kitchen, her attention given to filling a water pitcher. Finally, she turned back to the girl. "I'll stop harping on it if you promise that the next time you talk to Lena you really talk. None of this 'yes' and 'no' nonsense. Give her some response other than one-word answers."

Katie sighed and rose from the couch. "Sure, the next time

she calls I'll talk. Doesn't mean I'm not mad." The girl straightened her shorts that were sticking to her backside and tightened the ponytail at the base of her neck. "I think I'll bike to town after lunch."

"You know, you could walk across the street and introduce yourself to Becky and Ronnie Morris." The woman pointed toward the window.

Katie moved to the window and separated the blinds. A boy and a girl, close to her age, were washing a car in the driveway. "Do you know them?" she asked, turning to get a better look. The boy wasn't too bad looking, with reddish hair and pale skin. He wore swimming trunks that hung a little low on his waist. Katie noticed an even lighter strip of skin just about the waistband and she wondered if he burnt easily with his complexion. The girl was pretty with the same reddish hair pulled into a bun on top of her head. She wore a swimsuit top and a pair of cut-off shorts. The boy squirted her with the water hose causing the girl to squeal and duck behind the car.

"I've spoken to them a few times." Maggie emptied the remaining water in the pitcher on a lily by the front door. She glanced out the window, smiled, and shook her head. "That Ronnie is a jokester. When he gets with his cousin Danny, they are a pair to be reckoned with. He's been over there a couple of times since you've been here, but I think you were on the dock or in your room napping then."

Hmm, Katie thought, *two cute guys within walking distance. Summer's looking a little more interesting.*

"Anyhow, if you see a Chevy Nova drive up, that's Danny." Maggie circled around and head back to the kitchen. "That car of his is nice! Of course, what do I know about cars? Could be a piece of junk under the hood."

Katie raised her eyebrow at her aunt; she knew better. Maggie had been taking care of her own car for as long as anyone could remember. She was the tomboy in the family, never married, very independent.

"At any rate, you should get out of the house. Sure, you're here as a sort of punishment, but that doesn't mean you stop living. It just means that you start practicing better behavior. Make better choices." The woman brushed a hand down the girl's cheek. "I know you've got it in you to do that."

Katie felt the hard shell she'd erected around herself crack just a little. If her grandma could be just a little more like Maggie, Katie knew they wouldn't fight all the time. She exited the back door and paused, gazing out at the canal. "Thanks for having faith in me. I know when I showed up here last week, I was a bitc..." Katie stopped herself, remembering Maggie's rule about cussing. "A bit of a handful with all my problems. But it helps knowing that you understand, and you trust me. I just wish Grammy did." Katie wrapped her arms around the roof support and leaned against it.

"Honey, she will, just give her time," Aunt Maggie said, patting Katie's shoulder. "I think you need to start enjoying your summer break. Have some fun! But I've got work to do. What do you want for lunch? I have..."

Katie, lost in her own thoughts about her family issues and the rest of summer, didn't hear her aunt. She wandered down the porch steps leading to the dock.

Following the dock to its end, Katie seated herself on the warm pine boards. A small canal ran between her aunt's backyard and the only road into downtown Cypress Springs. The heat from the boards warmed her bottom quickly through the thin boxer shorts she wore. She dangled her feet over the edge of the dock, inches above the water of high tide, and looked down the road into Cypress Springs. From where she sat, Katie could see that there was no stop light on the only road in or out of the tiny town.

She stretched her arms behind her to support herself and tilted her face up to the bright, burning sun. Her legs, long and shapely, swung back and forth in a slow rhythm that mellowed Katie even more. Her aunt had tried to sound encouraging, but how much fun would she really be able to have in a town with not even one traffic light? *Yeah, this summer's going to be a blast.* Sarcasm tainted her thoughts and the words that followed. "I'll have *so much fun* in a town with no movie theater, no McDonald's, no--"

Her pity party was interrupted by a shout from a passing car.

"Whoa, baby!!"

Katie jerked her head up in time to see the blur of red hair ducking back into the passenger window of a blue, two door car that flew by. A car that looked vaguely familiar.

--no intelligent people worth making friends with. She finished the thought that was becoming a constant bother in her mind. "Boring, boring, boring. That's how this summer will be," Katie muttered, lifting herself from the dock and walked back toward the porch.

"So, why don't you do something about it?" Aunt Maggie called from the shadows of the porch. "I told you to have some fun. Make friends. That was the Nova I was talking about. Danny was driving, I imagine. They're probably going swimming in town." She followed Katie into the kitchen. "You should put on your swimsuit, ride the bike into town, and find those kids."

"I don't even begin to know where to look," Katie said, half-way trying to talk herself out of actually going out and meeting people.

"Honey, I'm sure that once you start riding around up there, you'll find it." The aroma of warm bread and herbs filled the room, and Katie peeked in the pot on the stove. Chicken noodle soup bubbled, emitting a mouth-watering smell that caused Katie's stomach to involuntarily growl. Maggie continued, "I mean, there's only so many places you can go in a town this small."

Katie shrugged, acknowledging the obvious truth.

"Have some lunch first." Maggie retrieved a bowl from the cabinet and ladled soup into it. She uncovered a loaf of bread resting on a cooling rack and sliced a couple of pieces off. Setting the bowl and bread on the table, she motioned for Katie to sit. "Then you can use that old bike in the side yard. Probably needs the tires aired up before you go, though. You know how to do that, right?"

Katie shook her head as she blew on a spoonful of soup.

"Then I'll show you how to do that too."

After scarfing down her food and changing into her swimsuit, Katie watched as Maggie aired up the tires. With a towel around her neck and a bottle of water and tube of sunscreen in the bike's basket, Katie took off down the two-lane highway toward town. Within minutes of pedaling, beads of perspiration ran down her back underneath the the thin, white tank top she wore as a cover-up.

The ride into town took less than ten minutes. The outskirts of the minute fishing town stretched in front of her. She slowed down near a single-lane, concrete bridge that connected a strip of land to her left to the main highway. The marker on it simply stated '417'. On the shoulder of the road was the same Chevy Nova that passed her earlier while she was on the dock. The canal that ran under the small bridge was murky but looked inviting as the sun beat down on her back. Splashing and yelling rose from the water below and her heart skipped a beat. *Is it him?* she thought, hopping from the bike and pushing it toward the bridge.

A few feet in front of her, two boys clambered up the embankment and dashed toward the overpass. Katie stopped and watched as the taller one climbed onto the railing and made a show of preparing to dive. He stepped to the edge of the rail and lifted his arms in front of him, parallel to the water below.

"Come on, dude," the other boy cried, "you said you'd show me how to do a back flip." He waited at the end of the bridge, his wet red hair poking out in all directions around is head.

"I know, just hold on," the first one said. "I got to get my balance." He shook his hair and drops of water sprayed around him. He turned his back to the water and inched a little closer to the edge.

Katie openly gawked at the gorgeous boy who stood high above the canal. Slick, salt water glistened on his bronze, muscular back and dripped teasingly from his shoulder-length, brown hair. He wore cut-off denim shorts that ended a couple of inches above his knees. He gave a backwards glance over his shoulder, judging the height one last time and his eyes caught Katie's gaze.

"Make it good, Danny," the redhead called to his friend. "You've got an audience."

Katie blushed and dropped her gaze, but not before she caught Danny's wink. A smile played on her lips as she watched the boy sprang backwards from the girder, twisting his body a full revolution before going head-first underwater.

Katie dropped the bike and rushed to the edge of the bridge, waiting for the boy to surface. His head bobbed up twenty feet from the base of the bridge. He swam to the bank of the canal and climbed out to sit beside his friend. Katie recognized the second boy as the passenger in the blue Nova from earlier. The two boys leaned their heads together in conversation and looked at Katie every now and then. *He must have been the driver*, Katie thought as she looked around for other people, feeling uncomfortable being the presumed topic of their private conversation.

Both boys stood up and walked toward Katie, who returned to her bike. Perspiration covered her body and the tank top she wore stuck to her skin like cling wrap. Through the thin undershirt, the hot pink and black bikini top could be seen. The boys stopped in front of Katie, each of them allowing their gaze to stroll over her body, pausing briefly at her chest. She crossed her arms in front of her, the bike leaning against her hip.

"Hey, I'm Ronnie," the shorter boy said. "And that's..."

"Danny. I heard." Katie lifted her chin in greeting.

"You new around here?" Danny asked. The sun had already dried the river water from his body and at this nearness, Katie noticed that his skin was a warm shade of creamed coffee.

"Just visiting my aunt for the summer," Katie replied, squinting at the glare from the water.

"Bummer, to get stuck here all summer," Ronnie said.

"You ain't lying," Danny agreed. "But I saw you yesterday, didn't I? Walking back into town on 334?"

"Yep." Katie brushed a hand across her forehead, wiping the sweat she'd gathered on her shorts.

The conversation fizzled. Finally, Ronnie piped up, "Well, it's hot as hell. Too hot to be standing around doing nothing. I'm hitting the water, man." With that, he ambled back to the bridge, brushing past Katie as he did. The salt water from his shorts smeared across her leg, creating goose bumps as a gentle gulf breeze blew by. She averted her eyes until she noticed Danny lift his head toward the sun and close his eyes. Then her attention was locked.

Danny reached up and swiped a few stray hairs stuck to his brow--not brown like she'd guessed, but dark blond. Sun-bleached highlights were scattered around his temples and trailing through the curls that he now shook the water from. She studied his face as he began finger-combing his curly locks, his eyes clamped tight against the burning sun. She took in his lean neck, square jaw, and perfectly bridged nose, a bit small for a boy. Then, her gaze fixed upon his beautifully seductive mouth. She had a thing for mouths, and full, moist-looking lips that were worth kissing fascinated her. His tongue slowly ran along the rim of his lips, licking away any traces of salt water. His mouth stretched into a smile, revealing small, gapped white teeth.

His face shifted and Katie's gaze was captured in his steel blue stare. At the revelation that she'd been caught ogling him, she dropped her gaze to stare at her feet.

"So, you know my name," he said, and Katie's attention jerked back to him. His piercing stare made her feel naked and vulnerable. And hot. "How about you tell me yours."

"Katie," she said, shifting her weight to her other foot. "Katie Dupree."

"Nice to meet you, Katie Dupree." He ran his hands down the front of his shorts and water trailed down his legs. "So how long is your sentence?"

"Huh?"

"How long are you staying here in our quaint fishing village?"

Katie was surprised at his questions and doubted that he even knew what the word 'quaint' meant. She was caught off guard.

"The whole summer. It *is* a punishment, sort of," Katie told him. She watched as he hopped around a little to shake some more of the salt water from his shorts.

"Cool, you'll be here for the Fourth of July parade and fireworks. Maybe I'll see you around." Danny started backing towards the bridge.

Great, Katie thought, *he's already getting bored with me.* "Hey, isn't that dangerous," she called as he climbed back onto the bridge railing. "That water doesn't look too deep."

"Yeah, it might be," Danny said. He turned himself to do another back flip. "But that's the way I like it." And with that, he flipped himself into the shallow canal leaving Katie to stare at the ripples from his splash. She waited and watched for him to resurface. Ronnie had made it back to the bank and was lying on his back with his eyes closed, hopefully ignoring their cutesy banter and hadn't noticed that Danny had yet to resurface. Twenty seconds went by, then thirty, and Danny still hadn't broke the surface. Katie got worried.

"Hey, does he usually stay down that long?" Katie yelled to Ronnie.

"He's fine," Ronnie responded unconcerned. "He dives here all the time." But he sat up, just the same. Nearly a minute had gone by when Ronnie finally showed any concern. He glanced over to the spot where Danny usually emerged and didn't see him. "He doesn't usually stay down *this* long, though," Ronnie said, just as Katie spotted Danny's body floating face down.

"Oh, my God," she cried, and instinct took over. Katie kicked off her flip-flops and dove into the canal fully clothed, pulling herself swiftly through the water with strong strokes. Ronnie had jumped in behind her, but she was used to fighting the waves of the Atlantic Ocean and her strokes were cleaner and more powerful. She reached Danny in a matter of seconds, with Ronnie right behind her. The water was only fifteen feet deep or so, but thick with silt and other river debris. When Katie turned Danny over to secure her arm around his torso and paddle him in to shore, she saw his face covered with mud and gunk.

Ronnie swam behind her, pushing Danny's body through the water. The distance to the shore was only about twenty feet, but with the added weight of a hundred and fifty plus pound body, she grew tired. As they reached the bank, Ronnie climbed out first and pulled Danny's limp body from the water.

"Oh, man! Don't be dead, bro!" he cried. "He's never done this before. He's always so careful. And such a strong swimmer." Ronnie was leaning over his friend and shaking his shoulder to revive him when Katie pulled herself from the water. The bank was steeper than it looked, and too much time would have been wasted had she swam all the way over to the ladder to climb out of the canal. She fell down beside Danny and Ronnie.

"Do you know CPR?" she barked. She tilted Danny's head back and checked for breathing and a pulse. She found a pulse in his neck, but not feeling any breath and not waiting for an answer from Ronnie, she pinched Danny's nose and began to blow air into his mouth.

Danny reached up and pulled her down on top of him,

turning her mouth-to-mouth resuscitation into a kiss, tongue and all. Katie fought with Danny to be released. She sat up abruptly, fuming from the scare that was a joke. Her thoughts were interrupted by hysterical laughter from both boys.

"You son of a bitch!" Katie yelled and shoved Danny. "You were faking?!" She stood, crossing her arms across her chest. The boys couldn't stop laughing. They rose to their feet and tried to calm themselves, but the cackles kept coming. "This was some sort of set up? A trick?" Both boys looked at each other, realizing that Katie wasn't laughing. "I thought he was dying," she said, tears welling in her eyes from anger and adrenaline. "I risked my life, jumping into that dirty water to save your sorry ass and this is all a prank?!"

"Hey, look, we were just goofing around," Danny said, trying hard to hold back his laughter. "We do this all the time. Most of the girls around here know what kind of idiots we are and don't think anything of it when we goof on them with something like this."

"Yeah, well, I'm not like most girls from around here." She stomped back to her bike and stripped to her bathing suit. Wrapping her towel around herself, she squeezed water from her ponytail.

"I didn't think you'd actually jump in to save me. It was just a joke. No need to be pissed..." Danny had followed her and grabbed her arm to stop her.

Katie had heard enough, though. Without thinking, she drew back and with all her might slapped Danny across the cheek. She spun away from him to steady the bike, shaking her hand from the sting of her slap. Danny rubbed his face, a red handprint forming above the bronze skin.

"You stupid bitch," Ronnie yelled, and lunged at Katie. The bike stood between them, and the boy was stopped by Danny grabbing his arm. Ronnie backed up, his fists clenched at his sides. "What the hell is your problem? It was just a joke!"

"Cool it, Ron," Danny said. He had caught his breath and a tight grin playing on his lips. He eyed Katie through his penetrating steel gaze. "I deserved it," he continued. "That was a bogus trick to play on you. Sorry. I never thought you'd jump in to try and save me. No other girl has done that before."

"Yeah, well, I guess I'm not like other girls," Katie replied. She didn't feel like sticking around anymore, especially with Ronnie so angry and her not knowing these two guys that well. She dropped the towel and pulled on her clothes over her wet suit. She righted the bike and straddled the seat.

"I can tell. Most girls don't have a swing like that," Danny said. He opened his mouth wide, stretching his jaw and shifting it side to side. "Hey, don't leave yet. I'm really am sorry for scaring you." He stood beside her but didn't make a move to stop her.

As she rode away, Katie heard Ronnie say, "Don't, man. It sounds like you're begging. And you ain't all about that." Once she had put some distance between her and the bridge, Katie glanced back over her shoulder and saw Danny and Ronnie leaning against the Nova, apparently talking with the gestures they were making. She couldn't hear what they were saying, but she had a pretty good idea that they were laughing it up at her expense.

She turned onto her aunt's road and minutes later rested the bike against the side of the house. Katie didn't go inside right away, but instead sat on the porch swing trying to sort out all the emotions flooding through her. She should have been furious at Danny for pulling a stunt like that, but he actually seemed remorseful, *after* she hit him. And what was that? She had never hit anybody before like that in her life. Of course, she'd never been that irate before, either. A plethora of emotions swept over her and tears that had threatened before returned. She wiped them away as the back porch door squeaked open. Maggie lumbered through the side yard in the ugliest pair of work shoes that Katie had ever seen.

"I thought I heard something hit the side of the house," Maggie called. When she turned the corner into the front yard and got a look at Katie's wet clothes and dirty knees, concern crossed her face. "What happened? Did you fall in a creek?" she asked.

"Something like that," Katie said. She really didn't want to talk about it. It was sort of embarrassing to be played like that. Thankfully, her aunt didn't press the issue.

"But you're okay?" she asked, making sure that Katie wasn't hurt.

"Yeah, I'm okay."

"Well, when you're ready, you can get a shower and help me with the laundry." Maggie turned and walked back around the corner of the house leaving Katie on the front porch to continue sorting through her feelings of the day's events.

CHAPTER 4
The Gossip

ELEVEN YEARS AGO

Katie

A couple of hours later, Katie sat on the back porch with Maggie folding the laundry just taken off the line. "Why do you hang these out instead of using your dryer?" She asked as the woman popped a towel in front of her then folded it into a neat rectangle.

"The dryer makes the house hotter," she explained. "Plus, just-from-the-line towels smell so fresh." She held one to her nose and inhaled deeply.

Katie sniffed the one in her lap, but not noticing a special scent, shrugged and continued folding.

"So, tell me about the bike ride?" Maggie asked.

Katie paused her movement, though the events from earlier had been on a continual loop in her mind for hours. "Oh, it was okay," Katie replied, coolly. "I met a couple of kids. The ones in the Nova that drove by earlier." Maggie stepped into the yard and plucked more clothes from the line. Katie continued, "But you probably guessed that."

"I figured you'd run into them," Maggie said. She took a

seat in the empty rocker and brought a basket of peas to rest in front of her. As Katie folded the laundry, Maggie shelled peas. The two worked in comfortable silence for a few moments before Maggie picked the conversation back up. "Danny is an okay boy, but that Ronnie is one to watch out for. I don't want you with him alone, ya hear?"

"Don't worry." Katie snorted. "I don't think either one of them will be having much to do with me..." Katie trailed off at the memory of the gorgeous guy she had both rescued and smacked just hours before.

"Like I said, Danny's not that bad," Maggie said. "A little misguided, but he's trying hard to shed his parents' reputation." Katie thought she heard a note of sympathy in her aunt's voice. "But he *is* a typical boy."

"He was diving off the bridge down there. The one leading into town," Katie said. She didn't go into the details of the rest of the encounter. Not the muscular hardness of his body, or his gorgeous aquamarine eyes, or the nonchalant way he carried himself. Or the way he scared the hell out of her then laughed at her gullibility.

"He's a dare devil, that's for sure." Maggie smiled at Katie. "And handsome too, right?" Katie blushed at her aunt's comment. "But don't let his looks fool you. He's a sweet talker, that one, with lots of girls waiting for him to give her the time of day."

"Are there many girls that live in town," Katie asked, keeping her tone matter-of-fact, "you know, anybody he's going with, seeing?"

Maggie emptied her bowl of peas into a larger container by her feet. "Not that I know of offhand. But that doesn't mean anything. I don't think that boy can settle with one girl."

"Why do you say that?" This bit of news stung Katie, and she realized that the boy had already embedded himself in her subconscious.

"Well, there was this one time," Maggie said, starting a

second bowl of peas, "when I was down at Dinwittie's picking up some supplies, Danny strolled in covered in grass clippings and dirt. He does lawns for the rental properties there in town. Anyway, I was behind him in line, and I overheard him sweet talking the cashier, this twenty-year-old local gal, telling her how beautiful her smile was, and that he'd like to get together later on when she gets off work. By the time he'd paid for his groceries, he had her phone number and had made a plan to meet her after work."

"That doesn't sound so bad," Katie said. Her basket of clothes was done, so she grabbed a handful of peas to snap.

"It wouldn't be, but that boy is only seventeen. And I know full good and well, Annaleigh Davis is at least twenty. I remember the graduation announcement they put on the side of the Sugar Shack for her a few years ago." She paused here to drop some hulls into the grocery bag. "I still don't know what a grown woman would want with a seventeen-year-old boy."

"Is that it? What's his story anyway?" Katie dropped her handful of snaps into her aunt's bowl and grabbed another handful. "That's not too bad. Yeah, the woman is older but not by that much."

"I guess it has to do with his upbringing. His parents aren't what you'd label parents of the year. It's sad, really. They're the reason he lives on his own now."

"He lives alone?" Katie's mouth fell open. "And he's only seventeen?" It was hard for her to imagine living alone at such a young age, being totally responsible for yourself, your food, your clothes, everything!

"Yep, just seventeen," Maggie replied. "His parents aren't the most upstanding citizens of Cypress Springs. And their dirty dealings nearly destroyed those boys."

"There's more than one?" Katie couldn't picture any more like him.

"Actually, he has an older brother, Jimmy," Maggie responded, "and a younger sister, Lisa. She's about your age."

Katie thought having a girlfriend to hang out with this summer would be fun. Her Grammy had forbidden Katie to call any of her friends in Jacksonville while she stayed with her aunt, and Maggie was upholding that decree. "So, the other two live with their parents?"

"Lisa still does, but Jimmy's much older, moved out a long time ago. And before he graduated from high school. Danny hasn't graduated yet either." Maggie paused in her work. "Come to think of it, that boy has been living on his own since he was fifteen. He got himself to school until he was sixteen. By law, he had to go until then. But once he turned sixteen, he quit school and started working for first this person then that one. Anyone who'd let him, he'd work like a dog for them just to get enough to get by. Don't know where he got his strong work ethic from. It sure wasn't his parents."

Katie drew her feet under her and waited to hear more. This new information put a new light on Danny. Not only was he good looking, he was a little dangerous. He lived on his own, had been taking care of himself for some time. Much more mature than any of the kids she hung out with in Jacksonville. But still, she'd met him diving from a bridge into shallow water; not very bright. And the stunt he had pulled was enough to make her question his sanity.

"But what did his parents do that made him leave home at such a young age?" Katie still couldn't imagine a home life that would force her to move out at fifteen. Even though her Grammy drove her crazy with her old-fashioned ways, Katie had still never seriously contemplated leaving home. And even if she had thought of running away, where would she go? How would she take care of herself? No, home was never too bad for her to have to leave.

"Well, they're alcoholics for one. At least they used to be when those kids were younger. The dad, Ed Carter, would go on a drunk sometimes for a whole weekend and those boys would take off to any safe place they could find. Lisa, the girl, had it better. Their mom, Valerie, worshiped that little girl. Even to this day, Lisa has had it so much easier than those boys. So, when Ed came home drunk, Lisa just stayed out of his way, but the boys had to disappear until he sobered up. Mind you, all this I'm telling you is common knowledge around town. Nobody really knows how bad it was in that house, but it was bad enough for those boys to leave. They still see their parents around town, but they don't go out of their way to spend time with them." Maggie stopped the story there, digging for a new batch of peas to shell.

"Do you think they were beaten?" Katie asked. How horrible to feel so unsafe in your own home with your own parents. She was having a hard time sitting still now. Her interest in Danny had evolved from anger to curiosity to yearning to pity. And now she just couldn't sit still.

"Oh, no, I don't think so," Maggie answered. "To be sure, if anyone suspected abuse going on in that house, someone would have called CFS. No, I think those boys got ordinary whippins like every other child who misbehaved, and there was only that one time that Jimmy got it bad for going to his aunt and uncle for school clothes for those kids. But I think I heard from somewhere that their Aunt Linda threatened to call the cops on them and take those kids away if Valerie and Ed ever hurt them anymore. That was another thing. Ed and Valerie got state money for having those kids as dependents and him not being able to work before he got his settlement. Now, that court case is a story!" Maggie huffed out a breath of disgust and rolled her eyes.

Katie sat silently, intently listening to the life history of Danny Carter. The more she heard about him, the more she admired him, despite his earlier antics. She still felt sorry for the home life he had grown up in, but he was taking care of himself now. And from what Maggie was saying, Danny hadn't let much of his troubled childhood affect him. Family history was coffee talk gossip in such a small town.

"So, you see, Katie," Maggie finished, "that boy may be only a couple of years older than you, but he's lived a whole lifetime more. I want you to be particular around him. I don't mind y'all being friends and hanging around together, especially with his sister and some of the other local kids, but don't set yourself up for a letdown. He may not be interested in you, you being so much younger and all. And it might not be in your best interest to get mixed up with him, what with the life he's had."

"Well, you've got nothing to worry about, Aunt Maggie," Katie insisted. "I don't think either of those boys will be coming around. I don't think I'm their type." Katie rose from her seat and stretched. "I think I'm going to get a slice of that watermelon I saw in the fridge and go read on the swing." She let herself in the house, and after salting the melon slice, she grabbed her book and settled on the front porch swing.

Sitting on the swing, she mulled over this new information about Danny Carter. He was virtually a grown man, though only seventeen. But he behaved so juvenile, jumping from a bridge to go swimming, openly teasing a total stranger like herself, pulling that drowning stunt at Cane's Creek bridge, speeding down the road in his Chevy Nova. Katie was sure he wouldn't want to have anything to do with her, as young and sheltered as she was. Toeing the ground, the swing swayed gently, and she finished her watermelon in three quick bites. She chunked the rind in the retention ditch between Maggie house and her neighbors and swiped her sticky hands on her still damp shirt. She was debating with herself as to whether she even wanted to try to get Danny's attention with only eight weeks left of her stay when the rumble of exhaust pipes broke into her thoughts.

The Nova pulled into the Morrises' driveway and out climbed Danny, Ronnie and two girls. Katie watched as the group went inside the small river house and exited a few minutes later. Ronnie had changed into a different pair of shorts and a tank top. He slid a pair of sunglasses over his nose. If they noticed Katie sitting just a few yards away, they didn't show it.

The girls hurried to the Nova, glancing back at Danny and Ronnie who stood on the porch talking to some unseen person in the house. A thin green line of jealousy slunk through Katie. She didn't know why she should feel so proprietary about a boy who wasn't even a thing yet. She just felt like she should be one of the girls hopping in the front seat beside Danny to ride off in that car. The girls, though, climbed in the backseat, and Ronnie pushed the passenger seat back into position to hop up front. Danny paused at the driver's door, as if he'd forgotten something, and Katie heard him say, "I'll be right back."

Then he dashed across the road to her front yard.

CHAPTER 5
Swimming

ELEVEN YEARS AGO

Danny

Danny stretched into the driver's window to crank the car and adjust the radio volume. He had changed into thin, gray athletic shorts that were cooler than his denim ones, but it was still too hot for a shirt. As he emerged from the car, he turned toward Maggie Baxter's house. Katie was sitting on the porch swing. He jogged across the narrow, dirt road and jumped the three steps with one quick bound. Katie stood up, her eyebrows arched in surprise.

"Hey," Danny said. "I'm really sorry about earlier. Listen, we're going swimming in town and seeing as how you're new around here, I thought you might like to come with us instead of hanging out with your folks."

"It's my aunt," Katie said, her gaze darting all around. If Danny had to guess, she was nervous. "And haven't y'all had enough swimming for one day?"

"Sweetheart, ain't no such thing." If he thought his presence was affecting her, laying on the charm and tossing in a pet name really amped up her fidgeting. "But, seriously, do you think she'll let you come?"

Katie squinted around him to the car and the sound of music wafting from the Nova. Ronnie was leaning out the window, motioning for Danny. "I, uh, it um..." Katie stammered as she glanced back at Maggie's front door. A screech from the car brought both of their attention to the Nova across the road. Danny's sister, Lisa, and cousin, Becky, shot looks of annoyance through the rear window at him.

"It looks like your friend Ronnie is ready to go," Katie said crossing her arms over her chest. "And won't your girlfriend get upset with you for asking me to tag along?"

Danny cackled at her response. Girls were so strange sometimes. This was only the second time he had even seen Katie and here she was already acting jealous. The look on her face made it clear that his laughter was only fueling her annoyance. "Sorry," he said, stifling a snicker, "but neither of them's my girlfriend. The blonde is my sister, and the redhead is my cousin. So, you want to go or not?" At that, the screen door squeaked open, and Maggie stepped out. Danny ducked his head at the sight of her aunt.

"I think it'll be alright, Katie, if you want to go," Maggie said. "How's it going, Danny?" Maggie smiled at the pair, but her friendliness did little to squelch Danny's distrust of adults.

"It's alright," Danny answered. "I was, uh, just asking her if she wanted to go swimming with us." Danny jerked his head in the direction of the car and the kids.

Maggie looked across the street at the passengers. She waved at Ronnie, who waved back then ducked into the front seat. "Where are y'all going?" she asked, nodding at the car.

Danny looked up and rubbed the back of his neck. "We were going into town to Salt Creek. You know, the swimming hole there." Beads of sweat formed on his forehead more from the scrutiny than the Florida humidity.

"Like I said, I think it'd be okay," Maggie said. "Katie, if you want you can go. Go change back into your swimsuit."

"I've already got it on," Katie said. She smiled at Danny who glanced at her attire. The thin shirt did little to conceal the string bikini top. He felt a stir in his groin with the thought of seeing her in that bikini again. Danny cleared his throat and looked at the porch floor. He was dying for a cigarette, but he'd been trying to quit for a week.

Maggie finally cut them loose from her scrutiny. "Be careful, then. And don't be out too late." She looked hard at Danny who nodded slightly, understanding. He didn't know much about Maggie Baxter, just that she lived alone in the river house, drove an old, beat-up pick up truck, and wore men's work clothes most of the time. He didn't remember ever seeing a man around her house, hinting at the rumors that Maggie might be a lesbian. At least the old hens in the town liked to spread that gossip. It didn't matter to Danny. Maggie had never given him cause to be rude to her, it was just his way. He didn't trust adults. His own parents had created that mistrust; therefore, he didn't really have a need for any of them.

Katie slipped on her flip-flops and followed Danny to his car. He opened the driver's side door and motioned for Katie to get in. Once they were out of the driveway, he introduced Katie to everyone. Turning right onto 342, he followed the many short winding roads through the small town to a small creek that branched off from the Cypress River. He pulled the car off the side of the road as far as he could. The parking spot was next to a sloping grassy area and a small bridge that crossed over the creek. The one-car bridge connected the main road to his yard--a small lot and a travel trailer hidden by the overgrowth here up front. The only landmark noticeable from the outside was a tall, metal pole topped with a sunflower yellow bird house.

"What's that over there?" Katie asked, pointing to the island. Trees and brush blocked the view, but clearly a road led to something back there.

"That's Danny's place," Ronnie said. "*Fantasy Island*, where all the girls' fantasies come true. Huh, bro?" Ronnie reached over Katie to punch Danny in the shoulder. Danny shot a hard look at Ronnie.

"Don't listen to him. He's just talking shit." Danny got out of the car and left the door open for Katie. He walked to the water's edge and bent down to dunk his head in. He slung his head up, water flying over him and into the air. The water ran down his bare chest, glistening in the sun.

"I have a trailer over there that I rent from Mr. Tillman, the man I work for," Danny told Katie. Not many outsiders knew about his lifestyle. Only the townies with their gossiping ways turned his life into fodder for the cows who had nothing better to do than chew on his family history. The one good thing about living where he did was that nobody could see what went on at his place. The trees and the brush hid it pretty well. If he felt like peeing in the front yard, he could. *Hell, if I wanted to walk through my trailer butt naked I could,* Danny thought.

And the girls! Man, if there was one great perk about being on his own, it was all the attention he got from the local girls. They dug the fact that he had his own space and it was so boss that he could have anybody he wanted over and nobody to tell him otherwise. His weekends were filled with sweet talk and sweeter nights, both of which were as hollow as a straw. He knew he used girls as much as they used him, but he was waiting for the one that mattered before he got serious.

Katie appeared at his side, drawing him from his thoughts. Ronnie, Becky, and Lisa wasted no time scurrying from the car and stripping down to their bathing suits. Screaming laughter caught his attention as Ronnie threw his sister into the creek. Danny watched as Katie stood back a little, looking unsure.

"Go ahead. Jump in." Danny motioned toward the creek. "It'll cool you off." He let his gaze sweep over her before turning back to his car. He shut all the doors that his friends had left open and went to the trunk.

When he looked up, Katie was standing by the driver's door, her bottom lip caught in her teeth.

"How about a drink?" he asked, reaching into a cooler in the trunk.

Katie jumped at the sound of his voice. "I don't drink," she stated.

"Aw, come on, everybody drinks." Danny snorted. This girl was too much. She left the door wide open for his teasing. "What'll it be? Bud or Mick? Here, have one." He tossed a can at Katie who instinctively grabbed for it.

"I told you..." Katie again, a note of anger in her voice. She turned the can over to see the Pepsi logo on it. Her already tan face darkened, and Danny laughed.

"I'm only seventeen," Danny said. "I don't drink either, except for sodas. Occasionally tea, if it's made right. But I don't drink beer, usually." He went to stand beside her, watching the other three splash in the creek.

"I just thought," Katie said. "Well, you know what I thought."

He watched from the corner of his eye as she popped the top on the soda can, trying to avoid looking at him. He glanced over at the yelling from the creek.

"Want to get wet?" he asked. The innuendo was intentional. He knew that sex talk made girls squirm or act different than they normally would. Hopefully, this would loosen Katie up some. She was wound too tight.

"I want to go swimming," she responded. "If that's what you meant." She shimmied out of her cut-offs, and Danny couldn't ignore the effect her nearly naked body was having on him. He heard a long, loud whistle come from Ronnie and a flame of jealousy flickered under his skin. He knew what a dog his cousin was when it came to girls. Lisa and Becky simply rolled their eyes and kept splashing.

Danny ran from the car and dove into the creek right next

to Katie. He stayed under a very long time before emerging right beside the girl. He grabbed her waist, lifted her, and threw her far out over the water. She landed full force in the middle of the creek that was deeper than it looked. Danny knew from experience that the current was a little stronger in the middle. He waited fro her to bob up, and watched with admiration as her strong, even strokes brought her to Danny's side.

Most girlie-girls would have been angry for Danny getting their hair wet. Katie, smiling, wiping water from her eyes, jumped up from the water with her hands on Danny's head to shove him under. He grabbed her wrists as he went under to pull her down with him. They wrestled and played for a long time. The earlier events and all the anger surrounding them slipped away. The boys took turns with the girls on their shoulders having chicken fights. It was awkward at first trying to get Katie up on his shoulders, but once Danny got her up there, they couldn't be dethroned. The group of friends splashed and swam until, en mass, they climbed onto the bank, tired and out of breath.

"Danny, did you bring anything to eat?" Lisa asked. "I'm hungry."

"No, only sodas," he replied. "And I'd tell you let's go to my place and get something, but I haven't been to the store yet. My fridge is empty." Danny and Ronnie laid out on the grassy bank, but Becky brought towels from the car for the girls to share.

"Otto's is only a mile or so," Lisa said. "Becky, you want to walk up there with me for some chips or something?" Becky sat up on her elbow considering the idea, and must have decided she was getting hungry, too.

"Sure," she answered. "Katie?"

"Nah, I'm tired after all that fighting," Katie answered. She stretched out on the soft grass and closed her eyes.

"Well, you two ain't walking up there by yourselves," Danny said, rising from his spot. "Hop in, I'll take you." Lisa looked knowingly at Becky who looked at Ronnie.

"Hey, man," Ronnie said. "Why don't you just let me drive them up there? There's no need for all of us to go."

"You know I don't let anyone drive my car," Danny said. "Besides, remember the reason you don't have your car still? Hmm?" Danny gave him a shrewd look that implied the discussion was over.

"Okay, okay. I'll walk with them up there. You two better behave," he said. The three teens left the pair lying on the bank. The sun was low on the western horizon, but far from setting and the heat was still obnoxious. A breath of a breeze stirred the marsh grasses every now and again as the two lay silently beside each other. After a while Danny spoke up.

"So, how did you end up here in Cypress Springs?" he asked rolling on his side toward her. She was resting on her stomach and Danny admired her tan legs and tight butt. Not many girls around here had a body like hers.

"I hopped a Greyhound," Katie replied jokingly. "Seriously, I got in trouble with my grandma--I live with her--and she sent me here for the summer." Katie raised up on her elbows to look at Danny.

"It must have been one hellacious mistake for her to send you here."

"I got caught sneaking through my bedroom window at three a.m. Grammy was pissed," Katie said.

"Oh, you're a regular wild child then," Danny countered, locking eyes with her.

"Well, I, uh," Katie stammered. He watched as she flipped herself over on her back.

Danny laughed. "I'm just trippin'. You don't look that wild."

"Like you'd know," Katie snapped, shooting him a look from the shade of her upheld hand.

"Yeah, I would," Danny said. "I've seen some pretty wild girls living on my own. I had the cops come out to my place one night for a girl who got so drunk she stripped naked and rode my broom down the road like a hobby horse singing *Freebird* at the top of her lungs. The townies had a field day with that. My parents were even embarrassed, and there ain't much that embarrasses them." He could tell by her open mouth and wide eyes that he'd shocked her.

"Nope. Never done that before."

"What? Got drunk, got naked, or sang Lynard Skynard songs?" Danny reached out and poked Katie in the side. Her skin was so soft and damp now from the humidity.

"Well, I've been drunk a few times and I've been naked a couple of times, and I've sang Lynard Skynard before, but not all at the same time." Katie reached over and brushed Danny's hair out of his face. "But, hey, summer's just started." Her hand rested on his shoulder. Danny reached up and took her hand in his and gently kissed the end of her fingertips.

"Yep, summer's just heating up." He watched as his words and his touch made the girl blush. He was beginning to enjoy getting her flustered just to see the glow on her face.

"From the look you gave me earlier today at the bridge, I'd have guessed you've never been around before," Danny said. "And when you pushed me away when I kissed you..." He trailed off, letting go of her hand and rolling on his stomach to rest right next to Katie.

"Duh. I just told you I just got here, last week," Katie answered. "And let's not go there with that kiss. That stunt you pulled was lowdown."

"You're right. Sorry. But I don't mean around *here*," Danny signaled with his hand, "I mean *around*, like with a guy."

"That's a little personal, don't you think?" Katie snatched his sunglasses from in front of him and put them on her face. The over-sized aviators hid half her face, but Danny knew she was trying to hide something else. He could easily guess that this girl wasn't as wild and experienced as she pretended to be.

"You tell me." He leaned over and nudged her with his shoulder. Just the brush of her base skin on his sent a rush of heat through his body. He'd been with plenty of girls all over Dixie County, but there was something about this girl that he couldn't quite pin down.

"What about you," she said, breaking into his thoughts. "Why are you living alone at seventeen?"

"Let's just say my childhood wasn't exactly a fairytale one." He looked out over the small creek watching some marsh birds peck along the edge of the grass. "My folks would have been the evil stepparents in the fairytale, if you know what I mean."

"Yeah." Lying there next to him, he watched as she pulled at the grass blades poking over the edge of the blanket they shared. "I mean, when my parents divorced my dad didn't come around that much anymore. Then, when he remarried, he just didn't seem to have time for us anymore. He spent all his time with his new wife and step kids. Then my mom died..." Katie didn't finish her sentence and Danny squinted over at her.

"Your mom died?" He hoped he didn't sound as shocked as he seemed. As useless as his parents were to him, at least they were still around, for his sister's sake. Lisa, being the baby, was the princess. His parents doted on her, especially their mom. Katie, though, had lost the chance of a close relationship with her mom. "Bummer," he mumbled. "How old were you?"

"Just twelve." Katie wiped her eyes and forced a smile. "She died of cancer."

"What did you do?"

"What do you mean *What did I do*? I cried, I got angry, I became a dare devil." Katie rolled her eyes at that last comment. "Well, at least for me."

"Sorry." An awkward silence fell over them. Though he barely knew her, he wanted to wrap his arms around her and protect her. Ease her heartache and wipe away her tears. Or at least offer his shoulder.

"It's okay, you didn't know. Anyway, my dad gave us to my Grammy to raise. Me and my sisters, Holly and Shannon."

"That blows. He didn't even want to take care of you after your mom died."

"I guess not. But Grammy's been more of a parent than my dad has anyway for a really long time. We moved in with her after the divorce. And she promised my mom on her deathbed that we three girls would stay together."

"How old are your sisters?"

"Holly is thirteen and Shannon is ten."

"And how old are you?"

The question seemed to catch her off guard, and Danny secretly smiled at the effect he had on her.

"I'm fifteen."

"So young. Still a baby," he teased, trying to lighten the mood the only way he knew how. "I bet you haven't even been kissed before."

"Try me." Her answer surprised both of them. She turned on her side, propping herself up on her elbow, the tip of her tongue wetting her lips. She leaned in a little and Danny watched as she let her eyelids drift shut and her mouth pucker.

For a hot minute, he considered rolling on top of her and and seeing how far she'd let him go. Then he thought better of it. The girl had just poured out her heart to him, cried for god's sake! He wouldn't be that much of a dick to try to feel her up after that. Still, he wasn't above a little teasing. He leaned in, as if to meet her, and whispered, "Nah, better not. Not like this. Not after everything you just..." he waved his hand between them.

"Yeah. Right." She drew away and sat up. Stretching her legs in front of her, she glanced behind her down the road the trio had left on.

Danny drank in her profile. Her face was turned away

from him, staring down the road that led away from his island. He was dying to reach out and touch her but didn't out of a sense of decency. This girl had just shared something very personal with him, and god help her, she was trying so hard to be this wild, reckless thing. But he could tell, with as many girls as he'd known, Katie was still a cherry.

And cherries weren't his style. He liked girls that had been around and knew how to show him a good time. Ever since that Halloween night he'd lost his virginity to an older girl, he'd been spoiled to girls with experience. Ones he didn't have to be gentle with. He'd only had a couple of cherries, and they had cried when they realized what they had done. As one girl described it, in the back seat of his Nova, tears rolling down her cheeks, she'd just given away the one gift God had given her to save for her future husband and she could never get it back. It was a line of bull that Danny knew was meant to make him feel guilty and sucker him into a commitment. He'd had rolled his eyes and reminded her it wasn't God's name she had been calling out fifteen minutes earlier.

Now he was faced with a dilemma. He'd just shot her down and probably hurt her feelings, typical. Should he be nice and console her? Make her feel special and probably get lucky later on? Or should he let it go? Was she worth his time? She did try to save his life earlier. Still, as rebellious as she pretended to be, she wasn't ready for all of him.

"Hey." Danny poked her leg. "You mad at me?" He could tell she was but gave her the chance to say it. He wasn't one to play head games. Teasing, yeah, he'd do that, but manipulation? Not so much. He usually came right out and said what was on his mind. He liked that quality in people. Maybe that's why he didn't hate his parents as much as he should for all the bullshit they'd put him through. At least they were truthful about why they took his money and hocked his stuff. If they'd lied about it on top of stealing, he would have hated them much more.

Katie turned to him, her eyebrows arching over those mesmerizing brown eyes. "Should I be? I mean, you haven't really done anything to me. Not that you would. Boys like you are all the same. You like naked, drunk girls who throw themselves at you. And besides, you're right, I barely know you. Why would I want you to kiss me, a complete stranger..."

Her rambling was interrupted by his mouth on hers. He eased her onto the ground and covered half her body with his. Her lips were full and soft and tasted like salt water from the creek. He'd be lying to himself if he said he wasn't shocked by the move. He hadn't planned it, and Katie hadn't expected it. Still, it felt right.

Her arms wound around his neck, her fingers softly combing through his damp hair. His lips parted slightly and his tongue touched the very edge of her lip teasingly as he lifted up on one elbow, his other hand resting on her hip.

"It was the only way to get you to shut up," Danny said. "Was that what you wanted?" Her face was flushed and her body was warm. From the sun or their heat, he couldn't tell.

"Boy, you're cocky," she said. She tilted her head to block the sun. "But it was pretty good."

"Just pretty good?" Danny asked. "Not great, not amazing, not totally rad? Just pretty good?"

"Well, I'm not the most experienced, remember?" Katie said, a smirk playing on her lips. "But you're better than most."

"That's more like it. I think we need to try that again."

"Your call, but I won't stop you."

Danny leaned down to kiss her again. Their mouths met, slow and exploring. His body again pressed to hers, pinning her down with his weight. He could tell she was getting into it, her body arching to meet his, be closer to him. His hand, on her hip, began fiddling with the string tie of her bikini bottom. He almost had it untied when she pushed him away and sat up quickly.

"No, not that. Not yet," she said, her breathing rapid. "I don't really know you, remember? And you're going too fast." Danny sat up and looked at her as the girl double-knotted each side of her swimsuit ties.

"It's all good," Danny said, though having her underneath him, even for those few moments had made his body burn. "I bet Ronnie and the girls will be back any minute." As if on cue, the three teens appeared around the curve in the road, laughing some joke unknown to Danny and Katie. As they approached, their laughter softened.

"I hope, for your sake buddy, we interrupted something." Ronnie snorted.

"Don't be a dick, Ron," Lisa said, shoving her cousin. "That's crude."

"I was just teasing." Ronnie placed a hand on his chest, as if wounded by her words. "Katie can take a joke, right?"

"Sure," Katie said. "Besides, what would there be to interrupt?" She jumped up from her spot and shot a look at Danny. Walking quickly to the creek, she slipped into the water and swam away from the shore.

Lisa and Becky followed her into the creek as the guys sat on the bank.

"Seriously," Ronnie said, slapping his cousin's shoulder, "We interrupted something, didn't we? Did she let you cop a feel?" He glanced at the girls splashing in the creek. "Man, what I wouldn't give to have a handful of that ass." He held his hand in front of him, squeezing his fingers open and shut.

"Dude, shut up! You act like you're hard up." Danny snatched up the glasses Katie had dropped and settled them over his eyes. "And Lisa's right. It's crude to talk like that about her, especially when you don't even know her."

"And you do? We just met her today."

"Yeah, well, Let's just say I know more than you, and you really should keep those comments to yourself."

He didn't know what had come over him. Usually, Danny would have joined in with sizing up a girl and rating his

63

chances of a conquest. But He didn't feel like doing that with Katie. She'd shared something with him that touched his soul, and he didn't want her to get hurt. His gaze swept over the creek in front of them and he watched with longing as Katie climbed from the creek.

"Guess it's time to go," Ronnie said, rising from his seat. He trudged toward the car, and Danny could tell his cousin was a little bummed. Becky was already out of the creek and drying off with her tee shirt as Danny and Lisa joined Ronnie at the car. Katie had nothing to dry off with so she began shaking her arms to shed the water.

"Here," Danny said, handing her a towel. "I use them as seat covers. They'll dry."

"Thanks."

"I've got to go to the store to get some stuff for lunch this week and get ready for work tomorrow," Danny explained. He watched as Katie leaned over to dry her legs. Her breasts fell forward in her bikini top, and Danny felt his groin tighten.

Done with the towel, she handed it back to Danny and picked up her clothes. She slipped her clothes on over her swimsuit and pulled her hair up into a ponytail.

"Y'all ready?" Danny circled the car and opened the door for Katie. The other girls climbed in the back behind as Ronnie shifted the front seat forward. Katie slid across the front seat to again sit between the boys.

Danny maneuvered the car onto the road and headed east out of town. It was slow going on the bumpy, narrow road and every time the car dipped into a rut, Katie's shoulder brushed against Danny. It surprised him how that simple touch affected him. Made him wonder what it'd be like if they were alone, at night, in his back seat...

The drive back to the Morris's ended too soon. Everyone piled out of the car and Lisa and Becky dashed off giggling into the house. They turned on the steps and waved back at Katie. "See ya around," Lisa called.

Katie waved back. "Well, thanks for inviting me." She stood next to Danny as Ronnie lingered by the car.

"Dude," Danny said, cutting a look at his cousin. The redheaded boy ambled off toward the back of the house.

"Anytime." Danny turned his attention back to Katie. The pair stood there in silence, the awkwardness growing. With any other girl, Danny would have eased her up against his car in the growing twilight and let his lips and his hands say his goodbyes. For some reason, though, he didn't want to treat Katie like any other girl. Hell, she'd tried to save his life earlier and she'd shared her family trauma with him. That alone made him realize he would have to handle her softer, more gently.

"Well, see ya later," she said, backing away from him to cross the road.

"Yeah, see ya," Danny replied. He watched her turn toward her aunt's house. She'd gotten five feet when he called to her. "Katie, wait." She stopped and faced him, a soft, quizzical look on her sweet face.

He met her on the edge of the yard and pulled her to him. Wrapping one arm around her waist, drawing her body against his, he leaned down and pressed his mouth to hers. The kiss was slow and soft. He held back a little, not wanting to scare her off, but also not wanting to lose himself in the moment.

It might be dusk, but anyone watching would pass judgment. He just didn't want that sort of baggage already in this new...whatever it was going on with him and this girl he'd just met.

"Wow," Katie said, blinking up at him. "I didn't see that coming."

"Yeah, well, I sort of just do what hits me in the moment." He smiled down at her and gave her hand a squeeze. Then he backed up. "I'll see you around."

Katie nodded, smiled, and headed to her aunt's house. She glanced back at him once, as he expected she would, and he puckered his lips and blew a kiss to her. Something he knew made a girl feel special.

Once she was on the porch, he crossed his cousins' yard to their front door, the image of this new, sweet girl taking up way too much headspace.

CHAPTER 6
Sitting on the Dock

ELEVEN YEARS AGO

Katie

It was nearly a week later when Katie saw Danny again. She had seen him in passing, driving his Nova down SR349 as she lay out on the dock overlooking the canal. He'd honk sometimes as he sped past. She had seen his car across the road at Ronnie's house a couple of times also, and she would sit on the front porch swing, hoping that Danny would come over and talk to her. But he always waved and drove away quickly. Katie was getting frustrated and beginning to wonder if she had imagined the interest Danny had shown her the week before at the swimming hole. His kisses had faded slowly but not the feelings stirred up by them. Katie was beginning to understand what her aunt had meant by Danny being different. He did his own thing and didn't seem concerned with anyone else. Just when she had almost given up on ever seeing him again other than fleetingly, he showed up on Maggie's porch Friday evening.

The knock at the door reverberated from the walls of the small river house. It was a quarter after nine and well past sunset. Katie was just getting into a *Dallas* rerun. The evening was like any other evening since Katie arrived in Cypress Springs--warm and boring. There wasn't even a breath of air blowing in from the gulf and any movement made perspiration bead up on Katie's body causing her clothes to cling to her all the more. She slowly lifted herself from the couch and dropped the remote on the coffee table. She shuffled across the tiny livingroom to answer the door.

"I've got it, Aunt Maggie," Katie called into the bedroom. Her aunt was already in bed, not sleeping, but watching her shows on the TV in her room so Katie could watch an MTV rockumentary in the living room at 10:00. Since it was nearly pitch-black outside, the knock at the door was a surprise to Katie. She reached for the door handle as she pulled at her shorts that clung to her thighs. Her auburn hair, as usual, was pulled up into a ponytail except for the few stray strands that stubbornly stuck to her neck like wet tissue. Katie let out an exasperated sigh at the interruption but changed her tune at the sight of the gorgeous, golden face of Danny.

Katie never expected him to show up at her aunt's front door, and especially at this time of night. Now he was standing in front of her, mirroring her smile. She crossed her arms in front of her as his gaze swept over her. Though she wasn't embarrassed about what she was wearing--her usual thin, white undershirt and comfy boy boxers--she wished she had known he was coming by. She would have done her hair or chosen a different shirt that wasn't *so* revealing.

She blushed at the thought and the look on his face in the warm porch light. He wore a half-smile half-smoulder and Katie's tummy fluttered. What was it about this guy, a near stranger, that made her so self-conscious and giddy at the same time? She didn't want to take the time to think about it now. Just that he was here, on her front doorstep, was enough. That's what she would focus on.

His forehead glistened from the humidity. He shrugged his shoulder to try to catch the sweat on his shirt sleeve. "Hi," he said, speaking so low that Katie wasn't sure if she heard him.

"Hey." She leaned against the open door, her heart racing. *Should I invite him in? Go on the porch with him?* With any other guy from home, she would have snuck out on the porch and maybe down the road before her Grammy even noticed.

Maggie, though, was younger and more aware. "Who is it, Katie?" She called from her bedroom door. She stood there in her robe, eying the two teens. Usually, she would have been in the living room with Katie watching *Dallas*. But she'd told Katie she was extra tired today after helping a friend in town with moving, so she'd went to her bedroom early. Now, she tied the sash of her robe and stepped into the room. "Evening, Danny."

"Hey," Danny said. He looked down at his shoes and took a step back on the porch.

"It's a little late for you to be stopping by, isn't it?" Maggie asked him. She shuffled into the kitchen for a glass of milk.

"I was across the road at Ronnie's and thought I'd come over and say hey to Katie," Danny explained.

Katie watched the exchange, unsure if she should intervene or not. Danny kicked at one of the dozen acorns that had fallen on the front porch, and she could swear this confident boy whom she'd spent last Saturday swimming and flirting with was nervous.

"Well, don't be long," Maggie said. She cut a look at the pair before smiling and slipping back into her room. After hearing the door shut behind her, Katie stepped out onto the porch. Her whole body was warm, but she couldn't tell if it was from embarrassment, the humidity, or being so close to Danny. Out of habit, Katie plopped down in the porch swing. Danny leaned against a banister, nudging a strip of loose porch wood with the toe of his sneaker.

"Sorry I haven't stopped by 'til now. I've been busy," he offered. He shrugged and tossed to the ground a piece of leaf he had been twisting between his fingers. He shoved his hands in his pockets, his eyes finally catching hers.

"That's okay," Katie said. For days, parts of her had waged war against each other--jealousy over who or what had kept Danny away and anger that she might not be important enough for him to come over. He'd been to Ronnie's a half-dozen times over the last week, sometimes staying for hours, but he didn't walk over to talk to her.

She also saw him when he drove out of Cypress Springs some afternoons. He'd honk and wave to her as she sat on the dock, leaving her to wonder where he was going and who he was meeting up with.

Now, here he was apologizing for being too busy, but she didn't know if she bought it.

"So, I don't have to work tomorrow." He stared at her in that soul-piercing way he had, and Katie dropped her gaze. "Wanna go up to Ace's and shoot some pool?"

"I don't know if Aunt Maggie will let me go, especially this late at night. She says there are some real sketchy dudes that hang out up there." Katie glanced up at Danny and watched a flicker of disappointment skitter across his face, surprised that her response affected him at all. Besides, the idea of a crowded, smoky pool hall wasn't what she had in mind when she thought of spending time with Danny. Still, if they got to be together..."I could ask her," Katie suggested.

"Nah, she'll probably say no." He shoved his hands deeper in his pockets, straightening his arms in an upper body stretch.

Katie admired the tight muscles of his upper arms and noticed for the first time a box rolled up in the sleeve of his T-shirt. "Want to go out on the dock?" she suggested. The dock was somewhat private, being a good forty feet from its end over the canal to the back porch. If Maggie wanted to spy on them, she'd have ample opportunity, not that Katie expected them to do anything worthy of needing a babysitter. She highly doubted that Maggie would be doing any spying at this late hour, anyhow.

"I guess." Danny shrugged his shoulders. He pushed himself off the banister and moved toward the steps.

Katie opened the front door. "Come on through. I just have to grab a shirt and we can go out the back door. It's okay; Aunt Maggie's in her room."

"Nah, I'll just meet you around back," he said, bounding down the steps and shuffling into the shadow of the bungalow.

"Okay, I'll meet you out back then." Katie shut the door and went to her room in search of a pullover to hide her sleep attire. She found her jersey night shirt that she had brought to Cypress Springs just in case one of those rare cool nights happened to be carried in on a gulf breeze. She fully intended on stripping back down to her tank top and shorts once she was on the dock with Danny. She'd learned long ago that boys liked skin, and she loved the feel of the thin cotton on her body with this Florida heat. Pulling the shirt over her head, she stopped by her aunt's room to tell her good night. Surprisingly, Maggie was already half-asleep, drowsily watching one of the innumerable crime dramas that always attracted people her age. The work in the yard and on the porch must have taken its toll on her.

"'Night, Aunt Maggie," Katie said. "I'm going out the back door, so I'll lock the front. Don't lock me out."

"Okay, honey," Maggie answered, her voice slurring slightly.

Katie smiled, realizing her aunt was on the verge of a long, deep sleep. *Good,* the girl thought, *no one to check up on us.* Katie pulled the bedroom door closed then tip-toed through the kitchen and out the back door. She stopped on the back porch to close the door, careful not to let it squeak.

As she waited for her eyes to adjust to the darkness, she took a couple of deep, calming breaths. This was the first time she and Danny would be alone, and though she wasn't necessarily scared, she was a little nervous. She didn't have much experience with boys, much less ones with his life experience.

It was a new moon, which meant no moon to speak of, and the darkness that Katie stepped out into was palpable. The only light was a streetlamp across the canal on SR 349, partially blocked by an overhang of trees. The humidity made the night seem that much more clingy and intrusive. Katie couldn't make out Danny's shape in the dark, and for a brief second, the distressing thought of him leaving entered her mind. She tossed the idea aside along with her stifling cover-up. That's when she noticed a tiny, orange light near to the ground. Katie was confused for a moment, then realized the orange dot was the tip of a lit cigarette. The sight and smell of it was indistinguishable, and she couldn't decide how she felt about Danny smoking.

Katie walked cautiously toward the darkened silhouette of the oak tree. "I didn't know you smoked," Katie said. She didn't mind other people smoking, but she had no desire to do it. Still, watching others smoke, like her friends back home and now Danny, made it look so worldly and cool. She edged her way to the oak tree and sat down next to him. The cool, shaded ground under her permeated through her thin shorts.

"I didn't know you were so immodest," Danny returned playfully, reaching out and lightly stroking her thigh to make his point.

He pulled his hand back, and the tingle where his pinky had traced a line along Katie's leg slowly faded. She scanned the yard as a distraction and noticed that his legs were a couple of inches longer than hers. Katie could make out very little in the dark, but she recalled that Danny had on a pair of Rustler jeans and a plain blue T-shirt. His tennis shoes were last year's fashion and really ratty looking, but she liked simple guys.

"Ain't those clothes a little less than your aunt lets you wear in public?" Danny asked mischievously, drawing her from her thoughts. She nudged Danny's leg playfully with her knee, enticing him to touch her leg again. She felt her face heat up and was thankful for the darkness.

She looked toward the gulf, into the black sky that was dotted with thousands of stars. From the corner of her eye, she saw Danny staring down at the canal. He looked so relaxed as he sucked on the cigarette to draw out whatever it was that made him feel so calm. She tried to be inconspicuous as she watched his lips, barely recognizable from the rest of his silhouetted face, gently pucker and blow out the smoke that lifted away on a subtle breeze. That whisper of a breeze blew every now and then giving her goose bumps. At least that's what she told herself. With each breath, Danny's elbow brushed against her bare arm causing her stomach to flip-flop. Finally, unable to control the desire she felt, she jumped from her seat by the tree. She looked down at Danny and caught a fleeting look of surprise on his face.

"I'm going to sit on the dock," she said, walking across the yard. "Come on." She didn't wait for him but heard the crunch of grass and the shuffle of steps as he rose and followed her.

At the end of the dock, Katie bent to light a candle in a pail. As she stood, she caught Danny's eye. His gaze swept over her body and a rush of heat traveled through her. She gave a tug on her shorts before sitting opposite him on the dock. She squatted to situate herself next to a piling and caught a glimpse of Danny as he tugged to adjust the front of his jeans. Another wave of warmth washed over her, and she focused on getting comfortable.

"The stars are pretty," she said, tilting her head back to get a better look. "They're so bright and clear out here." Trying to focus on some innocuous subject did little to keep her mind off the cute boy who sat just feet away from her. She wondered why he sat so far from her. She wanted to feel the caress of his hand on her skin again and debated about moving next to him. Would that be too obvious? Katie folded her hands in her lap and sighed, thinking better of it.

"Yeah, maybe we'll see one shooting across the sky if we're out here long enough," Danny answered. He looked up at the sky, and Katie chanced a glance at his silhouette.

He sat so relaxed, leaned back on the dock support, his head tossed back to stare up at the night sky. The blue t-shirt was pulled tight across his chest, outlining those muscles and those of his shoulders. A breeze blew and the strands of hair around his face fluttered. Katie caught her breath when he suddenly looked directly at her.

"How about some music?" She jumped up from her spot to hurry to the back porch. She needed the distraction. Sitting there with Danny had her thinking all kinds of improper thoughts. She grabbed the cassette player and a handful of tapes she'd brought with her then returned to the dock. Setting the device between them, she flipped on the radio. Raw, obnoxious new wave tunes shredded the silence that separated Danny and Katie, and both jumped at the radio to turn it down.

As their hands touched over the knob, Danny took hers in his and gave a gentle tug. "You don't have to sit so far away," he said, extinguishing the cigarette Katie hadn't noticed. "I don't bite. Well, not unless you want me to." A devilish smile played on his lips, and he scooted over to make room against the pole for Katie.

She busied herself with choosing a tape. The distraction did little to keep her mind off the pressure of Danny's leg against hers. "So, what'll it be--Night Ranger? Aerosmith? Or how about a mix tape?" she asked, waving the cassettes in front of her.

"Whichever. Dealer's choice."

She chose the mixed tape, recorded from countless hours of listening to the Sunday morning *Top Forty Countdown*. After the initial hum of the forwarding cassette, *In Your Eyes* by Peter Gabriel flowed softly into the night. Katie leaned back on the piling and listened as the mellow tune drifted on another gentle breeze. Even with the added pressure of first impressions with a boy she hardly knew, Katie felt more relaxed than she had since she left Jacksonville.

She listened to the melody intermingling with crickets chirping and frogs singing and felt peaceful for the first time in a long time. Closing her eyes, she thought of her mom, gone now three years, and her sisters back in Jacksonville. She remembered the last day of junior high, only two weeks ago, and thought about the end of summer. She'd start tenth grade in the fall. Time was moving so fast. She sighed at the thought.

Her worry over starting high school led to dreams of her future. As the music played on and the lyrics to *Four in the Morning* rang out, her mind drifted to imaginings of prom and graduation day, all night college parties and late-night study sessions. But all of that was years away. Tonight, she was sitting next to an absolutely gorgeous guy. Maybe Danny would be part of her future. *Not likely with three hundred miles between us and only two months to get to know each other,* she thought. But still, they did have two months...

CHAPTER 7
Dating Independence

ELEVEN YEARS AGO

Danny

The mood breaker came with the piano intro and opening lines of *Sister Christian* by Night Ranger. Katie turned her head from him and he heard a long, low breath push from her lips. Danny hoped she wasn't crying; he didn't really know how to deal with girls crying. He set his hand on her thigh, trying to offer comfort in a touch, but her leg tensed under his fingers. Taking it as a rejection, he withdrew his hand. Disappointed, he picked up the cigarette he had ground out earlier and relit it. After the last drag, he flicked the butt into the canal. Frustrated, he rose and walked to the end on the dock.

He stopped at the edge and stared up at the night sky, digging his hands into his front pockets. His clenched fists strained against the pocket cloth. The tension in his biceps and triceps made his arms ache as he held the pose to push out all the frustration. He longed to touch Katie. He'd held back because he didn't want to scare her, to push her too far. But with her right next to him, almost in his lap, he couldn't resist her soft, smooth leg that lay next to his. He really wanted to glide his hands under her shirt and stroke her bare stomach and move upward...but she was inexperienced. He could tell. Someone with any knowledge of women could tell a cherry from a peach.

Maybe he was wasting his time. Maybe he didn't know what the hell he was thinking. Maybe she wasn't interested in him at all.

"God, Danny," Katie snapped, her voice right behind him. "Do you even want to be here with me?" Danny turned to face her. "I mean," she continued, "You pull away every time I get close to you." She crossed her arms, waiting.

"Me?" He flattened his palm against his chest, authentic surprise in his voice. The question came out of left field. "You jump up or tense up every time I touch you. Do you even want me here, Katie?" His face was masked, an attempt to conceal the pain of rejection. So far, his life had been one long exercise in accepting rejection. Living his whole life in Cypress Springs, with all the judgmental so-called do gooders, had taught him to build walls. He thought Katie would be different. That he could be himself around her.

He watched in the dim light as the stern look on her face softened. He hated that look--pity. He debated leaving the dock, the yard, and her, but Katie laid a hand on his arm. Her voice came out in a soft murmur.

"All I've thought about the last two weeks is you." She stepped closer. He didn't move, didn't try to stop her. She slid her arms around his waist, pulling him to her, as she rested her cheek on his shoulder.

He dropped his head and inhaled sharply. Her scent filled his nostrils--fruity shampoo, tanning lotion, and the smell of attraction. Yes, desire had a scent that was raw and warm and salty.

"Danny, I don't know what you're used to, but I'm not ready for, well..." Her words drifted off and she rubbed her cheek against his chest. Then she pulled back and looked up at him. "I won't do everything you--"

"I know," he interrupted her. He bent his head to drop a kiss on her forehead. His embrace tightened, and the warmth of her body near his had him wishing he was bare chested and in shorts. How stupid it was for him to get dressed up to impress her when it was so damn hot! Being this close to her was torture, especially knowing she wasn't ready for more than kisses and the occasional fondling. Maybe not even that much, but he was certainly willing to put in the time to find out.

His own sexual experience had started early, at thirteen, in a neighbor's garage with a girl four years older than him. It wasn't what he expected, just something to say he'd *done it*. And other encounters since then weren't that earth shaking either. Maybe what his older brother Jimmy had told him once was true--being in love made sex different, special. Jimmy had threatened to beat Danny's ass if word ever got out about their *talk*. Danny had kept quiet, but Jimmy left home shortly after graduation and hadn't visited much in the last four years.

Danny's heartbeat quickened as did his breathing when he felt Katie's lips brush his neck. Her hands found their way under the back hem of his tee shirt, and he trembled slightly at Katie's touch on his naked skin. His hands followed suit and began tracing small circles on her warm, soft sides.

"Is this all you want?" Danny asked her, bending closer to Katie's ear to gently kiss the side of her temple. He scattered a few more kisses on her cheek, on her ear, in her hair. His hands continued their circular path, growing wider, from hip to rib cage. He could feel the outline of her panties' waistband through the thin material of the shorts. Though his longing was urging him to push a little further, he chose to take his time with Katie. She wasn't like the local girls he knew, who'd jump in bed with anyone who treated them halfway decent. Danny could tell she was different, special.

"For right now," Katie murmured, "I'm content with

holding." She eased up on tiptoe to let her words and breath drift into his ear. Her voice turned playful as she added, "and some kissing and touching, too." Danny felt a small squeeze on his rear just as her lips found their way to his mouth.

Danny enthusiastically returned her kiss. He felt her soft lips on his mouth open slightly to lick and suck on his lower lip. His hands that had been chaste up to this point, deftly slid into the back of her boxers. A firm grip and a tug had her body pressed to his. A gasp followed by a sigh fluttered across his lips before their kiss continued.

Bare skin met his touch where conventional underwear should have been. A small piece of T-shaped cloth ran from hip to hip making up the back of her thong panties. A smile played on his lips at the thought of this naive girl pretending to be a wild child. How far was she willing to go? And how far would he be willing to push her without running the risk of losing her?

Katie pulled away and stepped back. "You're going just a little too fast," she said. She bent to switch cassettes, then sat next to a piling.

Danny couldn't see her face, but her hands fidgeted in her lap. Frustrated, he ambled to the opposite side of the dock to compose himself. *Great, now she's mad,* he thought. *How could I have read her signals wrong?* Moments from the last two weeks played in his mind, up until the recent foreplay on the dock. She'd started it by sliding her hand under his shirt hem. And once he felt the type of panties she had on, he was lost.

He unzipped his jeans to rearrange himself. The throbbing in his pants from unrealized sex bugged the hell out of him. Though he'd sworn to never to convince a girl to do more than she wanted, he would rather not even get started if there wasn't going to be a follow through. He zipped his jeans, adjusted his attitude, and turned to face Katie. She was still sitting against the piling, looking down the canal toward the gulf. He could only see her silhouette against the horizon.

"You're mad at me, aren't you?" Katie asked, not looking up at him. "You guys usually are, but I'm not ready to go where that was leading." She brushed her hand across her cheek.

Danny couldn't tell if she was brushing away a gnat or a tear. He wanted to be sympathetic, but the girl had to know that her actions could cause reactions that might not end up the way she expected. Not every guy would be a gentleman like him and stop when she said no. Especially if that no came in signals and not words.

"I'm not *mad*," he said, emphasizing the last word, but keeping his voice calm, "I'm just...frustrated, and a little disappointed." *Damn, am I disappointed!* "I like you Katie, a lot. And I don't want you to get the wrong idea, but if you move like that on a guy, he's going to try more, just to see how far he'll get."

"Most guys just keep pushing and pushing until I give in and let them touch me," she said. She glanced up at him and smile sadly. "I end up feeling...*ashamed*, but I get tired of the pressure. I give in. I thought that when I say no, they're supposed to stop."

"They..., I mean, we are, but it's really hard," Danny said. He knelt down beside her on the dock and looked her in the eye. "Look at yourself, Katie. Look how you're dressed out here with me. God, I can't help but want to touch you, *everywhere.* I'm not saying it's your fault, I'm just saying cut me some slack. You're pretty, and I really want you. But you're trying too hard to be sexy and all. You've got to understand that giving off the signals will make us think you want more than just a kiss and a light pet." His lips curled into a crooked smile, and he jostled her leg to coerce a smile from her. "Let's wait before we go any further."

"I like you holding me and us kissing," Katie said.

Her voice was so soft Danny barely heard her. His smile softened and sat down beside her, his hand resting lightly on her thigh.

She blinked and Danny caught the glistening in her eyes. "We could do that--kiss, hold--but if we get too excited, I'm going to stop it. I don't know if I'm ready for more." She looked at him expectantly.

Danny shifted to let his feet dangle over the edge of the dock. He'd lived in Cypress Springs nearly his whole life and most girls around here were easy. He hadn't yet found one that would turn him down for sex if he really pushed. He wanted Katie, but was she worth waiting for? He didn't know, but he thought so.

"What the hell," he said turning to face her. "I can settle for kissing and holding, and you let me know when you're ready for more." Then he leaned over and kissed Katie fully on the lips; a soft, slow kiss that told her he's wait, at least for a while.

CHAPTER 8
The Fourth of July

ELEVEN YEARS AGO

Katie

Two weeks after their first "date" on the dock, Katie was preparing for Cypress Spring's Fourth of July Celebration. Lisa, Danny's sister, and Katie had become good friends in the short time Katie had been at her aunt's house, and all Lisa could talk about for the past week was the Fourth of July fireworks. She'd described the boat parade in such detail that Katie wondered if it would live up to the hype. Lisa also assured her that the fireworks were the best among the five surrounding counties.

"To get a better light show," Lisa had told her as they painted their toes one late afternoon, "you'd have to drive south to Tampa or east to Gainesville."

The pair sat in chairs on Becky Morris's front porch. Becky had gone inside at the summons of her mother, and Lisa leaned closer to Katie, her voice low. "You know the real reason I'm so excited about this weekend?"

Katie glanced up and shrugged.

"I get to see Mark for a few hours without my parents

gawking at us." She shoved the brush into the polish bottle. "Do you know how hard it is," she said, her hands waving emphatically in front of her, "to want to kiss your boyfriend and your parents are literally in the next room. They could walk around the corner at any second and catch you."

"God," Katie said rolling her eyes in sympathy. "I'd be mortified if Aunt Maggie came out on the back porch while Danny and I--" She clamped her mouth shut, remembering who she was talking to.

"While you and my brother what?" Lisa shook the bottle and unscrewed the cap.

"Nothing. Never mind." Katie busied herself with polishing the toes on her other foot. She couldn't tell her new friend about the pulse-racing moments she and her brother shared out on her aunt's dark dock.

"What?!" Lisa insisted. "Come on, share some dirt about my brother."

"I don't think so." Grateful for the twilight that hid her deepening blush, Katie rose from the rocker and carefully slid her flip-flops on. "I've got to head in before these mosquitoes carry me off."

"Sure you do." Lisa clicked her tongue and dabbed one final coat on her pinky toe.

"Tell Becky I said bye." With that, Katie stepped off the porch and crossed the street to her aunt's house.

Two days later, Katie was waiting on the front porch for Danny. He'd promised to be there to get her by 4:30. Though the drive was only six minutes to the parade route, he'd explained how bad the traffic would be. Finding a parking spot would be near impossible, but he told her he had to work. One afternoon lawn job that paid extra because of the holiday. He couldn't turn it down.

So, she sat on the porch swing patiently waiting, and heard the familiar rumble of his car as it turned into the neighborhood. After grabbing her purse from the swing and poking her head in to say goodbye to Maggie, Katie climbed into the front seat next to Danny.

Once in the car, he kissed her properly, and she felt the heat of his gaze travel over her body. "You like my choice of outfit for the night," she asked.

"Definitely." He swung his arm across the seat back and let his hand graze her bare shoulder. "I'm just surprised Maggie let you out dressed like that."

"Well, the shorts aren't that short." She fiddled with the frayed hem. "The halter top, though, I covered with a regular tee shirt."

"And where's that?"

"Under the bushes in the side yard."

"You little sneak." He gave her shoulder a squeeze and Katie settled in closer to him for the short ride into town.

They parked in the last empty spot at Cypress River Grill and Hotel. The hotel had a dock that ran through a marshy area to an opening near the mouth of the Cypress River where it met the gulf. After exiting the car, Danny took Katie's hand and tried to cut a path through the crowd to the dock. It was no use; there wasn't any place to stand, much less see the boat parade. The couple returned to the parking lot the way they came.

With the start of the parade just moments away, Katie could sense Danny's frustration rising. In the short time she'd known him, she could tell when his patience was running thin. As he fidgeted in front of her, Katie's anxiety rose. She didn't want something as irrelevant as a boat parade to ruin her first legitimate date with Danny.

Suddenly, Danny snapped his fingers. "I got it," Danny exclaimed. He grabbed Katie's hand and tugged her away from the parking lot toward a small trail in the woods. "Are you up for a small adventure?"

"Sure, I guess. But I thought we..." She pointed back to the crowd at the restaurant, many of whom wouldn't even be able to see the boats.

"Do you trust me," he asked.

"Yeah, I trust you."

"Then follow me." He led her through scrubby underbrush that was mushy underfoot, helping her over tree roots and around palmetto bushes poking out into the path. An official with a loudspeaker announced that the parade would begin in five minutes. A whoop went up from the crowd, and Danny urged her on. The brush opened up in front of them into a small hammock of trees on the bank of the river, one humongous cypress tree rose tall above the bank. Katie noticed strips of wood nailed to the trunk leading up to an enormous branch that hung out over the river.

"Sometimes when we can sneak back here, Ronnie and I climb up there and dive off into the river," Danny said, pointing to the branch that stretched out over the water.

If she had to guess, the branch was at least a good twenty feet above the water's surface.

"You want me to climb up there?" she asked, hesitation echoing in her voice.

"If you want a good view of the parade," Danny said. "It's safe. Trust me." He stepped onto the first rung, bouncing a little to prove its strength, then pulled on the second and third rung. Both held strong. He stopped on the fourth one up and turned to offer a hand to Katie.

"I don't know." She eyed the steps warily. "What if I slip or you accidentally let go of my hand?" Danny hopped from his perch to land beside her.

"You want to go up first? I'll be behind you to catch you before you fall. You can land on me."

Still unsure, Katie finally relented. "Well, okay, if you promise to catch me if I start to fall."

"Cross my heart." He smiled and made a quick X over his

left collar bone. "But we have to hurry. Once you reach the rung closest to the limb, swing your foot out to step up on the branch and that's where we'll be able to sit out over the water and watch the parade."

Up the tree they went as the announcer blew the horn to start the parade. Katie glanced down river, then shimmied up the trunk. She reached the low-hanging branch easily and scooted out as far as she dared to give Danny room to sit. He slid into the spot behind her, and she leaned back against him for a better view of the river. She felt his arm slide around her waist. That, combined with the pressure of his chest against her back and his signature scent filling her nostrils, made Katie breathless with anticipation for what the rest of the night would hold.

The pair watched as one boat after another glided past them. Each vessel was more spectacular than the last, and had Katie been a judge, she wouldn't have been able to decide a winner. One boat even had its complete hull painted to look like an American Flag with an eagle ripping through the center of it. Lights that ran in succession lit up the deck and masts, and a neon sign that flashed *God Bless America* hung from the upper deck. The participants on that boat wore patriotic tee shirts, hats, and bandannas and blared Lee Greenwood's *Proud To Be An American* from its loudspeaker.

As the parade wrapped up, the pair maneuvered their way back down the tree. Danny took her hand and led her back down the path toward the crowded parking lot.

"Wasn't that better than fighting this crowd," he asked, waving his free hand at the glut of people.

"Absolutely." Katie hurried to keep up with him and to avoiding getting squished among the strangers.

As the couple reached the Nova, a line of traffic was already forming. "And now to get to the park." Danny inched his way out of his parking space and nudged between a pick-up and a convertible. Waving a thank you to the drivers, he muttered, "This is going to be a freaking nightmare."

And he wasn't wrong. It seemed that everyone who'd watched the boat parade was heading to Coleman Park for the fireworks. It didn't help that there was only one road into and out of Cypress Springs. Forty-five minutes after they got in the car, they climbed out of it to find a place to throw down a blanket for the evening.

It was useless though. Too many people were at the park. The noise of conversations, the screams and laughter of kids running, the blaring music--it bombarded Katie and her head began to throb. She put up a hand to shade her eyes.

"What's wrong?" Danny faced her, putting himself between her and the crowd. "You look like you're going to puke."

"I'm not much for crowds this big. And the noise." As if on cue, a blast from a car horn right behind her made Katie jump. She leaned into Danny, welcoming his body as a shield.

"You wanna go?"

"Where?"

"We could head to Frosty's now." He shrugged.

"But we'd miss the fireworks." Katie leaned in closer to be heard over the commotion.

"You look like you're feeling bad," Danny said, "and I don't want you feeling bad later." He pulled her closer to him and kissed her forehead. "We could ride over to my house for a little while. Watch the fireworks from there."

"What about Lisa and the others?" Katie asked. Lisa was supposed to stay with Danny until he took her home later that evening.

"My parents are here," he tipped his head in their direction. "I'll just tell Lisa we're running up the road because it's too loud and we'll be back to get her in a little while. Hang on."

As he left her to go talk to his sister, Katie thought about spending the next hour alone with Danny. Despite the crowd and the noise ratcheting up her headache, the thought of finally being alone with Danny lightened her sour mood.

As she waited by the Nova, she wondered what Danny's home looked like. She knew it was a travel trailer that one would use to go camping and that it was on a tiny little island near the mouth of the Cypress River. How neat could it be with a seventeen-year-old living there alone?

Danny returned and the pair climbed back into the car. "Why don't you slide closer?" Danny asked as patting the spot beside him. Katie scooted toward him, straddling the stick shift. He started the car and glanced at his side mirror. "I told Lisa that I'd pick her up across the street at 9:15 to beat the crowd." The engine revved and gravel flew as Danny accelerated quickly onto SR 349.

Katie's heart raced as the car sped back into town. This is what being around Danny did to her. She felt invincible with him, like she could handle anything. She hadn't felt that way since her mom died three years ago. It still hurt to think about it, but she blinked back the tears and focused on the present.

Katie was drawn from her thoughts by the touch of Danny's pinky finger slipping under the fringe of her shorts. After shifting into fourth, his hand came to rest on her upper thigh. The touch of his hand on her leg sent ripples of excitement through her. She didn't dare move, or hardly breathe, fearful that he would remove his hand from her thigh. The tension was thick in the narrow front seat, but Katie opened her knees a tiny bit, a subtle invitation. Her steady breathing returned when Danny's hand left her leg to downshift. He swung the car onto the one-lane road leading to his island.

A streetlight snapped on with a buzz and cast a pale glow on the small, vintage trailer. Katie wasn't good with measurements, but if she had to guess, the trailer was maybe 25 foot long. Tiny one by two-foot windows dotted the front side. The two-toned brown and white aluminum siding needed a good scrubbing. Even in the twilight, Katie could make out leaves and something that looked like fishing net hanging from a back corner. She would have felt pity and embarrassment for anyone having to live here, but for some strange reason it suited Danny. It was exactly what she expected his home to be like. The yard, though neat and mowed, wasn't well maintained. No flowers, no shrubs, nothing but the light pole, a single tree and sparse spots of Bermuda grass.

Danny cut the engine but didn't move from the car. "I know it doesn't look like much, and the inside ain't much better, but it's my home. I'm free here." His statement caught Katie off guard. He still hadn't said much about his previous home life and what drove him to leave his parents' home. She wondered what had been so awful that being totally responsible for oneself would be considered freedom. Her door opened. Danny leaned down and asked, "You coming?"

Katie slid out of the car and, taking his hand and followed him to the narrow, aluminum door. He unlocked the padlock on the outside of the trailer and held the door open. Stepping into the small living area, Katie was surprised at its tidiness. It had classic camper decor--brown tweed upholstery on the hide-a-bed couch, brown Formica cabinets, and gold counter tops. The carpet was worn thin, but not too stained. To the left of the living area was the small kitchenette with linoleum that appeared newly scrubbed. Katie expected to see dishes and clothes everywhere but was pleasantly surprised. Past the kitchen Katie saw a small door that was pulled closed.

"What's back there?" she asked. She had never been in a travel trailer before and was fascinated by how cute and useful everything was. Every nook and cranny was utilized for storage or function.

"Here, let me show you in case you need to, you know, go." Danny slid the door open exposing a small, tidy bedroom with an attached bathroom. The toilet was next to the shower and across from the sink. The bathroom itself appeared to measure only three by three feet. It left just enough room to turn around in. The bedroom was small also with a narrow twin-size bed that looked to be too short for Danny. The decor matched that of the living area and kitchenette but was exceptionally clean.

"It's so neat," Katie said returning to the living area. She sat down on the couch.

"You want something to drink?" Danny asked, turning back to the kitchenette. "I've got soda or water."

"Sure, whichever." She noticed that there weren't any pictures of anyone or art hung up anywhere. But this was a guy who lived here. He probably didn't have any pictures to decorate with. Danny brought her a can of soda and sat down beside her.

"So, what do ya think?" he asked. He smiled in satisfaction and glanced around his tiny home on wheels. "It ain't much, but it's mine. As long as I make rent each month."

"It's small, but cool," Katie said.

"Yeah, I don't need much room with it being just me," Danny answered.

"It's so clean," Katie commented.

"I'm really hardly ever here, so it doesn't get too dirty," Danny said. "Plus, if you'd seen what I grew up in, you'd probably get the idea why I keep it so clean." His face clouded briefly, then he was back to his smart-aleck self. "Bet you thought I lived in a dump, being so young and all?" His steel blue gaze landed fully on her, and Katie looked away. She couldn't get used to his forward stare. It was so penetrating, it forced the truth from her.

"I thought, uh, yeah," she stammered, "maybe it'd be more messy." She stared at her Coke can, rubbing the condensation from the rim with her finger. "You don't have any pictures of your family, or anybody," she commented. Her room at home had pictures of her mom and her sisters, and posters of her favorite band, Duran Duran, covered one whole wall above her bed. Even her room at her Aunt Maggie's had some pictures of her family that she'd brought and scattered around.

"No, I guess I don't think about things like that," he answered, looking around the small living area. "You got any pictures of yourself I could have?"

"You want a picture of me? For what?" Katie asked.

"Duh, to hang up in here," Danny said.

"What about your mom and dad, or Lisa?"

"I get along with Lisa okay, but I don't want photos of my parents reminding me of why I left home." Danny took a sip of his Coke. "Besides, if I wanted to see them, I could go over to their house, right?"

"I guess."

"So, I'll just put up pictures of people I want to look at on a daily basis."

Katie blushed. "I'll see what I can find at Aunt Maggie's. If I don't have any here, I'll mail you some."

"So, the fireworks don't start for about another hour," Danny pointed out. "What do you want to do until then?"

Katie's mind reeled. There was plenty she could guess that he wanted to do, and some of it she wouldn't mind. She started fidgeting with a loose string on his couch cushion. "I don't know. What do you want to do?" It was a loaded question, she knew, but she couldn't think of anything else to say. She snuck a glance at his face only to find him staring right at her, his expression was hard to read.

"I don't know," he echoed. "We could play cards or listen to music. I'd say let's watch TV, but I only get two channels. You hungry?"

"Not really."

"So you just want to sit here?"

"No, you got any good tapes?"

"I just bought Whitesnake's new one." Danny got up and walked quickly to his bedroom, returning with a radio/cassette combo and the Whitesnake cassette, plus a few others. "Get this. It's called *Slide It In.* Puts it right out there, don't they?"

Katie saw the look on his face. *God, is all guys think about is sex?* She avoided his gaze by reading the play list on the cassette jacket. "Slow and Easy" was one song she knew; it played a lot on the rock station back home.

He popped in the tape and raw guitar chords filled the silence. The song began and the couple let the first song play through before Katie suggested something less suggestive.

"You got Night Ranger or Heart?" Katie asked, looking at the tapes he's brought from his room. She located *Midnight Madness*, dropped it into the cassette player. She fast forwarded the tape, stopping it and starting it again, until the opening piano melody to "Sister Christian" wafted from the speaker. Katie fell back onto the couch next to Danny listening to the lyrics of the song. A sense of calm settled over her. Music did that to her--her mood usually matched the mood of the song she chose. And right now, she wanted to be calm and relaxed. The noise in her head that had followed them from the park was finally slipping away.

Danny lifted his arm over her her head for her to rest on his shoulder. It felt so comfortable sitting there with him, without the distraction of other people. She snuggled in closer to him and a sigh escaped her lips.

"What's wrong," Danny asked, his voice low and close to her ear.

"I don't know," Katie replied, as sadness swept over her. "I guess I might be missing home." *Or actually, my mom,* she thought.

"You'll be back there before you know it." He gave her a little squeeze, his fingers brushing along her shoulder. He pressed his mouth on the top of her head, and Katie heard him inhale.

"I guess," Katie said, mentally shaking herself. There was no way she was going to sit here and mope when she had this hot guy being all caring and understanding about her homesickness. She sat up. "You got anything for a headache? Maybe that'll help me feel better."

Danny rose from the couch and rifled through a kitchen cabinet before pulling out a bottle of Tylenol. "Here," he said, handing her the bottle.

Katie took two tablets, popped them in her mouth, and took a swig from her Coke that was nearly empty. She refused to be in a crappy mood when she should be having some fun with this gorgeous boy. Their romance hadn't progressed much beyond kissing and caressing, but every time they were together Katie came that much closer to giving herself to him. It was a struggle to remain chaste and she still didn't know if she was ready for a more adult relationship.

"Thanks. That should help." She set the bottle on the counter and switched the music again to something more upbeat. "Why don't you find us the cards so we can practice playing poker to beat the others later on," Katie said.

"You *do* know we're playing strip poker," Danny said.

"Won't that be weird with your sister here?"

"She won't be in *here*," he indicated his living area, leaving her to guess that they'd called dibs on the bedroom.

"Oh, well, um..." she stuttered, searching for words.

"No, not that," Danny replied. "I think Mark is taking her for a ride later. God, Katie, she's my little sister. I wouldn't let that happen here."

Katie blushed. "That's good, I guess." She watched as he shuffled the deck of cards.

"I don't play cards without some stakes. What are we playing for?"

"Not clothes. Not yet," she said. The idea of stripping in front of near strangers was weird, but if everyone else did it Katie guessed she could do it, too.

"How about for pennies?" Danny got up and brought out a jar of change from his room.

"Fine, but you'll have to tell me again exactly how to score." They played for a while until Katie got the hang of it. She was actually pretty good. She didn't bluff well, but when she had a good hand she knew how to hide it. It was nearing 9 o'clock when they finally put the cards up and Danny returned the penny jar to his bedroom. Katie stood up to stretch and was surprised by Danny's arms wrapping around her waist from behind. He slowly rocked her back and forth to the rhythm of the music, his body pressed against hers.

Turning around in his arms, she kissed him on the mouth. He pulled her tightly to him, stroking her back with his hands. They swayed to the couch where Danny lowered her onto her back. He covered her body with his, kissing her neck, her cheek, her ear. Nothing about tonight had hinted that this would happen, but Katie should have expected it. They had been pushing boundaries ever since she got here. It was just a matter of time before they got to this point.

Her hands glided up and down his back, finally grabbing the end of his tee shirt to tug it over his head. She threw it in a ball on the floor and caressed his bare skin. His scent--salt and sun--drifted around him. He slid a hand under the edge of her shirt, grazing her rib cage then the hem of her bra. Katie stiffened and pushed his hand away.

"Not yet," she whispered, aware that this was becoming her summer theme song. They had spent many days and nights together over the last few weeks, and each time it became more and more difficult to hold him off. Not because he pushed too hard, but because her own resolve was weakening. She was falling in love, real love, for the first time and wanted to experience physical intimacy with someone she loved, with someone who loved her back.

She knew Danny had already been with many girls. The way he and Ronnie joked around when they thought they were out of earshot was as illuminating as it was embarrassing. And hearing some of the more raucous things they shared made Katie wonder if she'd ever be able to compare to his past.

Just as she was building up the nerve to guide his hand

back to her bra hem, Danny removed his hand himself and settled it on her waist. The fabric that separated his hand from her bare skin did little to quash her budding desire. He began caressing her breast on top of her shirt, and she nearly lost herself to the feeling. When she felt his hardened desire press against her thigh, she knew she'd have to end the make out session. Otherwise, she didn't know if she'd be able to stop them once the clothes came off.

"What time is it," she asked, her breath shallow and soft from the kisses.

Danny leaned over to fish the alarm clock from the floor. "Five till nine. The fireworks will start in a few minutes. We could go outside and watch them, but the mosquitoes will be bad." He rose from the couch and pulled Katie up with him. He kissed her one last time, and Katie got the distinct impression that this wasn't the end of their tryst.

"I'll be right back," he said, ambling through the kitchen to the bedroom.

Katie heard the water turn on then off. She wandered to the tiny fridge and found another soda.

A few minutes later, Danny returned, his hair combed, and smelling like aftershave and mouth wash. He went to the refrigerator and got himself a drink before turning back to her.

"You don't have any bug spray, do you? I really don't feel like being eat up by mosquitoes."

"Let me look." Danny dug around under his tiny sink and produced an old, partially rusted can of Off! "It's better than nothing," he said, offering her the can. They stepped out of the trailer and took turns spraying themselves, finishing up just as the first BOOM exploded the night air.

Katie hopped on the trunk of the Nova. Danny leaned against the car next to her lighting the cigarette he had retrieved from pack behind his sun visor. His torso disappeared through the car's window and when he returned, the radio was on playing patriotic music. As country songs from The Charlie Daniels Band and Lee Greenwood bellowed out into the night, bursts of color, each more spectacular than the last, lit up the night sky. The show ended with a finale of multiple explosions that painted the sky in reds, whites, and blues in the form of an American flag as the National Anthem played.

The couple listened in silence as the last of the anthem's lyrics faded away. Katie cleared her throat and felt Danny's hand on her knee, his gentle touch a reflection of how she felt in that moment--proud, fortunate, awestruck.

After a moment, he gave her leg a light pat. "You ready?" He helped her from her perch, and they slid into the front seat of his car.

As they sped away toward the park to get Lisa, Katie hoped the rest of her summer would be just as perfect as this day had been.

CHAPTER 9
Danny's Confession

ELEVEN YEARS AGO

Katie

The Frosty's was packed with cars. Many of them were filled with teens who'd just come from Coleman Park and the Fourth of July celebration. Mark was waiting for Lisa outside his truck when Danny pulled up. Katie felt out of place. As soon as Danny parked, his car became the hub for many kids to gather and hang out. It seemed to Katie that everybody knew Danny. Some people were around Katie's age, but most of them were Danny's age or older. To calm her anxiety, Katie left the group to get some ice cream and a drink.

Inside Frosty's was just as busy as the parking lot, and it took Katie nearly fifteen minutes to get her order. When she left the store, she noticed the crowd around the Nova had thinned. There were fewer people near the car, but one girl in particular made Katie uncomfortable. As she approached the crowd, Katie noticed a tall, thin woman leaning against Danny with her arm around his neck. The scene was so intimate that Katie felt embarrassed and awkward for interrupting their conversation.

"Hey, I, uh, got some ice cream," she faltered, her nervousness apparent in her voice. The woman turned toward Katie, dipping her head so it nearly rested on Danny's shoulder. She left her arm around Danny's neck and smirked at Katie. Danny looked up at Katie, not realizing what the scene truly looked like, but hearing her concern in her voice.

"Hey, Katie this is Angel, an old... *friend*," Danny said. The way he drug out the word friend made it seem like the relationship was much more. He stood up and shrugged Angel's arm from his shoulder. That didn't hinder the woman's flirtations. She kept her body pressed to his side, still maintaining the sexy, secretive smile.

"Hey," Katie said. Angel nodded at her, seeming to size up the competition. The conversation lulled in a moment of awkward silence.

Finally, Angel sighed and stood. "I'll see you around, baby," she purred. Her hand glided up to Danny's cheek. She brushed her fingers along his stubbled jaw then turned his face toward her and kissed him on the mouth. A lingering kiss that Danny seemed in no hurry to end.

Blood rushed to Katie's face. Her gaze fell as tears sprung in her eyes. She didn't wait for an explanation but turned and ran back inside the restaurant to the bathroom.

Once inside, she locked herself in the largest stall and let the tears flow freely. *How dumb could I be*, she berated herself, *to think that I was so special to a boy I barely know?* She slammed the side of her fist against the partition between her stall and the one beside her. She felt a scream building inside her, but fought its release until just a long, low grumble escaped her lips.

"Hey, are you okay in there?" A woman's voice called from the other side of the door.

Katie clamped her mouth shut. There was no way she was going to spill her sob story to a stranger. She sat there in silence on the toilet, waited the woman out, until the woman gave up and left. Katie heard the whoosh of the door opening then closing and listened a moment longer. Alone, she let the tears fall freely again, the embarrassment and rejection washing over her in waves. She blew her nose and flushed the tissue, then grew silent again as she heard the door swing open.

"Katie, are you in here?"

She heard Lisa's voice call out to her. She didn't reply. She didn't want to see the pity on her friend's face. Besides, Lisa would probably try to explain away her brother's actions. Then that would create a whole other issue. *Because how can I be friends with somebody who thinks cheating is okay*, she reasoned.

She saw Lisa's shadow under the stall door and heard the girl moving from stall to stall. The shadow stopped in front of Katie's stall.

"Look, I know you're in here." Lisa paused. "My brother's an idiot sometimes, but I know he didn't really mean to hurt you. He just doesn't think things through. And he doesn't see things the way everyone else does. We've told you, he's been on his own for a while."

"But that doesn't make it all right to kiss another woman in front of me," Katie answered through the door. She sniffled and wiped her nose again before exiting the stall.

"I know," Lisa said, "but that's just the way he is. Maybe he doesn't think you two are serious?"

"I mean, God, doesn't he know how stupid I feel now?"

"Not unless you tell him."

"Oh, no, I don't want to go back out there with that...*woman*, hanging all over him and me standing there like a moron."

"Oh no, she's already moved on to some other helpless Bozo. Danny sent me in here to get you. He wants to talk to you. He's outside waiting for you."

Katie washed her face and dried her hands. Her eyes were still red from the crying. *But at least my face isn't all red and blotchy*, she thought. She sighed at the thought of talking to him, but he was her ride home. So she'd have to talk to him eventually. "Fine." The two girls walked out of the bathroom.

Danny was sitting at a booth talking to some guys when Katie came out. She glanced at him, catching his eye, then walked out the side door of the restaurant to the car. Mark, Ronnie, Becky, and a few other people she didn't know were standing by Mark's truck, near Danny's car. Their conversation halted and they avoided looking her way as Katie opened the passenger door and slid in.

Danny was just seconds behind her and reached the car as she shut the door. He poked his head in the driver's window. "I didn't know Angel's kissing me was such a big deal. She does it to everybody."

"Well, that makes it all better then, huh?" She couldn't help being sarcastic. She crossed her arms in front of her and avoided looking at him. The image of the scantily dressed, overly sexualized woman hanging on him brought tears of anger to her eyes. She blinked hard to hold them back and imagined being home with her sisters, swimming at the local pool and hanging out with her friends. There was no way in hell she'd ever be sent away from home for this long if she could ever help it.

Danny opened the car door and fell behind the wheel. From the corner of her eye, she saw him reach across the distance between them. She kept her eyes forward, ignoring the gesture. When she didn't offer her hand, he withdrew his and started the car. "Fine. I guess I deserve that."

"Just take me home, Danny." She fought to keep her voice level.

"Why?" He paused in shifting the gear and turned to face her. "It's only 9:30. We were gonna go back to my place and play cards."

"Really?" She turned her hardest glare at him, not shying away from his steel blue gaze. "You just want to go on with the night like nothing happened?"

Danny sighed, shut the engine, and got out of the car. Katie watched as he walked over to Mark's truck and talk to the man.

Dammit, she thought, *he really is just going on with the night's plans and not giving a shit about what just happened.* She grabbed her purse and dug through it searching for a quarter for the pay phone. When her search produced no money at all, her body started to shake. There was no way in hell she was spending the rest of the night in Frosty's parking lot while Danny pretended like everything was fine. If nothing else, she would go inside Frosty's and beg the manager to let her call her aunt to come get her. She grabbed the door handle to get out just as he slid back behind the wheel.

"Where are you going? I thought you wanted to go home."

She released the handle and settled her hands in her lap. Letting Danny drive her home would keep her aunt from having to come get her. And the subsequent conversation with Maggie that would happen on the ride home.

"I guess they're all mad at me for ruining the night," Katie said. She didn't really want to talk to Danny, but she couldn't help but feel responsible for the change in plans.

"It's not ruined," Danny said. He started the car, waved at the group and pulled onto the highway toward Cypress Springs. Neither of them said much in the ten-minute ride, but Katie looked surprised when Danny flew past her aunt's house.

"I told you I wanted to go home," Katie said. The ride had calmed her some, knowing that she would soon be back in the comfortable surroundings of her aunt's bungalow. Now, her body vibrated with anger and worry. *Where is he taking me?*

"Yeah, I know, but we have to talk," Danny answered. "In private. Without all of our friends around or in a crowded parking lot." His fingers wrapped tightly around the steering wheel, the muscles in his arm pulled taut like cords of iron. "There are some things you need to know. Before this goes any further."

Katie settled her purse in her lap, ready to jump from the car the moment it stopped if need be.

Danny turned down the narrow road leading to his trailer. Instead of heading to his home, he pulled off the road near a shallow wash out. Cutting the engine, he took out a cigarette.

Katie gripped the door handle, readying herself to flee, but his calm demeanor didn't cause any alarms to go off in her head. So, she sat in silence, waiting for him to explain why he had humiliated her in front of their friends.

"Look, I know you're pissed," he said matter-of-factly. "I didn't think about how it would look to you." He lit the cigarette and blew the smoke out of the cracked window. "I've only ever had one serious...*girlfriend* before now."

She listened as he seemed to pick his words carefully. But the one word that stood out to her was 'girlfriend'. Was that what she was to him? Her heart softened a tiny bit, but she still kept her guard up.

"And even that was so fucked up I don't know how we lasted as long as we did."

"And that was, what's her name. Angel?"

"God. No." Danny screwed up his face as if disgusted, then took another hit from the cigarette. "She's partly to blame for all this." He waved a hand in front of his body.

"For what?"

"For how I see all of my relationships as casual. For how I usually focus on getting just one thing from a girl. For how I have many girls that are friends" --he emphasized the word friend-- "but only one, maybe two that were girlfriends." He cast a sideways glance at her before flicking the spent butt out the window.

"She was practically dry humping you, Danny." Katie heard her words laced with disgust but couldn't stop herself.

"And you let her kiss you. On the mouth. How'd you think I would react?"

"Pissed. Like you are now." He fiddled with the radio and found a top forty station. Each of them got caught up in their own thoughts, but Danny was the one who broke the silence. "It's not like you and I are *going* together or anything. I mean, you're leaving in two weeks, for Christ's sake."

"Don't you think I know that." Katie ducked her head, willing the tears away. "Then I'll be gone, and you can kiss, or do *whatever*, with whoever you want. I'll just be some summer fling you'll forget while Angel can pounce on you anytime she wants." The idea of that woman draped all over Danny caused Katie's ire to notch up a level. Her voice rose with her anger, and with her anger came the tears. *I'll be damned if I let him see me cry, though.* She turned away from him, but the move didn't go unnoticed.

Danny reached out and stroked her cheek. "Katie, baby, please..." Pain echoed in his voice. "What do you want me to say? You want me to swear my undying loyalty to you, even though we're hundreds of miles apart leading totally different lives?"

"It's only 150 miles." She sniffled and let out a half-laugh half-snort at the ridiculousness of her statement.

"Girl, seriously?"

"But knowing you're here. And she's here. And y'all are here together." The southern twang of her voice thickened as her annoyance heightened.

"Angel is part of my past. And there's nothing I can do about that. Plus, like I was trying to tell you, she's part of the reason I am the way I am." He tightened his lips and squeezed the steering wheel, twisting his hands back and forth along the leather cover. He smacked the dash with his open palm and climbed from the car. Drawing another cigarette from the pack he lit it and took a long drag before releasing a stream of smoke into the night air.

Katie sat alone in the front seat, her frustration with

Danny competing with her curiosity about the hold this Angel woman had on him. Realizing he wasn't getting back in the car anytime soon, she joined him outside.

"OK, I'll bite. What do you mean Angel is the reason you are the way you are?" She scooted up onto the hood and stared out across the small creek they were parked next to.

Danny finished his third cigarette and sent the butt flying off into the darkness. The orange tip streaked through the inky night and landed near the stream. Sighing, he moved to stand next to her.

"You know I haven't lived a typical teenage life," he began. "I was pretty messed up pretty early on. And my parents were only part of the reason." He paused here, and Katie heard him take a ragged breath. She didn't say anything, just gave him the space he needed to tell her what he had to say.

"Angel was my first." He kept his eyes on the ground and Katie kept her gaze on her lap. "Not only that, but she was seventeen and I was just about to turn fourteen. So, technically I think I was molested, but what boy doesn't want a fine, older woman for his first?" He gave a small hmph, trying to make light of the incident, but Katie caught the hint of sadness behind the attempted bravado.

She felt so bad for him. She wanted to reach out, to put her arms around him, but she didn't dare. "How?" she asked. "How, when, did it...happen?" She nearly whispered, wanting to give him the space he needed but also wanting to understand.

"It was Halloween night, and I was spending the night with my friend, Keith, after trick or treating. There was more tricking than treating that night, at least until Angel showed up. She was one of Newton's most notorious sluts who came to Keith's sister's sleepover. Why, I don't know. I didn't even think Sarah knew her." He paused here, fiddling with his shirt hem.

"Anyhow, Keith and I were camping out in a tent in the

back yard, and in the middle of the night, when we were all supposed to be asleep, I went inside to get a Coke. And Angel walked into the kitchen wearing only a thin tank top and these tiny black panties. I was surprised, to say the least, and felt like the luckiest son of a bitch alive. I had a half-naked woman standing right in front of me. And she didn't act embarrassed or try to cover herself. In fact, she strutted right over to me, took the soda from my hand and drank half of it."

"Wow," Katie whispered. She reached out for him, to pat his shoulder, but withdrew her hand when he turned from her. "What happened next?"

Danny took out another cigarette and lit it. After a couple of drags he picked up his story again. "She waggled her finger at me and told me she had something to show me. And I followed her out the screen door and into the utility shed in the garage. I said, 'So what is it?' and she pressed me against the washing machine and kissed me. At first, I thought, 'man, I hit the jackpot!' But then I felt her hand between my legs, rubbing me, you know. And I couldn't help but to get...*hard*.

He paused here, swallowing, and Katie equally angry and sad for the little boy lost that night. She didn't want to hear anymore, but like a highway car wreck, she couldn't turn away. She sat quietly, giving him the time to finish the story at his own pace.

"I won't gross you out with all the gory details. But for a first time, I guess it was OK. I mean, she knew what she was doing, which was a good thing, I guess, 'cause I sure as hell didn't. But after it happened, I went back to the tent with this guilty feeling, like I did something wrong. I mean, I know I wasn't supposed to fuck the town whore against my best friend's washing machine, but it was more than that. I knew I was too young to do it, and she was too old to do it with me."

"Did you tell anybody?"

"Hell, no. What was I supposed to say? Who would I tell?

Besides, it's supposed to be every teenage boy's dream, right?" In the dim light of a distant streetlamp, she saw him shrug as if to discard the feelings of betrayal. Then, his whole demeanor changed. He became the carefree boy she was falling in love with. He ran his hands over his face, then cast a generous grin her way. He moved to stand in front of her and took her hands in his. "Anyway, that was how I learned what drives you women crazy," he said playfully. He dragged her hand down his chest and stomach, dangerously close to his crotch, until she blushed and pulled away. Headlights flooded them as he leaned over to kiss her. Mark's truck pulled up next to the Nova.

"You two done tonguin' each other so we can play cards?" It was Ronnie who yelled from the back of the pickup. "I'm gonna kick your ass in poker tonight, man," he shouted as the truck lurched toward the trailer.

Danny helped Katie slide down from the hood, and they climbed back into the car. "I'm sorry for flipping out earlier," Katie said. "I know we're not *together* together, but you really hurt me tonight. If you just want this to be casual, let me know now so I can at least be ready if this ever happens again."

"It won't ever happen again," Danny told her. "And for as long as you're here in Cypress Springs, it's just you and me." He kissed her again securely on the mouth, started the engine, and drove toward his tiny trailer and their friends.

They carried on that night like nothing had happened, and no one in the group brought it up. Even though Katie told him she'd let it go, she couldn't shake the feeling that other relationships from his past would come back to haunt them.

CHAPTER 10
The End of Summer

ELEVEN YEARS AGO

Danny

Katie's comment stuck with him the rest of that night. And he couldn't shake it for the two weeks after the Dairy Queen incident. He worked hard over that time to convince her that she was the only one he was interested in, which was unusual for him. With all of his past flings, he had kept it totally casual, noncommittal. And he liked it that way. *But is that I want with Katie, just a casual relationship?* He could see himself wanting to be with her indefinitely. He didn't know if it was her innocence or her strength or a combination of the two that drew him to her. But as the summer and her time in Cypress Springs came to a close, he found himself on edge more often. And he knew it had something to do with her leaving.

Danny finished the pressure washing job he had that morning and drove to Maggie's house. His sister had spent the night with their cousin, Becky, across the road from Maggie's. When he slammed his car door, the two of them, followed by Ronnie, came into the yard.

"Hey, doofus," Lisa called. "Wanna take us down to Salt Creek so we don't have to walk in this heat?"

Katie emerged from the house, a cloth bag on her shoulder, and met Danny in the yard. She threw her arms around his neck, receiving the quick kiss he offered.

"Yeah, I guess so," he said, looking down at Katie. "I mean, if you don't mind. I know we were going to go by ourselves."

She smiled up at him. "I don't mind." She rose up on tiptoe and whispered in his ear, "We can be alone later tonight."

A wave of warmth washed over him at the suggestion, and he opened the door for her to climb in. After the rest crowded into the back seat, he drove them into Cypress Springs and turned left onto the main entrance to the small strip of land that housed most of the town. As they crossed one of the many small bridges that connected the area, Katie rested a hand on his arm.

"I want to try bridge jumping," she said, looking across him to one of the canals out his window.

Danny pulled off the road to face her. "Are you sure?"

"Maggie will be pissed if she finds out," Ronnie said.

"He's right," Danny said. "She might not let you go off with me anymore."

"Then she can't find out." Katie craned her head at the threesome in the back.

"We're not going to tell her," Lisa said, glancing first at Becky then at Ronnie. "Right?"

"Why are you looking at me?" Ronnie's look of surprise caused everyone in the car to laugh.

"Because," Becky responded, "you're the one who can't keep his fat mouth shut."

"Just find a place that nobody will really see us, though," Katie said, biting her bottom lip. "I mean, I don't want it getting back to her, just in case."

The look of excitement and concern flashed across her

face, and Danny debated if the idea was a good one. "I don't know," he said, putting the car in park. "Maybe we shouldn't chance it. You've got to be a good swimmer to dive into the creeks around here. If it's not deep enough, you could get hurt. Too strong a current and you could get pulled under."

"Did you forget? She's the one who pulled your ass out at 417 last month," Ronnie said. "That was epic!" He covered his mouth as loud laughter escaped. With a sharp look from Danny, Ronnie clamped his lips shut and sat back in the seat.

"I think I can hold my own," Katie said. "Like Ronnie said, I did pull your fake butt out of the canal my first week here."

"Come on, bro," Lisa said, nudging his shoulder. "Let her try it once. We've all done it."

"Yeah," Becky added, "it'll be something she can brag about at school next week." The car grew quiet at her comment.

Danny pulled back onto the road and followed it further onto the island. A few minutes later, they parked at the southern entrance that connected to an old, unused logging road. The river here wasn't too wide but had one of the deepest spots on the island, so Danny thought it'd be a good place for Katie's first jump. The current was the only thing that worried him.

Everyone clambered out of the car and set up a makeshift picnic area on the side of the creek. Though it was after lunch, the teens had brought snacks, drinks, and a battery-operated radio. Finding a top forty station broadcasting from Gainesville, the group spread out on the grassy, sun-splashed bank.

A few minutes later, Danny led Katie to the concrete connector and helped her climb up on the guard rail. The two stood above the creek, looking twenty feet down to the water below. "Are you sure you want to do this?"

Katie swallowed, her hand in his, and scooted her toes closer to the railing's edge. "Yeah, I'm sure."

"Okay, so it's not as bad as it looks." Danny ran his thumb over the top of her hand, a comforting gesture he hoped registered. Just seven weeks ago, she was pulling him from the water in an attempt to rescue him from what she thought was a drowning. He'd played a dirty trick on her, but it worked. It had led to their spending nearly every moment together that he wasn't working.

Now, she stood next to him above the water, her hand in his, ready to jump in. He could feel the tension in her grip and gave her hand a squeeze. He'd done this sort of thing ever since he'd learned to swim. Jumping off one bridge or another in the small coastal community was no big deal to him. He always waited until high tide, and none of the bridges were more than twenty feet above the water. The overpass they stood on now wasn't more than fifteen feet long and lower than most that connected the many parts of the small island to each other.

"When we jump, I've got to let go of your hand so we both can swim," he said turning to face her. "And there is a bit of current, so when you hit the water, start kicking and aim for that bank over there." He pointed to where their friends waited. Catching her gaze, he gave her arm a shake. "Look, you don't have to do this if you don't want to."

"No, I do," she said. "I mean, you seem to have so much fun when you do it, so why not?" She nodded her head and smiled up at him. "Yeah, I'm ready. Let's go."

"Yeah! You got this Katie," Becky yelled from the shore. Lisa and Ronnie stood beside her in anticipation of the couple's jump.

"On the count of three," Danny said, nodding for Katie's okay.

"On three," she said.

"One. Two. THREE." Danny jerked her arm, and the two leapt from the railing into the air. A second later he released her hand, and they hit the water. He kicked to the surface and searched for Katie, finding her ten feet away pushing toward the shore. He followed her and came up behind her as she reached the canal's steep edge.

"It wasn't that bad, huh?" Ronnie said, extending a hand to help her up the embankment as Danny gave her a push from behind.

He pulled himself from the water, and the two sat on the blanket spread out on the grassy incline.

Katie laughed and reclined back, breathing deep. "That was fun, but the current is stronger than I thought it'd be."

"Wanna go again?" Danny said. He glanced over at her, the droplets of water glistening on her nearly naked body. She wore the same pink and black bikini from the first day he'd seen her riding a bike down State Road 349. He jerked his head toward a squawking marsh bird achingly aware that if he stared much longer, he'd have to jump back in the water to hide his rising desire.

Katie sat up beside him. "I think I'll stick to the swimming holes. I don't have to work so hard there to keep my head above water." She reached across him and grabbed his t-shirt to tug over her head.

He loved that she felt comfortable enough to do that. Ever since the night of the Fireworks Festival, he'd been working hard to make sure that she felt safe around him. He'd let his usual, noncommittal ways hurt her that night when Angel had kissed him. He hadn't seen the big deal then, but after talking to her later that night, he realized how wrong he'd been. He'd vowed not to hurt her again.

He gave her leg a nudge then jumped up from his seat. "Then you sit here with the girls while Ronnie and I go a few more times." He smacked Ronnie in the stomach and took off running across the bank to the bridge.

They dove from the bridge and swam in the canal while the girls lay out in the sun. Katie jumped from the crossover once more with him, but the tide was going out, so the group called it a day. They all squeezed into the Nova, tired but content, and headed home.

Danny pulled into Ronnie and Becky's driveway and let them and Lisa out.

"I'm going to call Mom real quick to see if I can spend the night," Lisa said as she climbed from the back seat. "Wait for me?"

"Sure," Danny replied. Katie sat next to him and fiddled with the radio as the three entered the house. He turned toward her. "You want me to come over later tonight?"

"Do you have time? I thought you had to change the string in your weed whacker."

"I do, but that takes no time at all. I could come over after, say eight-thirty?" His hand rested on her knee, and she set the radio on a Journey song. "We could hang out on the dock. I'll bring some Twinkies and beef jerky."

She slid closer to him. "You know what happens when we sit on the dock?"

"We get eat up by mosquitoes?" He teased. He knew damn well what happened on the dock. It was something he looked forward to each time he came to Maggie Baxter's house. Making out with Katie, enjoying her body pressed to his, dreaming of the time when he would leave this town and all the prejudices against him behind, was the perfect end to any day.

"Well, that too," she replied, running her hand up his thigh. It stopped short of reaching his crotch. For a girl who was still a virgin, she sure had a way of making him hot. "I'll bring the sweet tea and the bug spray." Her fingers made tiny circles on his thigh, creeping closer and closer to his crotch.

The door to the house slammed, and Danny grabbed her hand in his, pushing it into the space between them. Lisa jogged to the car and leaned in the back window, grabbing her bag.

"Mom said I could stay." She waved at the two of them and bounded back to the house.

"Then I'll be over a little after dark," he said releasing Katie's hand. "I've got to finish the Winchester's yard before the renters arrive tomorrow. After I replace the weed whacker string"

She slid across the seat, gathering her clothes and reaching to remove his shirt that she still wore.

"Keep it," he said. "I'll get later." He leaned across the seat and kissed her. He wanted it to deepen, but it was the middle of the day, and anyone could come outside and catch them in a heated moment. No, he would wait for the cover of night to show her just how bad his urge for her was. He pulled back and patted her knee.

Katie smiled and opened the passenger door. She shut it behind her and strode across the dirt road to her aunt's house. Danny watched her from his rear-view mirror, tamping down the building desire he felt. It'd have to wait until tonight.

At half past nine, Danny climbed the steps to Maggie's house. A shaft of light sliced through the dusky twilight as Katie stepped out. She wore a short, flowered dress that felt smooth under his touch. She filled the space between them, pressing herself to him as his hands spanned her waist. Her mouth met his in a quick, promising kiss.

After a moment, they parted. "Where's your car," she asked, glancing behind him.

"I walked over from across the highway." He bent to kiss her again, his fingers finding the back of her neck, lacing in her hair as he took his time with her mouth. This was their last night together and he wanted to savor it.

When he finally released her, she took his hand like she had so many nights this summer to lead him around back to the dock.

"Let's go somewhere else tonight," Danny said, his voice

husky. "I want your last night here to be special." His words cast a sadness over the couple.

Katie bit her bottom lip before stepping in the house for a pair of shoes, then she followed him to his waiting car and they sped down the highway out of town.

Halfway between Cypress Springs and Newton, Danny turned off on a gravel road and slowed as he wound his way among the overgrown forest on each side. Only the headlights and the full moon illuminated the road in front of them. They rode in a tense silence, each lost in their own thoughts.

Finally, Katie spoke up. "Where are we going?"

"This place I found a few months ago while I was looking for a new fishing spot." He took a left and a few hundred yards further the woods thinned. In the center of the clearing stood an unmanned fire tower. Cutting the lights, he parked under the tower and turned to Katie. "If you're up for the climb, there's an amazing view from the top. And the moon's bright enough, we'll probably be able to see all the way to the river."

"What if we get caught?" Katie said. She slid out of the car and took his hand, looking up at the vague outline against a star-scattered, indigo sky.

"I've been by here a few times this summer, and I've never seen anyone here," he said, opening his trunk and pulling out a large towel. "We might need this to sit on up there." He took her hand and gave a gentle tug. "There *is* a caution sign" --he lifted the chain as best he could for her to go under-- "but I've been up there, just to check it out, in case I could talk you into coming with me one time."

She ducked under the chain, her eyes cutting a skeptical look at the stairs.

"I promise," he said, seeing her hesitation, "I wouldn't take you up there if I thought it wasn't safe." He waited until she was ready, then they began the ascent together with Katie in the lead.

They stopped a couple of times for each to catch their breath, and after a few moments, they reached the top. The door into the tower room was built into the floor. Danny stepped around her to give the door a shove with his shoulder. It opened and Danny pushed it wide enough for Katie to enter. Then he followed her in and dropped the door back into position.

The room they climbed into was a twenty-by-twenty square. The wooden floor covered a metal base. Knotted pine boards ran the length of each wall to hip height. The rest of each wall was screen mesh reaching up to the roof.

"Oh, man," Katie said, turning around to get a three-sixty view of the entire, unfurnished room. "They used this for a fire watch?" She moved cautiously around the room in the haze of the full moon as it illuminated the space a little.

"Yeah, I think it belonged to the Forestry division before a logging company bought the land and this tower." He watched as she picked her way to the room's outer edge and scanned the horizon. Her small frame, with her hair blowing in the gentle night breeze, was a silhouette against the midnight blue sky.

"It's beautiful up here," she said craning her neck to search the horizon. "I'm glad you talked me into it."

"I wanted your last night to be something you remembered," he said as he made his way over to her.

Her back to him, he circled his arms around her waist, his face dipping into her hair. The soft floral scent he associated with her permeated his senses, and he pulled her against him.

"I'll remember everything about this summer," she said, leaning back. "But this is pretty awesome." She waved her hand at the expanse below.

Danny dropped his mouth to the dip where her neck met her shoulder and kissed her. The skin there was warm against his lips. He felt her body give a little shudder at his touch, and a fire sprang in his groin. He loved that he could draw such a response from her.

117

She turned in his embrace and met his mouth with her own. Her lips were soft and inviting and Danny let his tongue flick out and run a trail along the rim of her bottom lip. She opened her mouth, and Danny took the provided opportunity. He thrust his tongue into her mouth, indulging in the taste of cinnamon and getting drunk on the feeling of her in his arms.

After a moment, they parted, and Katie turned from him. "You said we could see the river from here?"

He shifted, searching through the dim light. "It's hard to find it at night," he said, "but if anyone is night fishing you might see the light of their boat." They stood together scanning the western horizon until Katie jarred.

"Look." She pointed to a bobbing orb past the tree line and due west. "Is that a boat?"

Danny strained to make out the light's source. "Probably. It's low enough and in the right vicinity." He scooted closer to her, his hand resting on her hip. "So, is all you want to do tonight is to watch for boats on the river?" He hadn't thought about anything other than getting her alone on her last night in town. Maybe making out some. When she turned to face him, even in the dim light, he could see the desire in her eyes, and his need for her ignited.

He took her hand and led her to the middle of the room, pausing long enough to spread out the towel. They lowered themselves to the floor, lying side by side as their mouths met again in a fit of hunger. He rolled her over on her back and settled above her as his hands roamed her body.

"So, this is why you wanted me to sneak out with you," she said, her voice breathy as he trailed kisses across her throat.

He lifted his head to meet her gaze. "No, I just wanted to be with you, but this doesn't suck." He lowered his head for his mouth to continue its course.

Her fingers kneaded in the flesh under his shoulder blades, and he felt her mouth latch onto his shoulder. The sweet sting of suction fanned his yearning to get her naked and get inside her. *Whoa, D*, he said to himself, *slow down or you'll scare her.* He wiggled his shoulder, and she released him.

"You left a mark?" He turned his head to see if he could catch a glimpse of the strawberry.

She craned her head and licked the spot she'd just released. "Just a little one." Her lips were swollen from their kissing. "Now, you find a spot and leave your mark for me to remember this night. I'll be able to look at it on the ride home."

"Um, not where I'm going to put it." He watched her brows wrinkle as he pulled the edge of her dress collar down to expose the top of her bra. Raising an eyebrow, he waited for her say so to continue. She shrugged a shoulder and released a jagged breath as his fingers pulled the top of her bra back to reveal a tiny, taut nipple.

He ran the tip of his tongue over the little bud and another shudder raced through her. He took the kernel in his mouth and rolled it around on his tongue before giving his full attention to sucking it.

Katie's breathing was shallow, and soft moans mingled with whispered affirmations. Her eyelashes fluttered against her cheeks, and Danny watched her face as he gently bit down on the tiny nub. Her mouth expanded into a rounded O, and she arched her back to meet him. He released her nipple and found a section right above it to latch onto. He sucked the bit of flesh between his teeth and felt her shiver in response.

A moment later, he licked the spot but didn't cover her breast back up. Admiring his handiwork, he trailed his thumb over the dark mark against her paler skin. Her fingers played in his hair, then she gave a small tug, urging him to meet her mouth again for more foreplay.

His body rested easily on top of her, and he slipped a leg between hers, resting his hip on hers. "Katie, girl," he said, his breathing labored. "We've, uh, been here before. Just say the word, and I'll stop."

"I know you will," she said, her voice thick with desire. Her hand wove into his hair, and she pulled him back down to her. Wiggling beneath him she spread her legs wider, allowing him to press himself against her. Even through his shorts and her panties, he could feel the indentation of her sweet spot. His cock strained against the fabric of his clothes, and it was all he could do to keep himself from reaching down and freeing himself from this prison.

As their tongues explored, he began to grind against her. The feeling of his swollen member pressing into her, even through fabric, was maddening. He felt trapped between wanting to satisfy his own needs and not pushing her further than she was ready to go. His hand glided up her leg until it met the resistance of the elastic band of her panties. The silkiness of her skin sent another wave of lust through him, and he slid his fingers closer to juncture of her thighs.

A moan escaped her lips and he nearly lost it.

"Seriously," he whispered against her ear, "you're killing me." Course hair met his fingertips, and he glanced up to peer at her face. Her mouth with its swollen, dark lips released soft, short puffs of air. It was so hot to watch her reaction as his fingers played along the edge of her flower garden. But as he moved closer to her center, her brow creased, and he felt her body tense.

He rolled off of her and rearranged himself. Slowly, she sat up propping herself on her elbows.

"Why'd you stop?" She straightened her skirt and rose beside him, crossing her hands in her lap.

"Because you aren't ready." He turned to face her, brushing a strand of hair from her eyes. "And I'm not forcing myself on you. When it's time, we'll know it."

"You talk like we'll always be together. I'm leaving tomorrow Danny."

"I know. That's why I stopped." He turned the full

strength of his steel-blue gaze on her. She ducked her head. He knew the effect his full stare had on her. She seemed to never have gotten used to his directness. Finally, she peeked up at him and lifted her hand to finger the curls at the nape of his neck.

"But I wanted to."

"Wanted to what?"

"You know..." She waggled her eyebrows before letting her eyes dart to his crotch then back to his face.

"Make love? Have sex? Fuck?" At his last word, she withdrew her hand and turned from him. "If you can't say it, honey, you're not ready to do it."

"You don't have to be a jerk about it." The emotional distance between them doubled, and she crossed her legs in front of her, tucking the edge of her dress under her ankles.

He sighed, annoyed with himself for upsetting her, and softened his voice when he spoke again. "I'm sorry, baby. It's just I could tell by your reaction that it might have felt good--what I was doing--but you weren't ready to go all the way." He nudged her knee to get her to look at him and leaned over to kiss her fully on the lips.

"No," he continued, "now's not the right time for us to be having sex. The fact is you're leaving tomorrow morning and we don't know when we'll see each other again. You'll probably go home and get back to school and find yourself some boy there to fall in love with. And I'll be here, in Cypress Springs, doing what I do: working, swimming, raising hell, and missing you."

He could barely make out the smile that blossomed on her lips with his last words. The unspoken quandary they faced--her impending departure--was now out in the open. Tears rose in Katie's eyes and threatened to spill. "So, what next," she asked him.

"What do you mean? Do we pledge our undying love for each other and swear to never see anyone else," he asked in return. He didn't wait for a reply. "I can't promise that; I don't want you too, either, because we don't know what's going to happen in the future. I can tell you this--I do care about you. A lot. And I'll call you if you want, but I'm not much for writing. I want you to go back to Jacksonville, get through this next school year, and think about me every once in a while." He cradled her face in his hand and kissed her lips again gently. "And be careful who you hang out with. I'd hate to come up there and be thrown in jail for beating the shit out of someone who hurt you." Danny smiled and pulled her toward him. "Come here."

They stretched out again on the towel, and she rested her head on his chest. As they lay there staring through the mesh screen at the moon creeping over the tops of the trees, he wondered how he could make this girl his. Only time would tell.

CHAPTER 11
Getting Advice

PRESENT DAY

Katie

Sitting on the dock like she had so many years ago brought back so many memories. The nights she would sit out here with Danny and talk, and kiss, until the mosquitoes got so bad, they drove her inside.

As angry as she had been to be sent here, it ended up being the best time of her life. After Danny finally started coming over, she spent nearly every evening and many weekend days with him. What had started out as a serious punishment for her bad behavior had turned into the greatest gift. She'd found her soul mate, the man she wanted to spend her life with. Even at fifteen, she knew Danny was her forever.

Now, she debated the strength of their bond. He'd left her alone on their honeymoon. Driving away like he'd done other times, and she was left wondering what she could have done differently to prevent it.

"There's nothing I can do but love him," she said out loud. And she did love him. He was a good man, who loved her and their children, and worked at the shipyard in the fiery hulls of ships to provide for them. Sure, his behavior was a little quirky and erratic, but he'd never harmed her or the children. He just didn't know how to express his feelings effectively.

She gave a little laugh. "I sound like a shrink," she said, thinking of the psychologists that sat in on parent-teacher meetings at the school. Many of the destructive children were described like that. And Katie understood. Danny's childhood had been stunted. Forced to fend for himself at a young age, he didn't learn to express his frustration constructively. He had to always be looking over his shoulder, watching out for people who would take advantage of him.

Katie's chin dropped, and she fiddled with the hem of her shirt. Would she have allowed this relationship to continue had she known that his issues were so deep and hard to overcome? *Of course, I would.* The thought jumped in her head the second the question was raised. She loved him. He was worth the struggle, she just had to make him see it.

Her stomach rumbled and reminded her that she hadn't eaten real food in hours. Not that she'd been able to keep much down. The stress of the wedding, the tense ride to Cypress Springs, and the ongoing conflict with her husband didn't help her situation. And when would be a good time to tell him about her *situation*?

She rubbed her stomach and stood. The shade had been nice, but the Florida humidity made sitting on the dock any longer unbearable. She turned back toward the house and saw Maggie at the end of the dock.

"I was just coming to get you," she said. "I have a sandwich and some grapes for you. And I've aired out the house. No more smelling like collard greens and ham."

"Thanks, Aunt Maggie." Katie followed her into the kitchen and sat at the kitchen table.

"Did you get clear on anything out there?"

Katie took a bite of her sandwich and a sip of tea before

responding. "Just that we've got a lot of work to do if we're going to make this marriage work."

"So, you're sticking it out?" Maggie set the bag of grapes on the table in front of her and plucked one from the stem. "But then again, it is sort of too late to change your mind. You should have thought about that before you got married yesterday."

"That's true," Katie agreed. "And believe me, it's not like I haven't thought about how his past, *our* pasts, would affect our future. I just know that I love him, and he loves me. And I have to believe that's enough."

"Sometimes it is. Sometimes it isn't. It took y'all this long to realize you were meant to be together. Maybe that's a promising sign. Maybe, though, all that time apart was a warning that you didn't heed."

Katie took another bite of her sandwich, and a silence settled over the two women. Aunt Maggie always knew when to nudge Katie and when to leave her alone. Sitting with her, allowing her to be in the stillness of her own mind yet still available to talk, if need be, was something Katie appreciated about her aunt. Her grandma, Lena, would push and push until a decision was made. It had driven Katie to make rash decisions she'd later regretted.

She turned over the thought that all the failed attempts of the past were warnings to her about the instability of their relationship. She could see all the misfires as signals not to pursue anything with Danny. That their life together would be too hard, filled with struggles. But what life worth living wasn't?

Anyhow, that wasn't the way she saw it. All of the times they almost committed but didn't was preparing them. They had to learn what they *didn't* want to be ready to recognize and fully embrace what they *did* want when it appeared. And she knew, without a doubt, that she wanted him.

"You asked me once why I didn't keep a tighter rein on you while you stayed with me that summer, and I never did give you a clear answer." Maggie's voice broke through Katie's contemplations. "I believe," she continued, "in giving people the chance to learn from their own choices. Now, mind you, I never would have let you get into anything so serious that it'd ruin your life, but you had to make some choices when you were young that taught you consequences to your behavior."

"So, you had no problem with me seeing Danny, even though he was so much more...*worldly* than me?"

"Sweetie, he wasn't though." Maggie covered Katie's hand with her own. "I saw that you two needed someone and figured you could be that for each other. He may have been living like an adult for a while, but inside, he was just a lost little boy that needed to have someone believe in him."

Tears welled in Katie's eyes at the idea of her husband, so tough and protective, as a broken boy who had no one to trust. That her aunt could see it, and she believed enough in Katie's goodness to help Danny, was touching.

"I saw that you needed someone, too. Something neither I, nor your family, could provide for you. You needed to discover your own self, be your own person, make mistakes and learn from them." Maggie rose to refill the tea glasses. "And the same is true now."

Katie finished her lunch and rose to put the dishes in the sink.

"Tell me, how did you two finally get together? Have y'all been keeping in touch all these years?" Maggie moved the conversation to the front porch. Turning on the fan and settling into a rocking chair, she waited while Katie situated herself on the swing.

"Yeah, we kept in touch," Katie said. The excitement of finding postcards postmarked from Cypress Springs with nothing but his name and a smiley face on them, the short phone calls, the couple of short trips she'd taken to Cypress Springs all brought a smile to her lips and warmth to her heart. "It was hard, especially when he separated from his wife and was fighting for custody of his boys. We lost touch during his marriage and the divorce, but the last year or so, he'd call out of the blue and I'd think, maybe we had chance."

"Oh, yeah?" Maggie nodded, encouraging her to continue.

"It sounds stupid, now," Katie said, nudging the swing into motion, "but Danny got into a vocational program for single parents. That's where he learned to weld. And on the nights he was in school, I'd drive up and wait for him to take a break or wait until the class was over. I'd bring him some dinner and we'd park behind the building, just to talk and see each other."

"You drove an hour and a half just to spend a few minutes with him?" The astonishment in her aunt's voice was obvious, and Katie blushed at the ridiculousness of her actions.

"It was only a few of times, but yeah, I drove all the way from college, in Tallahassee just to see him. He had his boys and couldn't come see me without bringing them along. Plus, he worked so much on top of going to school. It was just easier for me to make the trip."

"Well, that just shows you how dedicated you are to him."

"Yeah, those were times when I had the most hope." Katie's eyes misted over again. *Man, my hormones are really running wild*, she thought. "Until I asked him to move to Tallahassee when he finished his training." She grew quiet and the swing slowed.

Maggie gave her a moment, then asked, "What'd he say?"

Katie turned toward her aunt. "He said he couldn't uproot his boys again." She swiped a hand across her cheek and continued, "He'd just moved out of Newton to be closer to his sister, who helped him with the boys, and didn't want to yank them out of a stable situation. Which was totally understandable."

"It was, but it wasn't fair to you." The phone rang inside, and Maggie rose to go answer it. "Be right back, honey."

Katie settled back in the swing, listening to the squeals of children down the road. She glanced over to the house that used to be occupied by Danny's aunt and uncle. It had been updated since the last time she'd seen it. The door opened and a young woman, close to her age stepped on the porch. Katie didn't recognize her but doubted that it could have been Becky Morris. From what she remembered, all of the Morris kids had moved away quickly after graduation.

The phone call was taking longer than Katie expected, and she needed to get back to the hotel. Once her aunt came back out, Katie decided to ask her for a ride. As she waited, her thoughts drifted to memories of those few carefree times she and Danny had met up. She had planned to attend his vocational commencement ceremony, but life had intervened again, and they lost touch once more.

WHILE YOU WERE GONE

CHAPTER 12
Katie's Graduation

EIGHT YEARS AGO

Katie

With her senior year in high school over, Katie was preparing for the next journey in her life--college. Her lifelong dream was to be a teacher, and her application to UNF had been accepted. She'd start in the fall, but for now, there lay a whole summer of fun and freedom as an adult with no real responsibilities except the part-time job she had at the daycare center.

Her graduation over, along with the family party her grammy had organized, Katie was preparing to meet her friends at a beach house one of the parent's had rented for the weekend. As she sat on the couch waiting for her friend Jennifer to arrive, a knock at the door had her jumping from her seat. She swung open the door. "It's about time. I..." Her words dried on her tongue. Standing in her entryway was Danny.

"What on earth?" Her heart raced with the flood of memories that bombarded her. Memories of the summer three years ago when she was exiled to tiny Cypress Springs as punishment for her teenage rebellion. Finally reviving herself, she lunged at Danny, hugging him fiercely. "I can't believe it."

"Well, believe it because here I am." He tightened his grip on her and Katie felt the nudge of his nose in her hair. His lips pressed a kiss against her temple before releasing her.

"Katie, honey, why don't you invite your young man in?" Lenora Mayfield called over her granddaughter's shoulder.

Katie stepped out of the doorway to allow Danny access to the small living room. As she guided him to the sofa, her stomach twisted into knots. Though they had spent one glorious summer together three years before, the last time she saw him, when he visited the summer of '86, had been disastrous. Still, Katie couldn't remember the exact circumstances and let the memory slip away. He was here now. That was all that mattered.

Danny sat on the edge of the sofa. Katie's younger sisters hovered nearby in kitchen entryway. He fidgeted with the hem of his t-shirt, a sure sign he was anxious. Katie sat next to him and offered a smile to ease his nervousness.

Lena, who had left the pair alone for a moment, returned from the kitchen with glasses of iced tea. "We're so glad you could make it down, even if you did miss all the festivities. The graduation was wonderful. I'm so proud of my girl." Lena brushed her hand over Katie's and smiled at her granddaughter.

"Yeah, well, I couldn't have made it to downtown Jacksonville if I'd wanted to," Danny said. "Too many one-way streets and all. I ain't used to big city traffic." He nodded a thank you for the tea and glanced sideways at Katie. "So, what are your plans tonight?"

"Some friends of mine are going out to the beach for a party, and Grammy said I could go if I'm back at a reasonable hour." Katie smiled at her grammy. Their relationship had mended over the last three years, but the matriarch still held a tight reign over the girls. Especially Katie. Actually, it was the trip to Cypress Springs that had made the biggest difference in Katie and her outlook. Now, a piece of that history sat in front of her with no explanation as to why he was there. Still, it made her heart happy.

"Hey, I have an idea." Her face lit up with the thought of spending more alone time with Danny. "Why don't you come to the party with me? We can catch up. You can meet some of my friends for a change."

Danny tilted his head, as if considering the idea. "I can't really stay that long. I just came to see you for a little bit."

"It was a long drive just to stay for *a little bit*," Katie pointed out. "Please, won't you come?" She stuck out her bottom lip and offered the big doe eyes that had won her many pool games against him that summer of '85. After a moment, he caved.

"Do you have a ride? To your party? I could drive you out there, but I can't stay long."

"I'll call Jennifer and tell her I'll meet her there." Katie jumped from the couch and disappeared into the kitchen to make the call. The call was quick and Katie returned to hear her grandma giving Danny strict orders.

"Now, Danny, I trust you'll take her straight there and make sure she meets her friends." The woman leaned in to emphasize her point.

"Yes, ma'am," Danny replied, his voice snagging on the words. He cleared his throat and smiled weakly at the elderly woman.

"Grammy!" Katie stood by her grandma's chair. "It'll be fine. You can trust Danny. I know you've heard me talk about him over the years."

"Of course." Lean stood and hugged her granddaughter. "Just because someone is trustworthy doesn't mean I won't worry." She gently squeezed Katie's face between her palms. "You're precious cargo." She kissed her granddaughter on the forehead and released her.

"We'll be fine." Katie picked up her boho purse and

backed toward the door. "Jennifer will bring me home later."

Before her grammy could reply, Katie pulled Danny out the door and the pair hurried to his car. oo many times had she ridden in that front seat, sitting right next to Danny, with the gear shift between her knees and his hand on her thigh. Sliding in the front seat, Katie caught her breath as memories washed over her. A sense of melancholy settled around her then, and she sighed as Danny slid behind the wheel.

"That was a quick escape." Danny started the car. "I didn't even get to thank her for the tea. She'll think I'm just some yahoo with no home training."

Katie cut her eyes at him.

"Hey, I might have practically raised myself, but I still know to be polite to old people."

The tension that had surrounded them since his arrival dissipated with the comment and the couple laughed.

As he backed out of the driveway and pulled onto the main road, he glanced over at Katie. "You look good," he said, his eyes traveling the length of her body. "I like the highlights." He touched her hair. He drove slowly down the residential street and brushed the fringed hem of her denim mini skirt. "And the clothes."

"Can you just pull over here for a second," Katie said, pointing to a newly paved entrance to a yet developed subdivision.

Danny obliged and put the car in park. He turned to her, the steel blue of his eyes meeting the light brown of hers.

Before she realized what she was doing, Katie leaned in and kissed Danny deeply. Two years was a long time and even then, the visit had ended badly. Still, he was here now, looking just as gorgeous as ever in his Levis and blue tee shirt. His hair was little longer, a little blonder, and a little curlier. His skin was still a deep bronze. *Probably from working outside*, Katie thought, as she pulled away from the kiss and looked him over.

Surprise registered on his face, but the look was

interrupted by a grin stretching across his full lips. He reached out to stroke her hair. His hand glided down her neck and pulled her back to him. He kissed her this time, more deeply, more desperately than before. His tongue edged its way into her partially opened mouth. A soft sigh escaped her. When they parted, his fingers continued to play softly her hair. He stared at her, as if trying to memorize her every feature.

"We better get going before your grandmother shows up behind us," Danny said, putting the Nova in gear and pulling back out onto the road.

The forty-five-minute drive to the beach was filled with questions and answers, each bringing back memories from the summer they'd fallen in love. Katie asked about his sister, Lisa, and Ronnie and Becky. Danny wanted to know about her feelings on the end of high school and which college Katie would be going to. Katie felt like she'd never tire of hearing his voice and peppered him with questions to keep him talking.

"So how much further?" Danny asked as he switched the channel on the radio.

"Not far now. So, why can't you stay for the party?"

"I've got to get back to Newton. That's where I live now."

"What's your hurry? You could stay for a while. You could spend the night and go back tomorrow." Katie looked slyly at him.

He slowed the car and turned into one of the beach access parking lots and cut the engine. The lot was deserted and remote and easily missed if a driver wasn't paying attention.

"I have to get back tonight. I can't stay." He paused, pulling a cigarette from the pack above his visor. "Because there's someone waiting for me back in Newton. That's what I came to tell you." He tilted his head to light the tip then inhaled deeply.

Katie's chest tightened and she couldn't catch her breath. *What an idiot I am*, she thought, *to believe he'd come here for me. To give us another chance.* She'd never forgotten him and always fantasized that one day they'd be together, that he was her *soul mate.* She swiped at her eyes with the back of her hand, turning away from him. W*hy? Why am I always the one to get screwed in life? First, my dad leaves. Then, Mom dies. Now this, with Danny? WHY???*

"Katie, look at me," he said gently turning her to face him. He ran his thumb under her downcast lashes. "I'm getting married. In a few weeks."

Katie sucked in her breath, the news like a punch to her gut. "What? Why?" The news was just too unbelievable. All the dreams she had of one day being with him were shattering right in front of her.

"Crystal's pregnant." He locked eyes with her, not even trying to dodge her stare.

Those steel blue eyes that had both unnerved her and made her feel truly seen once again bore into her. She felt the burn of that gaze straight to her core. Katie was the first to turn away and let the tears flow freely.

"After the last time we saw each other," he said, a certain timbre in his voice that she'd never heard, "I really thought it was over between us. You said so yourself. If I couldn't move here to be with you, then you didn't want to see me anymore. So I started running wild again, like before I met you. And Crystal was a girl I knew back when I went to Dixie High. Well, we sort of started seeing each other and before I knew it, she was pregnant."

"The one thing you'd tried to avoid all these years," Katie whispered. Her heart was breaking. Irrational thoughts ran through her mind--*If I'd only let him have me that last night in Cypress Springs at the cove, this wouldn't be happening. He'd be marrying me instead of her.*

"Yeah, I've been lucky up until now. But it's not that bad. I love her. Not like I do you. It's different. She's gonna have my baby."

"God," Katie cried. She got out of the car and walked to

the edge of the boardwalk. How could this be happening? He was her one. The only man she wanted to be with. She leaned over the railing, sniffling, trying to stop the tears. She felt his arms encircle her waist, and she turned to bury her head in his neck. "You don't have to marry her. This isn't the olden days. Her parents aren't going to force you into a shotgun wedding, are they?" She still couldn't look at him. She couldn't let him see her so broken.

"Katie, I love her," he repeated. "And it's time I grew up and took care of my responsibilities."

Katie laughed out loud. "You've been taking care of your responsibilities for years now, Danny. Ever since I knew you, you've been paying your own way."

"Yeah, and now I have a baby on the way. My child. And I'm nearly twenty-one. Old enough to do the right thing."

"And what about me? Us?" Katie looked up at him then.

He didn't say anything. He didn't have to.

She knew the answer. Before she could stop herself, her mouth was on his. Her hands grasped his shoulders and pulled him to her. She didn't care that he was getting married or having a baby with his new girlfriend. *In fact,* she thought, *if I'm never going to see him again, I'm going to make sure he remembers what he gave up.*

As their kiss deepened, she slid her hands down his back to the waistband of his jeans. The soft skin at the small of his back was so inviting. She didn't have much experience with guys, but she did know how to tempt them. The gentle touch of her fingers on his bare skin had him moaning under her lips.

For his part, Danny didn't try to stop her, didn't push her away. He held her body close to his, letting his hands roam freely over her soft curves. "Dammit woman," he said through gritted teeth. "What are you doing to me?"

"Making sure you remember." She flicked her tongue out, teasing him before taking his in her mouth to suckle and enjoy. She needed to do this, she reasoned. This was her goodbye, once and for all. She'd lose herself in him for this brief time, not giving a damn about the risk or the consequences.

She slid her hand into his waistband and felt the warm skin of his hip. Their bodies were so aligned she knew the instant he started getting hard. His reaction to her touch was an aphrodisiac and she wanted more. She wanted him.

As if reading her mind, he slid his hands up her waist, brushing them against her breasts as he lifted her up onto the railing. She wrapped her legs around his waist and pulled him to her. With their hands exploring, their mouths devouring each other's, it wasn't long before Danny lifted her from the railing and carried her to his backseat.

The sun was nearly gone. Only streaks of orange played along the western horizon. Danny flipped on the radio and Night Ranger floated softly around them.

Katie lay back in the seat pulling Danny down with her. His mouth found hers again, and her legs once again wrapped around his waist.

Neither of them mentioned Danny's predicament, or her party, or that this may be the last time they saw each other. The only thing that mattered was this moment--the two of them wrapped around each other in the back seat of his Nova.

Katie had imagined this very scene time and again ever since their last night together in Cypress Springs that summer. It didn't even matter how cliche it was to be in the back seat of his car, just that it was him. As his hand slid under her shirt and caressed her stomach, He pulled back long enough to look at her once more. His gaze told her that he, too, had been thinking of this meeting for a while.

She tugged at his tee shirt, pulling it over his head to reveal a bronze, sculpted chest she hadn't seen in years. She ran her hands over his chest, feeling the velvety soft hair on her palms.

Danny dropped his head to kiss her neck, her shoulder,

her ear, his breathing labored. He bent to lay kisses along the valley between her breasts and pulled her shirt up to expose her pink, front fastening push-up bra. Popping first one clasp, then the next, it was a matter of seconds before he would unburden her. With the last clasp pinched between his thumb and forefinger, he took her mouth in his again.

"Danny, you have to stop," she said, pushing him gently. "As badly as I want to, I'm not a homewrecker. Or a whore." She scooted back against the side panel and tugged at her skirt.

"I never said..."

"I know you didn't, but...well, I'm sort of feeling like you might be thinking it." She knew she'd initiated the whole thing with the first kiss, but somehow, she expected him to have more restraint, being older and all. *I guess I gave him too much credit.*

"Yeah. Well." Danny sat up opposite her, buttoning his jeans. "You're the one who wrapped your legs around me, ready to ride me like a hobby horse." He dropped his head against the back of the seat.

Never one to pull punches, his words stung. She had tempted him, but he was the one with a pregnant girlfriend waiting for him back in Newton. He had more to lose. He should have been the responsible one.

"I didn't see you telling me no." She fastened her bra hooks and pulled her shirt down. "And you're the one getting married next week. What'd you think? You could fuck me tonight and go back to her tomorrow as if nothing happened?" Katie reached for the seat release. Opening the door, she climbed out of the back seat. She straightened her halter straps and smoothed her hair. "You can't just drop this news on me and expect me to be okay with it."

Danny climbed out of the car, bringing his Marlboro pack with him. He lit the cigarette and flicked the match into the sand.

"I thought you wanted this, Katie, what with the way you

practically tackled me over there," he motioned toward the boardwalk railing. "You've really got to work on your subtlety."

"God, I do want it. I want you. I have for three long years, but not like this. If I'm going to be with you, it's gonna be just you and me. Forever." Katie realized the absurdity of her statement even as it slipped from her lips. They'd never be together now. He was marrying some other woman and starting a family with her. And she was about to start college. She looked longingly out over the dunes towards the ocean. The waves crashing in the distance soothed her. The breeze had lessened with the impending nightfall.

Danny appeared at Katie's side. His hand went to the nape of her neck, gently massaging there. She didn't pull away, instead closing her eyes and fighting back the tears that once again threatened. She was so tired of almost being his. Maybe they weren't meant to be. Katie turned to him, wiping at a stray tear.

"Look, I appreciate you coming all the way here in person to tell me this, but I don't think I can handle anymore. I love you, Danny. Always have and probably always will. I'm just tired of coming in second all the time." She reached for his hand, giving it a gentle squeeze before removing it from her neck. "I deserve to be first for once."

"I know. And I'm sorry I screwed things up for us." He pulled his hand away and shoved them both in his front pockets. "Come on." He jerked his head in the direction of the car. "I promised your grandma I'd get you safely to your party."

"Oh, it's just down the beach a ways. I think I'll walk. I need time to think." She stroked his cheek with her hand before leaning in the car window to grab her purse. "Besides, we'd just have to say goodbye again."

Danny snaked his arm around her waist, pulled her to him and kissed her. Quickly, he cleared his throat, got in the Nova, and drove away, never looking back.

Neither did Katie.

CHAPTER 13
Making a Living

FIVE YEARS AGO

Danny

It killed him inside, leaving Katie on the beach that day. As he drove back to Newton in the dark, his thoughts kept returning to their last night together three years ago. The game of 'what if?' played on a loop in his mind. What if they had slept together back then? Would his life be any different now? He would have had the knowledge that he was her first and she'd taken his heart, but life would have gone on. It's not like she would have moved to Cypress Springs or he to Jacksonville. None of it was possible at the time.

What if he hadn't gotten back together with Crystal? Would he had tried to move to Jacksonville to be with Katie? No, that wasn't a choice either. He couldn't show up at her house, with her grandma and sisters there, expecting to have a place to stay. He didn't even have a job lined up there. The only option that made sense was to stay near Cypress Springs.

He had a steady job at Lehman's Mill Work, a local lumber yard south of Newton. He had solid friends from work, especially Hal Montgomery, an older guy who was like the brother he always needed since his own brother Jimmy didn't have much to do with the family. And he had family here--a small support system in his sister and his cousins, plus some aunts and uncles who still checked up on him.

Now, he'd have his own little family. He was settling down with a girl he cared about. And she was having his baby.

Damn, he thought as he turned off I-10 in Sanderson. *I'm going to be a dad. I've really got to get my shit together.* He still had an hour and a half to go before he reached the tiny single-wide he and Crystal rented on the south end of Newton, but he made up his mind. It wouldn't do to keep living in the past. He had a child on the way and a woman at home waiting on him. Best to leave his adolescent crush in the past.

But that's the thing, he thought, *it wasn't just a crush. It was real. And I just fucked it up.*

It took nearly three years, a half-hearted marriage, and the birth of his second son to force Danny to realize this wasn't the life he'd wanted for himself. Sure, he loved his children; they were the reason he got up every morning and he didn't regret having them, but Crystal wasn't the type of mother they deserved. In the four years they'd been together, she'd been arrested twice for drug use. He'd kicked her out too many times to count, always to let her come home when she crawled back crying to him that she missed her boys. Promising that she was done with the drugs and she'd get her life together. His guilt overrode his better judgment and, each time, he took her back.

This last time, though, seemed to be working. Crystal spent the weekend in jail before her court appearance. Judge Walker had threatened her with removing the boys from the home if she got arrested one more time. Danny was furious. He wasn't about to lose hie boys because his wife was an addict. Crystal promised to get help and joined a free AA group at the church on the corner of their street. She met with them every Thursday night, but the worst part was her job. With her record, the only job she could get was at The Squirrel's Nest, a bar on the outskirts of Newton.

Danny had just walked in the door from work and plopped down on the couch when Crystal ran from the bedroom at the honk of a car horn outside.

"Shit, I'm going to be late," she cried as she tugged at the hem of her skirt.

"Who's that?" Danny asked, watching her slip on her heels. Crystal was wearing a tube top that barely covered her breasts and a miniskirt so short that Danny was sure she would catch cold from the draft. "And why do you have to wear such trashy clothes there?"

"I've told you before, it helps me get better tips," she said, leaning over to peek out the window. A blue Toyota coupe waited in the driveway for her. "That's Juliet, a girl that works with me. She promised to give me a ride if I pay her. You got ten bucks I can have until I get home?"

"I can drive you and save the ten bucks," Danny said reaching for his shoes.

"Who's going to stay with the kids, huh?" Crystal said, her hand outstretched. "Besides, my ride is already here. It's just easier this way."

"It'll take a minute for me to get my shoes back on. Go grab the boys."

"No. They've...already had their baths," she said, glancing down the hall. The car honked again, and Crystal went to the door to signal for it to wait. "Just give me the money to pay her, and you'll get it back tonight when I get home."

Reluctantly, Danny dug some bills from his wallet and gave them to her. "Speaking of the boys, where are they?"

"In the back room." She took the bills from him and tucked them in her top.

"I wish you'd find another place to work. The Squirrel's Nest is no place for the mother of my boys to be every night."

"We've already gone over this," she said wobbling toward the door. "There's nowhere else in this shitty little town that I'd make what I do in tips. You don't make enough to support all of us. So, unless you want me to trick on the street corner, the bar it is." She turned her back to Danny and bent over to straighten the back of her shoe. Danny was given a clear view of her thong-covered crotch.

"Dammit, Crystal go put some fucking clothes on!" He rose from his seat and stepped toward her. She flipped him off and scooted out the door. Danny reached the door just as she jumped in the passenger seat and the car sped away. He beat his fist on the interior wall as one of his boys ran down the hall naked and dripping.

"Daddy, you're home!" A slippery, four-year-old Trent threw his arms around Danny's legs. Shock registered in Danny's brain at the same moment as fear. He hurried down the hall and found Clay, the two-year-old playing in the bathtub. Lifting the child, Danny cursed his wife and and his life. *How the hell could she be so clueless?!* To leave the boys alone in the bathtub just to rush to work. And not even tell him where they were. What kind of mother was she?

After drying and dressing both boys, Danny made the three of them a quick dinner of noodles and sauce from a can. He locked the doors, put on a cartoon for the boys to watch, then took a quick shower. In the bedroom that he shared with his wife, he dug out a box from the far bottom corner of the closet. Sitting on the edge of the bed with his hair dripping and a towel wrapped around his waist, he lifted the lid and fingered the letters that lay on top. All of them were from Katie. She'd sent them over the years, describing her life with her sisters, times with her friends, and her life in college. Each letter ended the same--*with love, Katie*. Her neat, flowery script reminded him of her soft curves, her gentle voice, the smell of her hair.

As he sat there reminiscing, he felt a stirring in his groin. He hadn't desired Crystal, or any other woman for that matter, in a long while. It was still Katie that stoked a fire in him. One that he couldn't douse, even if he wanted to. Each letter he received, he had responded with a phone call. He'd once told her that he didn't write letters, but he'd recently taken to putting his thoughts down. Every time he wrote down what he was thinking, feeling, he'd end up tearing it to bits or crumpling it up and burying it in the trash can. What man writes out his feelings? That's what women did.

He stuck his head out the bedroom door to check on the boys. They were laying on the couch where he'd left them. A giggle from Trent wafted down the hall to him. Danny smiled softly at the thought of his boys and their happiness. That was all he really wanted was for them to be happy and to know that they were loved.

He returned to the bed and the box full of letters. Pulling the most recent one out, he unfolded it and a picture of Katie fell to the floor. Danny picked it up and took a good look at it. Her hair was dark, not the reddish color it had been that first summer together, and shorter than he remembered. She smiled in the photo, but her eyes seemed sad, like her life wasn't everything she thought it would be either.

Her sadness hurt him. He could still remember the look on her face when she saw Angel, an ex of his, kiss him at Frosty's. That was the moment he realized that he loved Katie. He'd never told her face to face that summer, but he'd felt it. And now he'd lost her. He was in a marriage of convenience with a woman who was too self-centered to realize her husband didn't love her, and there was little he could do without uprooting the boys.

Lifting one of the letters, he brushed it across his lips and thought of the last time he'd kissed her. It was a quick kiss of broken promises made by children. If she had asked him to stay that night of her graduation, he might have considered it, regardless of Crystal's pregnancy or Katie's college scholarship. He loved her. That would never change, but she'd done the right thing by walking away first. He had been too weak to.

He let out a huff of breath and dropped the letter into the box. Rummaging through the contents, he pulled out the stack of cash and counted it once more. He was surprised Crystal hadn't found it yet. Five thousand dollars was enough blow to kill a stable full of horses. But Danny had other plans for it. He wasn't quite sure what those plans were yet, but he knew he needed to save money. For a brighter future for his boys or as a means of escape, he didn't know. Still, he had it if he needed it.

Securing the lid on the box, he buried it back in the corner he'd taken it from. He found some underwear and shorts in a basket at the foot of his bed and got dressed. In the living room, he found his two boys asleep on either end of the couch. He carried them one by one to their beds, then returned to the couch to watch some TV before drifting off to sleep.

Sometime in the middle of the night Danny was awakened by the sound of the front door shutting.

"Why are you asleep on the couch, baby?" Crystal sat down beside him and placed her hand on his chest. She smelled like liquor and cigarette smoke. "Waiting up to see if I got home all right?"

He took her hand in his. "I don't know. I guess I just dozed off watching TV." The memory of her running from the house while the boys were in the bathtub came back to him, but he quashed the urge to fight with her. Thoughtless as she was, she was still the mother of his children. He had to remember that she hadn't been raised with good role models either. They were both new to this whole adulting-parenting-responsibility thing. It was scary, but this was his life. He wanted to make the best of it for his boys.

Crystal held out a ten-dollar bill. "Here's the money I owe you. I told you I'd make it back tonight in tips."

"Keep it," he said, giving her hand a soft push. "You might need it later on for gas."

She cocked her head and stared at him, her brow furrowing. "You feeling all right?" She touched her hand to his head then pulled it back.

"Yeah," he said sitting up beside her. "I'm just tired of struggling. And fighting with you. We got two boys together, Crystal. Responsibilities. We can't be just doing things we want anymore, especially not stupid, thoughtless shit that could hurt them." She opened her mouth to protest, but he held up his hand. "I mean it. I don't want to fight. I just want you to promise me...Promise that our boys will come first. Always."

"Yeah, sure, baby, whatever you say." She stood, her head down and moved away from the couch. "Our boys come first."

Danny rose next to her.

"Look, I'm sort of beat. My legs are killing me." She kicked her heels off in the corner. "I'm going to take some Tylenol and hit the sack." She moved in the direction of their bedroom, but Danny pulled her back to him. He bent his head and kissed her fully on the lips. She raised up on tiptoe to meet his kiss.

"How about I join you. I could massage your calves for you." He let his hand trail down from her neck to her waist.

"Yeah, sure," she said leading the way down the hall.

Danny followed her into the room, shedding his clothes as he shut the door. As Crystal stretched out on the bed in front of him, he hardened at the thought of sex. But it wasn't with the woman he desired.

CHAPTER 14
College Life

FIVE YEARS AGO

Katie

It had been two years since Katie had last seen Danny in person. She sent letters to him about once a month. And once a month, she got a phone call from him. They'd talk about their day-to-day lives and and their futures, but rarely did the conversation include a discussion of their future together. Katie couldn't blame him though. He had two boys now and a wife to support. It was borderline adulterous for him to even call her, though their talks never got too personal. Mostly they reminisced about the summer she'd spent with her aunt Maggie in Cypress Springs.

It was Katie's senior year of college that brought the most change for her. She'd been dating a guy introduced to her by her college roommate. They'd been a couple for nearly a year when he told her he'd was enlisting in the Army.

"Isn't that what most people do *before* they start college so the military can pay for it?" She said as he broke the news over dinner.

"Yeah, most people do," Brian replied, "but my parents

already had a college fund set up for me, and it wasn't until recently that I thought about the Army."

They were dining at Latielli's on Lake Ella and Brian was in a celebratory mood. "I'm not joining until I graduate," he said. "Besides, after twenty years I'll be able to retire and still be young enough to start a second career."

"I guess that's an idea." Katie set her fork down and turned her full attention on him. "What about us?" The question sounded whiny in her own ears. She wondered what Brian would make of it.

"What do you mean? We'll still be together." He swirled a piece of lobster in his dish of butter before lifting it to his mouth. After downing the bite, he continued, "You can come see me graduate basic. And once I'm stationed, we'll write and call each other."

So there it was. He'd planned his future without her. He hadn't mentioned that she would join him at his post, just that they'd write and call.

"Brian, where do you see us? In the future." She'd pushed her plate away and was now prepared for a full conversation that had been building for weeks. He skirted the issue of their future long enough. Tonight, she'd get answers.

"Come on Kate. What's all this fussing when we're out celebrating my decision to have a military career." He called her Kate when he wanted to put her off.

"I'm not fussing," she replied, her hands folded neatly in front of her on the table. "I just want an answer to a question you've been avoiding since the end of fall term. Do you see us together after graduation?"

His silence spoke volumes to her. He took the time to wipe his mouth and lay his cloth napkin across his plate before answering. "Truthfully," he paused, catching her stare, "I don't know. I thought settling down was what I wanted, but..."

Katie couldn't hear the rest of his explanation. A wave of nausea washed over her as the idea of a happily ever after with Brian slipped away. She covered her mouth and pointed toward the bathroom. "I've got to--" She rushed from the table and barely made it to the bathroom before the dinner she'd just enjoyed made a second appearance.

A few minutes later, after rinsing her mouth out, she rejoined Brian. The check was already at the table and Brian stood when she arrived.

"I'm ready if you are." He pushed his chair under as Katie grabbed her purse, then she followed him to the door.

The ride back to her apartment was silent as tears threatened to fall. They hadn't officially broken up, but with his unflinching decision to join the Army and not include her, it was basically a done deal.

He walked her to her door and kissed her cheek. "Get some rest. We'll talk about this tomorrow."

She wanted to scream at him, to hit something, to demand a reason for his sudden frigidity to their relationship. Instead, she slid the key in her lock, let herself in the apartment, and closed the door on him without another word.

It would have been romantic and poetic if he'd knocked on the door, demanding they talk about it then. Or declare that he'd made a mistake and he really wanted her to finish college then join him when he was stationed somewhere. That didn't happen though. She heard his car rev and pull away a few minutes later, then she threw herself on the couch and cried until she had a migraine.

The end of spring semester flew by with Katie finishing her internship at a local elementary school, earning her exemplary grades and a strong recommendation for future employers. She had no desire to stay in Tallahassee once she graduated, though. Her home was in Jacksonville. So was her family. Her relationship with Brian had essentially ended the night of their date over Spring Break, when he told her about his enlistment idea. The phone calls dried up. He avoided her on campus and at parties. He even went so far as to send his roommate to pick up the few items he'd left at her apartment.

As she pulled her overstuffed SUV into the driveway of her childhood home, her stomach clenched, and she flung open the door. She barely made it to the shrubs surrounding her grandma's flower bed before the remnants of a drive-thru lunch came up.

Oh, this is not good, Katie thought. That was the eighth time in six weeks that she'd vomited for no apparent reason. Thinking back over the last two months, she noted other health-related oddities that pointed to the one conclusion she was dreading. As she pulled a couple of bags from the back of her vehicle, she struggled to recall the last time she had her cycle. Not one to be regular, it didn't occur to her that there could be a problem. Her stomach tightened again, but this time from the suspicion that she might be pregnant.

The front door of the house flew open, and Shannon raced down the steps to greet her.

"You're finally here," the younger girl cried. It'd been nearly five months since Katie had last seen her sisters. They'd all been home for Christmas, but even a few months made a difference in her sister's appearance. The gangly adolescent she'd left in December, all elbows and ears, had transformed into a gorgeous young woman possessing poise and style. Gone were the Cindy Brady ponytails, athletic shorts, and boyish tank tops. The girl threw her arms around Katie, nearly knocking the bags from her grip. "Here, let me take those."

Katie released the bags to her sister and pulled two others to replace them. "Where's Holly?"

"She had to go to the high school to clear her senior debt." Shannon lugged the suitcases to the front porch and dropped them out of the way. The door opened again and Lena Mayfield appeared in the gap.

"Katie-did, you're home!" The older woman, who was nearing sixty-three, held out her arms to her eldest granddaughter.

Katie smiled at her grandma and fell into her embrace. Through all the times she and Grammy didn't see eye to eye on things, her grandmother's love for her was never in doubt.

"I did," Katie replied, "and I brought everything I couldn't sell or part with. I hope you have room in the shed for most of this, because until I get a job and an apartment, I have no place to put it."

"Once Holly gets home, your sisters will help you unload it all."

The three women went inside and catch up and wait for Holly to return. Katie's heart filled with contentment at being home, but the anxiety over her predicament rested on her shoulders like a hot, damp towel.

For two weeks, Katie hid the worry over her secret. Her missed cycle, the tenderness in her breasts, and nausea were sure signs of the obvious truth that she refused to acknowledge until after Holly's graduation. The commencement and after party was reminiscent of her own high school graduation four years earlier. As family and friends alike congratulated Holly on all her hard work, Katie slipped away to her room and pulled out old photos of that day four years ago. Shannon had surprised her a few days later with a picture she'd snapped of Katie and Danny. It was a side view. Katie didn't even know if Danny realized he was being photographed, but it was one of the few pictures she had of the two of them, or of him.

She sat on the bed, her stomach churning, her emotions a mess. *I should be out there celebrating Holly's accomplishment*, she thought. *Instead, I'm in here mourning over a lost love and the life we'll never have.*

Shaking her head, she wiped away the threatening tears with the back of her hand. "Woman, you've got to get it together. You're gonna have a baby. Maybe." She reached into the top drawer of the nightstand next to her bed and pulled out a small, rectangular box. Slipping into the bathroom, she opened the box, followed the directions and waited the three minutes for the results.

As she crept back into the bedroom with the test stick held delicately between her fore finger and thumb, Katie dropped onto the bed, dumbstruck. The test was positive. Now it was true. Real. She was going to have a baby. At twenty-two and jobless. She let out a soft, hoarse laugh. Of all the dumb luck, to be pregnant with a baby by a guy who's avoiding you.

A knock at the door caused her to jump. She opened the drawer and dropped the test in.

Shannon stuck her head in the room that used to be hers. "Grammy wanted me to come check on you. You okay?" The girl sat on the bed next to her.

"Yeah, sure," Katie said, running her hands over her hair to smooth it. "I think I got overheated out there and wanted to cool off."

"Yeah, I don't know why Grammy insisted on having Holly's party in the middle of the afternoon." Shannon rolled her eyes. "A barbecue for dinner would have been just as good."

"So, I guess you're next," Katie said, stroking her sister's arm affectionately. She remembered when Shannon was a toddler, and her mom was still strong enough to play with them on the floor until everyone was laughing. Soon, she'd have that same joyous opportunity.

"Are you sure you're okay. You don't look too good." Shannon's brow wrinkled as she searched her sister's face.

Katie cleared her throat and stood. "I'll be fine. Come on. Let's go get some watermelon. I saw Uncle Jeff stash a couple in the freezer on the back porch this morning. Hopefully they aren't frozen."

The two sisters exited the room to rejoin the party.

Four months later, Katie's baby bump was obvious. She'd told her grandma and sisters about the baby, getting a stern lecture from Grammy about being a single mom and the embarrassment that came with it. Her sisters were excited to be aunts and the opportunity to spoil a baby.

"Grammy, it's the nineties. Being a single mom ain't such a big deal anymore," Holly explained over Saturday morning breakfast, a week after the news broke.

"Isn't," Katie corrected. "And thanks for the support." She nudged her sister's shoulder as she sat at the table.

It'd been two months since she started work at Bonnelin Elementary, the same school the three girls had gone to. It took some finagling in the interview and a small white lie of a fake wedding band, but Katie landed the second-grade position. Mrs. Sturges, the principal, was understanding, since Katie's 'husband' was deployed, and her due date wasn't until mid-December. Katie's excellent grades, letters of recommendation, and portfolio had all played a part in her securing the coveted position. She didn't want to let some old-fashioned bias keep her from doing what she loved.

"I still say you and your young man should have gotten married," Lena said, pouring herself a cup of coffee and joining the girls at the table. "In my day that's what was expected."

"It's kind of hard to even discuss marriage when he's avoiding me." Katie slathered butter on a piece of toast and scarfed it down in three bites. Holly deposited scrambled eggs on her sister's plate, and Katie attacked the pile with gusto. "Besides," she mumbled between bites, "He knows and is choosing not to take responsibility."

"What do his parents say?" Lena asked.

Katie finished scooping the last of her eggs into her mouth, stalling a response. After washing them down with apple juice, she turned to her grandma. "They don't believe it's his." She swiped the paper towel across her lips and carried the dishes to the sink. "So, now you see. It's not even my choice to be single. Brian doesn't want anything to do with us." She rubbed her protruding belly and was rewarded with a healthy kick.

"Hey, I saw that!" Shannon cried. "All the way from over here. That's definitely a boy." The gender speculation was three to one, with Shannon being the only vote for male.

"We'll see," Katie said. She didn't care what the baby was as long as it was healthy. "So, what do y'all think about the names Carlie and Will?" The conversation turned to baby names and Katie was grateful for the dropped subject of Brian.

Now, though, the topic had come up with a vengeance. Second graders had a way of getting to the core of any subject, and the topic of baby's daddy was a common conversational piece in her classroom. Katie would come home exhausted from fielding questions about Mr. Dupree and, *when he was going to visit the classroom, because Ms. Jernigan's husband came to school last year and surprised her with flowers and a cake for her birthday.* She didn't know how much longer she could keep the charade up. Even her coworkers were questioning the whereabouts of her imaginary spouse. The excuse of him being deployed would only last so long. Thank goodness Thanksgiving break was just around the corner and she'd have some peace.

She'd heard nothing from Brian, either, which frustrated her even more. Essentially, he was making it known that he didn't want anything to do with her or the baby. The more she thought about it, the more comfortable she grew with the idea of raising her baby alone.

The house was empty as she unlocked the door, so she kicked off her shoes and went to her room for a short nap. She woke half-an hour later with shooting pains down her back and knew something wasn't right.

CHAPTER 15
Abandoned

FIVE YEARS AGO

Danny

Danny Carter pulled his old, beat-up Dodge Ram truck into the driveway and parked next to the single wide trailer that he shared with his wife Crystal and their two boys. Turning the engine off, he dragged himself from the cab and walked stiffly toward his home. His jeans and navy-blue t-shirt were sweat stained from the ten hour shift work at the mill. Though it was now half past four in the afternoon, the summer sun was high overhead, hanging in the clear blue sky, threatening to melt or burn anything that was unfortunate enough to find itself outside for longer than half-an-hour.

Danny's short light brown hair was plastered to his forehead and stuck in dark, stringy strands to the sides of his face. He swung his lunch box with each heavy step he took toward his home. The past six years of working seemingly endless hours to support a family appeared to be taking a toll on his as he sat on his front doorsteps. His back ached and he reached his hand absentmindedly to rub out the pain thinking, daydreaming really, of summers long past that were so carefree. "Man," Danny breathed out in a defeated voice, "what am I killing myself for? And missing these wonderful summer days when my boys are growing up so fast. We should be out in Cypress Springs fishing and swimming..."

His thoughts trailed off as he heaved himself up off the steps to enter the trailer. Danny pushed the front door shut behind him, letting his eyes adjust to the darkness of the small living room. He ambled over to the window AC unit to cool himself off. Pulling his t-shirt over his head, he tossed it on the floor. He closed his eyes to the cold stream of air as the sweaty skin of his forehead and bare chest turned to goose flesh. Feeling a little better, he made his way into the kitchen. He sat his lunch box on the counter and grabbed a beer. Days' old dishes were still in the sink unwashed. He turned up his nose at the sight and the smell of something spoiled.

"Crystal!" He yelled down the hall. "Why couldn't you wash the dishes today, huh?" He made his way down the hall, unbuttoning his jeans and pulling the top on his beer can.

He stopped halfway down the hall in the doorway of the bedroom his boys shared. Trent's toddler bed was unmade but covered with clothes and stuffed toys that fell from the bed and scattered onto the floor. Opposite Trent's bed was Clay's crib. Danny smiled at the thought of Crystal and himself going into the large baby store in Gainesville to buy the bedding for the crib. They hadn't known the gender at the time and bought a bedding ensemble with a very neutral yellow and green and bunny theme. And Clay loved it.

Danny turned from his children's room and continued down the hall to his bedroom. He expected to see Crystal in her bra and panties, her bleach blond hair pulled up in a pony bun with tendrils falling loosely down, strutting around the room to some suggestive song on the radio. Instead, the room looked like a disaster zone. Clothes were strewn all over the room or lying on the bed with the hangers still on them. Bottles of lotion and deodorant lay next to the dresser they shared. A strange feeling in the pit of his stomach pushed him to search the closet. He let out a sigh of relief when he felt the secret box he kept hidden in the furthest corner. He lifted it out, rifled through the contents to make sure nothing was missing then put it back.

Still, something was wrong. He felt it. The house was too messy. Of course, Crystal wasn't known for her housekeeping skills, and it was usually Danny that cleaned up around the trailer. But this mess in the bedroom was not part of the regular messiness of the home.

He left the bedroom and walked around the corner to the only bathroom that the four of them shared. Everything appeared normal. The bathroom displayed the same upheaval as the bedroom. Towels that the boys had used the night before were still lying on the floor. The boys' bathtub toys were in their nylon bag hanging from the tub spout. Danny's razor and shaving cream were just where he'd left them two days ago. Their toothbrushes were in the cup where they were supposed to be except for... The prickly feeling in Danny's gut turned into a churning that threatened to explode from his lips.

"Crystal," he yelled. He ran back to his bedroom, surveying the room. Every piece of clothing around the room was his. Not one single garment was Crystal's. He rushed to the bed and flipped through the hanged clothing. Nothing was hers. Danny turned from the room and hurried again to the bathroom. Crystal 's toothbrush was missing from the cup that housed his and the boys. He pulled open drawers that usually held Crystal 's feminine things, like deodorant, make up and such, only to find a few cotton balls and Q-tips. His brow wrinkled as he struggled to make sense of this. Then an even stranger, scarier thought emerged: *Where are my boys?*

"Oh, God, my boys," Danny said, hurrying from the bathroom to his sons' room. Pulling open drawers, he exhaled a sigh of relief at the sight of children's clothes stuffed into the dresser. Then the strange confusion gripped him again. What happened to Crystal and all of her things? He didn't want to believe the obvious: she had left them. Would a mother actually desert her own children?

Danny hurried to the living room, leaving the dresser drawers open, to call the sitter. He picked up the phone but slammed it back on the holder at the sound of a dead line. "Fuck!" He'd forgotten that their phone had been cut off the week before. "Fuck! Fuck! FUCK!" Without a phone, he'd have to drive to the sitter's house.

Grabbing his keys from the kitchen counter, he sprinted to his truck, not even thinking to lock the front door. *God, please let Felicia have my boys,* he pleaded silently as he jumped into his pickup and peeled from his driveway.

The whole way to Felicia's house Danny prayed that his boys were okay. The confusion that had gripped him earlier had turned to fear--fear of never seeing his sons again. For him, being a father was the best thing that ever happened to him. He loved his sons more than life itself, and he didn't know what he would do if his boys were taken from him.

"But only Crystal's things are gone," Danny reasoned aloud. The twenty-five-minute drive to the far west side of Trenton seemed like an eternity, and the only way this would be real and not a dream was if he could hear himself talking to himself. "Why, God, why would a mother leave her children," he asked as he barreled into Felicia's driveway. "Please, let them be here," he pleaded as he jumped from his truck, leaving the engine running and the door open.

Felicia, an old friend of Danny's family in her mid-thirties, met him at the front screen door.

"Are my boys here?" Danny asked walking in long strides to the front porch.

"Danny, what's the matter?" Felicia replied, her face

pinched with concern. "Of course,..." But the woman couldn't finish her statement because a small, blond three-year-old boy pushed past her, out the screened door and ran to Danny.

"Daddy," Trent cried as he threw his arms around Danny's neck as the man dropped to his knees.

He hugged the child fiercely. *Thank God,* he thought, clinging to the child as if he were the thing that his very life depended on. Danny felt two other small arms snake around his neck from behind and he turned to include Clay in this family group hug that now consisted of only three.

After leaving the sitter's, Danny swung by his sister's house to see if she could come over for a while to watch the boys. He needed to find Crystal and see what the hell was going on.

He pulled into his yard for the second time that day. His boys sat in the truck seat beside him — Trent with a look of fear on his face, and Clay asleep in his car seat. Danny cut the lights and the engine and heaved a heavy sigh. The thought of confronting Crystal was tiresome, but at least his boys wouldn't be involved. He didn't know where she was staying. With his phone turned off, he had no way of calling her mom or her sisters. And he didn't know when or if she was ever come back, with all of her stuff being gone and all. Going to her work would be the only way to get to the bottom of this mess right now.

Danny gently unbuckled Clay from his car seat to not disturb the sleeping child. But Clay jostled and cried out, "No, Daddy. Don't go!" He fiercely clung to Danny's neck, his tiny fingers knotted together. Trent, fearful also, stood close to his father waiting to be led to the door.

"Oh, no, buddy. It's all right. Daddy's not going anywhere." Danny hugged the boy close, stroking the toddler's soft, downy hair. "It'll be okay." He shut the truck door, nudged Trent toward the trailer, and started humming one of the boys' favorite children's songs.

Once inside, Danny hurriedly began a meager dinner of hot dogs and macaroni and cheese. After the boys were settled and eating, he heard a car outside and rushed to the door. With a wild hope that it might be Crystal, he was a little disappointed to see his sister's car in the drive. He hadn't explained the whole story earlier when he'd asked her to come watch the boys, So, he met her outside and told her the abbreviated version of the evening's events.

When the pair finally entered, Trent jumped from his seat and ran to his aunt Lisa. He threw his thin arms around her legs, squeezing tight. Lisa was like a second mother to the boys since their births. Crystal never really got the hang of parenting. She let her work and her friends dictate her time. Clay and Trent came second to that, and feared the boys could tell even at their young ages. He'd always suspected Crystal's first pregnancy was a means to snag him. Her second one, a way to make amends. And though he may have been able to forgive her for that, what pissed him off the most was how all this affected his boys.

Clay whined from his highchair, and Lisa tousled his hair. Kissing his head and pointing back to his food, she walked toward the bathroom to draw a bath for the boys.

"The new bubble bath is under the sink, I think," Danny called. "Sorry about the mess."

The boys loved to play in the bubbles, and Danny had told her that the warm water and fragrant lavender bubbles might calm the boys down some.

"Don't worry about it," Lisa said, returning to the living room. "After I get the boys down, I'll straighten up for you some."

"You don't need to do that--"

"No, it's fine," Lisa interrupted him. "It'll give me something to do. Besides, you've got enough to deal with." She lifted Clay from his highchair and lowered her voice. "So, you think she's at work?"

Danny tugged the toddler's shirt over his head and wiped the boy's mouth with his cheese-stained shirt. The child wiggled in Lisa's arms, wanting down. She gave the boy a stern look and hi calmed down.

"You're so good with them." He stroked Clay's hair, and the boy lay his head on his aunt's shoulder. *They deserve more,* he thought, and an image of Katie Dupree popped into his head. He hadn't seen her in a couple of years and was surprised that she would come to mind. If he'd had any sense that summer of '85, he would have done his damnedest to keep in touch with her. And his life might have been different. He shook his head to dislodge the thought.

"Did you hear me?" Lisa stared at him, concern reflecting in her eyes.

"No, sorry. What'd you say?"

"I said 'be careful'." She shifted Clay to her other hip. "Her work doesn't draw the best folks in town if you know what I mean."

Danny nodded. He knew the crowd that partied at The Squirrel's Nest on the weekend. He'd been by a few times after work with some of his friends from the mill. It was a local bar where most of the county's good ol' boys drove their four-by-fours into the spacious back field to knock a few drinks back before going home to knock around their girlfriends or wives. Danny hated the idea of Crystal waitressing there. He'd been totally opposed to the idea, but that didn't stop Crystal from asking her cousin's husband to hire her.

"I will," he replied. "Besides, it probably isn't that busy tonight." He wasn't looking forward to the drive across the county, or the fact that he'd be out late when he had work the next morning, but he wanted this done and over with. "I'll be back as soon as I can. Thanks for staying with them, Sis. Tell them I will be back to tuck them in soon."

He left as his sister carried Clay down the hall. As he pulled out of his drive, he tried to think of what he would say to Crystal when he saw her. *If* he saw her.

Traffic was light as he drove down Highway 441, and his thoughts were a jumble of memories from his childhood and images of his life now. He tried to make sense of why any mother would abuse or abandon her children. He remembered his relationship with his own mother. She didn't brutalize him, but she definitely didn't know how to be a loving, supportive parent. He brushed aside the ill-will he held for his mom and focused on Crystal and her damage.

Crystal had been his high school sweetheart, at least for the two years he'd spent at Dixie high before dropping out. Even at fourteen he could tell her home life was just as bad as his. Maybe that's what drew them to each other--two screw-ups from screwed up families.

He remembered the first time he had seen Crystal at Dixie Junior-Senior High School. She was wearing the poor girl's version of the Madonna outfit: a hot pink mesh muscle shirt over a black lace bra, black legging tights under too short cut-off jeans that barely covered her ass and tons of black jelly bracelets and junk jewelry that she had probably bought at the thrift store. Her dishwater blonde hair was teased up from her forehead and held in place with bobby pins and hair spray above her left ear while the remainder cascaded down the right side of her head to partially cover her face. She had on way too much make-up for a fourteen-year-old, he had thought when he saw her standing in front of the Dean's office.

Danny stood at the secretary's desk waiting to get a tardy pass when he overheard Dean Simpson leaving a message for Crystal's parents. He'd cut his eyes to peek at the girl sitting just outside his door. Obviously, she was out of dress code. Danny had thought it gutsy that she'd even made it out of her house, much less walking down the hall of Dixie JSH, dressed the way she was. He remembered some of the other kids in the office whispering to each other as they cut their eyes at Crystal. But he had to stifle a laugh when she flipped them off. She smiled at him, and that was the beginning of their story.

Danny slowed for a red light, and the memories of his early life with Crystal played on. After that first, silent exchange in the Dean's office, Danny found Crystal after school and the pair became inseparable. They spent every moment together until Danny's cousin, Ronnie, told him he'd caught Crystal going behind the football stadium with some senior. It happened during the Homecoming pep rally, and the guy was a known druggie. Danny didn't believe it at first. How could he not know? But that evening at the game, Crystal acted weird when Ken walked by, and Danny knew it was true. That should have been a sign of things to come, a warning to him. But he had loved her, and when they met again three years later at Frosty's in Newton, the old feelings came rushing back. He stupidly believed she had changed, that wasn't doing drugs or other guys. Then she got pregnant and swore the baby was his. That was June of '88, the last time Danny had seen Katie at her high school graduation.

God, Katie. Why did his thoughts always return to her? When was he going to let go of that part of his past?

The flashing neon light of the bar jarred Danny from his reminiscing, and he wondered how he had made it all the way there without realizing it. The drive from his house to the bar was a maze of turns and stop-and-gos that he didn't remember making.

The parking lot was half full of muscle cars, motorcycles,

and huge trucks. Danny didn't see Crystal's car in the front lot, so he pulled around back to look. Off in the far corner he spotted her Nissan. He parked his truck near the side entrance of the bar and got out. *What am I going to say to her?*

Danny pushed the door of the bar open, and a blanket of cigarette smoke mingled with pot smacked him in the face. He adjusted his eyes to the dimness of the bar and noticed that for so few cars in the front lot there were way more people in the building. He ambled over to the bar and noticed his cousin Ronnie with a cute red head he remembered from high school. He walked over and nodded at the bartender.

"Hey, Ronnie," Danny yelled over the music. Ronnie turned on the barstool, his arm still around Patty Jarvis, the red head. "You seen Crystal?" Danny asked. Ronnie pulled Patty close to him, whispered something in her ear, and she hurried away toward a booth full of people.

"Yeah, I've seen her, man," Ronnie yelled back. "You shouldn't bother with her anymore, Danny. She's no good." Ronnie lifted his shooter glass, tossed back the drink, slammed the glass down on the bar and waved to the bartender for another one.

"Ugh, how can you drink that shit," Danny asked.

"I remember a time a few years ago when you could toss 'em back with the best of us," Ronnie replied.

"Yeah, well, I've changed." Danny glanced around the room unimpressed. "Life happened and I became a father. So, you said you've seen Crystal. Where is she Ronnie? I need to talk to her, now." He turned back to his cousin. Ronnie stopped the shot midair, looked at the bartender, then set the drink down without taking a sip.

"I told you, man, she's no good. Forget about her." Ronnie lifted his glass to his lips and emptied it in one quick motion. He looked back at the bartender, exchanging a knowing look that didn't escape Danny.

"What's going on? What ain't you telling me? Where is

she?" Danny asked, his heart pounding harder in his chest. *Something's happened to her. She really is gone.*

"Look, man," Ronnie said. "She's here. She just took a cigarette break out back a few minutes before you got here."

"Fine," Danny said, letting out a breath he didn't realize he'd been holding. "I just need to talk to her. Find out what's going on." He started for the side door he had just entered.

"I don't think now's the best time for that." Ronnie grabbed his cousin's arm. "She's...not alone."

"Well, I wouldn't expect anything else from her right now," Danny said, jerking his arm from Ronnie's grip. His long strides carried him to the door quickly, with Ronnie nearly running at his heels to stop his exit.

"Bro, wait," Ronnie called as the door shut in his face.

Danny rushed around the corner of the building to the employee entrance in the back. Searching around the nearly empty back lot, Danny didn't see anyone outside the back door; but his eyes caught sight of a person standing next to a car parked beside Crystal's Nissan. Danny saw that the man's attention was on something in the back seat. His back was to Danny, which made it easy for Danny to ease up behind him without being noticed.

Great, Danny thought. *She's out here getting high with some local redneck.* As he slid up behind the guy, he heard the man moan.

"Oh, yeah, baby. Take it all in."

What the fuck?! Danny stopped short. *What did I just walk up on? A back seat bj?* He squinted, trying to get a look at the back seat, but grunts from the opposite side of the car drew his attention.

"Oh, fuck, yeah. How do you like that?" A man's voice bounced from the car into the night. "You like my big dick, don't you."

The man in front of Danny threw his head back and cursed. "Shut up Ray," he snarled. "You'll make her lose her concentration."

Danny was about to tiptoe back the way he had come, not wanting to disturb whatever was going on. Clearly, he was at the wrong car. As he took a step back, he noticed a floppy yellow bunny with a blue bandanna tied around its neck lying in the back window. His heart tightened and he felt his body turn cold. That was Clay's Wubbie, his comfort toy for when he rode in Crystal's car.

Danny leaned forward, peering into the back seat through the rear windshield. The sight caught him up short. Crystal was in the back seat of the car on her hands and knees. Her face was buried in the crotch of the man in front of Danny. Following Crystal's arched back to where her ass would be, Danny saw the torso of another man, his torso propped up on stiff arms above Crystal. From his movement and his previous comment, Danny knew. He knew the guy was fucking his wife.

"What the fuck are you doing?" Danny yelled. The guy standing closest to him jerked his   cock from Crystal's lips. As the man tried to button his pants. Danny let loose with a right swing that connected with the guy's nose. Blood gushed from the wound and the man fell to the ground, holding his nose as he tried to cover his exposed dick.

"You whore! You stupid, fucking whore!" Danny's words echoed in the silent night as he reached into the back seat and hauled his wife to her feet. "What the hell are you doing?!"

Crystal, surprised and confused, stared at her husband.

Danny glared at the guy on the far side of the car who rushed to fasten his pants. When he looked back at Crystal, he saw her exposed breasts and her panties were on the ground. He grabbed the only thing he saw to cover her with—Trent's superhero cape. He shoved it at her, pressing it to her chest.

"Get your shirt on, for Christ's sake." His stomach turned at the sight he'd just witnessed, and he felt like puking. It was one thing to watch a little porn every now and then to get in the mood. It was something altogether different to see your wife at the center of a threesome.

Crystal struggled to pull her blouse over her head. Clearly, she was on something.

"Danny?" She stared hard at him, but even in the dim light he could tell how dilated her pupils were. "What are you doing here? Didn't you get my letter?" Her words, however slurred, made sense. She raised her hand as if to stroke his cheek, but he pulled his head back. "I left you a note."

"I didn't find a note, Crystal." He took her by the upper arms to steady her. "Not that it matters after what I just saw."

She giggled, then hiccuped. "Yeah, about that." Tilting her head to the side, she smirked. "Consider it my notice."

"Your notice? What the fuck are you talking about?"

"My notice." She struggled to pull herself free from his grip, but Danny held tight. "I'm done. I'm tired of it all. Of you. Of those kids. Of that shitty little rat trap we live in. I'm done. I want more."

The two guys, nearly forgotten in the exchange between Danny and Crystal, began backing up toward the rear door of the bar.

"What do you mean 'you're done'?" Danny's fingers squeezed into her arms. Before he could stop himself, he began shaking her. "You're done with *those kids*? They're your *children*. How can you be *done* with them?"

"Stop it!" Crystal cried. "You're hurting me." Her head bobbled back and forth with each jolt. Her hip kept hitting the rear panel of the car and she nearly lost her balance.

"You make me sick!" Danny yelled. "What the hell were you thinking? You fucking whore!" He raised his hand to smack her across the cheek but stopped in midair. She was still the mother of his boys, and he'd never hit a woman in his life.

The two men halted their retreat and began making their way back to the car.

"Hey, man," the one with the bleeding nose said, "let her

go." He came up behind Danny and grabbed Danny's arm, pulling him away from Crystal.

Without word or warning, Danny drew back and slugged him again, busting open the gash he'd delivered just moments before. The guy fell to the ground again, his nose spewing blood. The friend, who'd been waiting on the fringe, charged at Danny who easily sidestepped the drunkard. When the man gained his footing and came at Danny a second time, Danny delivered a punch to the gut that made the man double over. A quick lift of his leg and Danny's knee connected with the guy's nose. Both men writhed on the ground, groans of agony and curses filling the air around them.

Fully aware now, Crystal stood beside Danny staring at the sight before her. "You son of a bitch," she screamed, turning on Danny, her hands flying, beating against his chest. "You can't just beat people up!"

Disgusted, Danny grabbed her arms and easily shoved her to the ground.

"Don't bother coming back to the trailer," he spat. "Your shit will be by the road if you want it." A crowd had gathered at the side door, but Danny was too furious to be embarrassed. "And don't come near my boys, either," he barked over his shoulder as he lumbered back to the bar. Ronnie met him at the door with an *I-told-you-so* look.

"Don't say it," Danny sighed, "just buy me a shot." And he entered the bar with his cousin, leaving Crystal groveling before the growing crowd.

CHAPTER 16
Carlie's Birth

FOUR YEARS AGO

Katie

Katie sat up in the dim room and swung her feet over the edge of the bed. The pain in her back lessened as she hunched over and didn't move too much. She rose to her feet to shuffle across the room. Flipping on the light switch, she found her purse in a chair and dug through it until she found a bottle of Tylenol. Though she didn't really like to take medicine because of the possible effects on the baby, the pain was a little more than she could bear.

She trudged down the hall to the bathroom and filled a cup with water. Tossing back the caplets and chasing them with the water, Katie studied her reflection in the mirror. Her skin was dull and pale. Her auburn hair, which was usually voluminous, was flatter than a tortilla. She sighed, hoping that the rest of her pregnancy would pass quickly so her body, which seemed to be betraying her, would return to some sense of normalcy.

She splashed some water on her cheeks and decided to make her way to the living room to see if her sisters or

Grammy were home yet. She kept a hand on the wall to provide stability, pausing to let out a long yawn. *And Thanksgiving is just a couple of weeks away,* she thought. *I'll be able to rest then, since it's a week-long break this year. And after that, three weeks until Christmas break.*

Seeing the light at the end of the tunnel seemed to give Katie a little more energy. She waddled into the front room and found her youngest sister, Holly, stretched out on her stomach on the floor watching *My So-Called Life.* Katie settled into the love seat and propped her feet up on a stool her grammy had bought her.

Lena came in from the kitchen with a bowl of popcorn and sat in her recliner. "Oh, Katie, you're up. I checked on you earlier, but you were sound asleep, and I didn't want to wake you. I know how tired you are after a long day with those children."

"Thanks Grammy." Katie accepted the bowl of popcorn Lena offered her.

"You want me to make you a plate? We have leftover spaghetti."

"That's okay," Katie said, shifting the bowl to the couch beside her. She'd learned a couple of weeks back that the baby didn't like anything to rest on her belly. Anytime Katie set a coffee mug or a bowl on her protruding stomach, the baby would become active underneath it. "The popcorn is enough right now."

"As long as you're eating enough," Lena replied, snuggling into her recliner and draping a cover over her lap. She glanced at the TV. "Shan, this isn't going to run into my shows, is it."

"No, Grammy," Shannon called over her shoulder. "You ask that every week, and every week I tell you the same thing. *Matlock* comes on at nine, so you let me watch this one before that, then I go do my homework before bed." Shannon glanced over her shoulder at Katie, giving her sister a knowing look.

Katie knew what the look meant--bedtime was after homework and phone calls to friends. She'd done the same thing at seventeen. She smiled at her little sister. "So, what's tonight's episode about?" She listened as Shannon gave a quick summary of what was to come. The two younger women focused on the TV, but Katie watched as her grandma flipped the page in the romance novel she was reading, biding her time until her detective show came on. Contentment wrapped around her even though a nudge of anxiety held tight.

The days until Thanksgiving break dragged by. Each day Katie grew a little more tired, especially with the now dull throb that was a constant in her lower back. *At least there's no more shooting pains,* she thought as she cleaned the chalkboard in her classroom. She'd convinced herself that the dull aches were normal. And there wasn't any bleeding, so there was nothing to worry about. Today had been especially tiresome with the children getting more and more excited about the upcoming breaks.

With the chalkboards cleaned and the next day's lessons laid out, Katie gathered her bags and ambled down the quiet hallway to the near-empty parking lot. The sun hung low in the west, and she glanced at her watch. Five-thirty?! How had the time gotten away from her? Grammy would be worried sick. The thought to call home and let her grandma know where she was struck her too late. The exit door slammed behind her as Katie swung around to try to catch it. Pulling on the handle, she realized it was locked. She sighed, then shrugged. Her house was just twenty minutes from the school, but with it being so late, she was sure to get an earful when she got home.

As she dropped her bags in the back seat then climbed into the driver's seat of her Honda, she counted the days until Thanksgiving break. Just six more days and she'd have a whole week off. Then, three weeks after that was a two-week Christmas break with her maternity leave starting right after the first of the year. Assuming the baby waited until its due date to arrive.

The drive home was uneventful, and Katie daydreamed about life with an infant. She had always wanted to be a mom, with a husband and a house of her own. She thought about Brian, so far away, both physically and emotionally, and sighed. A horn honked nearby, and she jumped. The memory of sitting outside the Frosty Queen in Newton flashed in her mind with drivers honking as they guided their cars up and down the strip in front of the restaurant. Danny Carter's beautiful face filled her thoughts as she remembered sitting next to him in his Nova, the feel of his thigh next to hers, one arm slung around her shoulder. Her heart fluttered and she sighed.

If things had worked out the way she wanted, she would have been sharing this moment of motherhood with Danny, not waiting for Brian to come around to the idea of being a father at twenty-five. She blinked, realizing a tear had traveled down her cheek and she swiped at it. Focusing her gaze on the landscape around her, Katie realized she had driven home on autopilot.

As she cut the engine, she noticed her sister Holly's car was in its usual spot next to their grandma's SUV. A tightening in her midsection had her massaging her protruding belly. At seven months pregnant and a first-time mom, every little pain or twinge caused a slight alarm. But this spasm was like so many others that had happened over the last week or so. Her OBGYN had explained that there'd be annoying aches as her body prepared for birth, that it was all normal. Still, it was uncomfortable and slowed her down.

Trudging up the paved walk, Katie thought about the

upcoming holiday break and the time she'd have to rest. Teaching second graders was exhausting during a normal year. Being pregnant just added to her weariness. Her youngest sister, Shannon, met her at the door and took her bag.

"Rough day?" the teen asked pulling the door behind Katie.

"No, not really. I think I've just reached the point where everything I do makes me tire out easier."

"Well, Grammy has dinner ready, and you can rest after you eat."

"I've got grading to do." Katie reached for her bag, but the pinch in her lower abdomen had her doubling over.

"Katie!" Shannon's voice rose in panic.

At the sound of the cry, Lena hurried from the kitchen. "Katie girl, sit down right now. Let's get your feet up." Along with the younger girl, Lena maneuvered Katie to the couch and tucked a couple of pillows under her propped feet.

"It's fine, Grammy," Katie objected, "I'm just tired."

"She grabbed at her belly, Grammy." Shannon tossed a look at her sister, daring her to contradict her. The glare softened to concern when Katie winced again.

Lena sat on the edge of the coffee table, her eyes darting between Katie's stomach and her face. "How long has this been going on?"

Katie inhaled and measured her words before speaking.

"Don't you dare feed me a story, Katie Christine." The woman stared at her granddaughter until the younger woman caved.

Katie sighed. "It started a couple of weeks ago. Nothing too bad at first; just little twinges in my hip joints. I thought it was just what Dr. Montoya said was my body preparing for birth. You know, my hips spreading. But then, the twinges became stabs in my lower belly and came on so fast, it took my breath away." Her whole body seemed to relax as she shared the weight of the burden she'd been carrying alone.

"And you didn't think to tell anyone?" Lena admonished. At the fringe of tears pooling in Katie's eyes, the woman softened. She took her granddaughter's hand. "I'm sorry, honey. I'm just worried for you and little life in there." She patted Katie's round midsection, and the baby gave a responsive nudge in return.

The two women smiled. "At least she's still active."

"Very active," Katie replied, her smile softening at the love she felt for this child she had yet to meet. A dart of pain wiped away the smile, and Katie sucked in a breath at its intensity.

"That's it," Lena said. "You're going to the ER." She rose from her seat. "I'm going to change, then I'll run you up there."

About to protest, Katie thought better of it. A sense of relief washed over her at allowing someone else to decide a course of action for her. As a first-time mother, all of this was new to her. She didn't know what was worth worrying about and what was insignificant. Still, she didn't want to inconvenience her grandma.

"No, Grammy," Katie objected. "I've been driving myself everywhere. I can drive to the ER."

"But what if you need me?"

"I'll call. It doesn't make sense for you to go up there and sit all evening."

"And what if they admit her," Shannon interjected, "Like they did that time Holly had a concussion from softball? She had to stay overnight, and we didn't know that until way after dark."

Katie watched her grandma's internal struggle. It had been hard on the older woman to raise three teenage girls after their mother died so young, but Lena Mayfield was strong and loving and fair. She finally nodded and moved to help Katie from the couch.

"You promise you'll go and let them check you out?"

Lena eyed her granddaughter. "I know you, Katie girl. Tough as a diamond and just as faceted. Don't go by yourself if you think you can't handle the news alone."

"I'll be fine. If there's anything you need to know that can't wait until I get home, I'll call you." Katie struggled to keep a smile on her face as the pain in her side increased. She let Shannon walk her to her car, and as she pulled from the drive, tears slid down her cheeks at the possibility of something being wrong with her baby.

The ER waiting room wasn't too busy yet, but it was early on a Friday afternoon. Katie registered and watched as other patients came and went. She knew she would have to patiently sit for a while, but after two hours and the pinches in her lower stomach getting more intense, she finally went back to the registration desk.

"Look, I don't mean to be a pain," Katie said, cradling her belly as the last stab of pain eased some, "but I've been here for nearly two hours. The pain hasn't gotten worse, but it has gotten more intense, and my baby's life could be in jeopardy. When can I see a doctor?"

"Ma'am, you're in the system," the clerk said, "as soon as a bay becomes available, we can get you back." He grabbed a folder from a row of them and flipped through the papers. He looked back up at Katie. "You wrote down that you haven't had any bleeding or any other discharge, so likely it isn't too serious. A doctor will be with you shortly."

Katie blinked back tears of frustration, wishing now that she'd let her grandma come with her. As unassuming as she was most of the time, her grammy wouldn't take no for an answer. She'd have gotten Katie a wheelchair and raised cane until someone took her granddaughter back. Katie, though, didn't have the same fight in her, especially not tonight. Her anxiety had her mind in a vice grip, imagining everything that might be wrong. Each worry was countered with a reasonable explanation which kept her emotional outbursts in check. She sighed, shot a look at the clerk, and ambled back to her seat.

Two minutes later, her name was called.

"Follow me, Ms. Dupree." A middle-aged woman in green scrubs led Katie down a corridor to an area to take her vitals. Then, around a corner and into a cubicle with a bed, monitors, a phone and TV tray, though there was no TV in the room. The nurse laid a gown on the end of the bed. "So, you're having abdominal pains? How far along are you?"

Katie answered the questions, along with others that followed, as she scanned the room for a chair to sit in. The nurse took her vitals--temperature, oxygen levels, and blood pressure--and marked them in the chart she carried.

"All right, if you'll slip this on" --the nurse indicated the hospital-gray gown-- "the doctor will be in shortly."

Waiting for the door to close before she undressed, Katie did everything she could to tamp down the rising anxiety. She knew it wasn't good for her, the baby, or her pregnancy. She'd read so many articles about how to have a normal, uneventful pregnancy, and understood that maternal anxiety can put stress the baby.

Once changed, she sat awkwardly on the edge of the too-tall bed. Thankfully, the side rail gave her a place to rest her feet. She glanced at the clock on the wall, read the pain chart with its silly faces to indicate different levels of pain, and wondered at the people who needed sad faces to express their discomfort. She finally settled on the fact that the faces might be of use to children instead of adults.

Finally, after what felt like an hour but was probably closer to thirty minutes, an olive-skinned woman not much older than Katie knocked then entered the cubicle. She flipped through pages on the clipboard she carried. "Hello,

Ms. Dupree, I'm Doctor Tan. I see your having some pain in your lower abdomen." She wore blue scrubs and a hospital badge, something Katie had been instructed by her primary care doctor to look for when visiting the hospital. Why that stuck in Katie's mind, she couldn't explain.

"Let's get you up on the bed so we can get a look at what's going on." The doctor offered a hand to Katie to help her onto the bed, but Katie brushed it away and scooted herself into the middle of the mattress. The head of the bed was slightly inclined, and Katie laid back against the pillow.

"I see you've listed some of your other symptoms as dizziness and occasional nausea. Do these last long? Or how do you alleviate them?" The doctor adjusted the top sheet over Katie's waist and lifted the gown above her belly. The nurse who had brought Katie back to the room reappeared carrying a towel and a squeeze bottle that Katie assumed was gel for the ultrasound machine.

"For the dizziness, I lay down for a bit until it goes away." Katie felt the ooze of the cold gel on her stomach and winced. The wand of the ultrasound device rolled over her stomach, and she heard the familiar beat of the baby's heart. She continued her explanation. "For the nausea, I take an antacid or drink milk. I try not to take too much medicine, even if it's something I'm allowed to take."

"That's good," Doctor Tan said as she studied the image on the screen. Katie didn't know if the doctor was referring to her answers or what she saw on the monitor. After a few tense, silent moments, the doctor set aside the wand and turned to Katie. "The good news is I didn't see anything that indicates a placental tear. The baby's heartbeat is strong, and she's moving around in her space that's getting smaller each week. The worrisome news is that your blood pressure is elevated, which may be a sign of preeclampsia. Your OBGYN has discussed that with you, yes?"

Katie nodded and blinked back tears. She'd worked so hard to keep her blood sugar and her blood pressure normal.

Anything to ensure a healthy pregnancy and delivery of a healthy baby. Now, something could derail all her efforts and put her baby's life and her life in jeopardy.

"It is something to be concerned about," the doctor continued, "but it's not something that can't be controlled. The nurse will get you a pamphlet explaining some precautions you should take to make sure this doesn't progress into ecclampsia, which, I'm sure you know, is much more serious."

Katie nodded. Her mind raced with the changes she knew were coming. At least the doctor didn't recommend bed rest. With four weeks left in the semester, she couldn't afford to take the time off. Plus, thanksgiving was a week away and she'd get a few days to rest then.

"If it's at all possible, I'd suggest you take it easy," Doctor Tan added. "If you work outside the home, now might be a good time to start thinking about your maternity leave and make arrangements to take the time off in your final month. Get some rest before the baby comes."

Katie felt her face fall. The idea of not working wasn't an option. She had to help support her household. Grammy did what she could with her social security and pension, but she and the sisters relied on Katie to add to the income. Still, Katie nodded at the doctor's suggestion.

"Do I have to stay overnight, or can I go home now?" she asked, tossing the sheet from her lap and tugging the gown down over her thighs.

"No, I think we can discharge you as long as you promise to take it easy. Slow down a bit and rest more." The doctor rose from the stool and handed the chart to the nurse. "Callie will be back with your discharge paperwork and that pamphlet. Good luck Ms. Dupree."

Two hours later, Katie was back home. She'd called her grandma when she got discharged, and the whole family was waiting for her when she arrived.

"I bet you haven't eaten anything since lunch," Lena said, ushering Katie to the dining room. The sisters followed, and the three young women sat at the table as Lena moved about the kitchen retrieving leftovers and heating them in the microwave. Five minutes later, she set a plate in front of Katie and joined the sisters.

Between bites, Katie related the hospital visit. Once finished with dinner, Shannon took her plate and washed it quickly while listening to the details of her sister's story.

"So, you need to rest," Lena said. Her hands twisted around each other, a sign the girls had learned indicated her worry. "Are you going to start your maternity leave early? Maybe after Thanksgiving?"

"Grammy, you know I can't do that," Katie objected. A twinge in her stomach made her wince, but she recovered quickly and continued her point. "I have obligations to my school, my students. And what about my bills? I have to cover them."

"What about your obligation to this child?" Lena took her granddaughter's hand. The woman's eyes softened as she stared into Katie's. The young woman noticed how similar her grandma's eyes were to her own deceased mother's, Lena's only child. "You just said the doctor told you to slow down for the baby's sake. You don't want to go into early labor and harm the baby, do you?"

"You know I don't. I just can't see a way to take an earlier leave." Katie rose from the stiff, wooden chair and moved toward the living room. The rest of the family followed. Holly, Katie's middle sister home for the weekend from college, had yet to speak. She sat next to Katie on the couch.

"Well, I think you need to do what you have to for your health," Holly said. Katie smiled at her sister's directness. Unlike Shannon, who went along with the easiest plan or what everybody else thought, Holly voiced her opinion, regardless of whether it was popular or not. Now that she had finished her sophomore year at the University of Florida, she was much more outspoken and confident. "Screw the bills. They'll get paid eventually."

"But it will mess up my credit," Katie replied. "And I eventually want to get my own place when I start my family. Maybe when Brian gets home from deployment." She propped her feet up on the coffee table and settled back against the sofa.

"You're still hanging onto that fantasy?" Holly asked. She didn't try to hide her feelings for the man who'd gotten her sister pregnant then denied the child was his.

Though Katie and Brian had dated for over two years in college, when he dropped out to join the Marines, their relationship imploded. When Katie found out she was expecting and told Brian, he became even more distant, insisting that the child might not be his since he'd left for boot camp when Katie found out. The truth of his denial hadn't yet reached Katie's innermost heart. She still held out hope that once Brian saw his daughter he'd be overcome with parental instinct and want to do the right thing--if not marry her, then at least be present in his child's life.

"Holly Michelle," Lena admonished. "Don't upset your sister. She needs to rest." She lifted Katie's feet to tuck a pillow underneath them. As the room grew quiet, with each woman momentarily in their own thoughts, the phone rang. Shannon jumped to answer it.

Probably for her anyway, Katie thought and settled her head against the couch cushion. She was about to close her eyes when her sister shoved the phone at her.

"It's for you," Shannon said, an odd look on her face. "Some guy."

Katie took the phone, her heart racing at the idea of Brian finally coming to his senses. "Hello?" she spoke tentatively into the receiver.

"Hey, Katie girl." The familiar nickname given to her by a boy long since left in her past was jarring, but the voice wasn't the same. It was thicker, more mature, more worldly, and it confounded Katie.

"Who is this?" Katie glanced at her sisters and shrugged. Her grandma had retreated to the kitchen and Katie heard water running in the sink.

"Who do you think this is?" The response sounded like a challenge, a dare, and so unlike Brian. But a familiarity in the tone tickled at the edge of Katie's memory. Still, she didn't have time for games.

"I don't know, but if you don't tell me who you are, I'm hanging up. I've had a crappy day and--"

"Whoa, ease up," the caller said. "I don't want to add to your shitty day. I just wanted to call and say hey. I haven't heard from you in a while."

"Danny?" The question was nearly whispered as Katie couldn't believe that after nearly three years he'd remembered her phone number.

"You got him."

Katie swung her feet from the couch to rise and shuffle to her room. "Oh my God. What are you up to? It's been forever since I heard from you. And you remembered my number? That's crazy."

"Well, truthfully, I asked Lisa for it, but yeah, I've been thinking about you a lot lately. How's it going?"

Katie swallowed. The last time she'd talked to Danny, he told her he was getting married and having a baby. Lisa, Danny's sister, had kept her up to date on his life over the past three years, but Katie hadn't talked to her in months. She didn't even know that Katie was pregnant. The fact that she'd now have to share that news with Danny herself made her stomach flutter. In response, the baby nudged her, and Katie noticed a little knot of a knee or elbow above her belly button.

"Hey, you still there? I know it's a shock, me calling you

out of the blue." Danny's voice held a note of concern, unusual for the carefree, happy-go-lucky boy she remembered.

"Yeah, I um...I was just lost in thought," Katie said. She sat at her small desk littered with papers needing graded. "And I'm surprised to hear from you. How are things going with...what's her name?"

Danny inhaled sharply.

Uh-oh, Katie thought, *I've hit a nerve.*

"Crystal. Her name is Crystal." Danny's voice was tight. Katie imagined his lips stretched into a thin line and his forehead wrinkled the way it used to get when a touchy subject was brought up. "And I left her. We're getting a divorce."

"Oh, no," Katie replied. Her heart ached for him. Though she hadn't talked to him in ages, he still held a special place in her heart. For her, he was her first love, and she'd loved him for a long time before finally accepting the reality that they lived in two different worlds. Ones that would never be reconciled. "I'm sorry. Do you want to talk about it?" She felt a little voyeuristic, not really enjoying the fact that his marriage was ending, but a teensy bit happy that he'd be single again.

Then her own critic chimed in. *What about Brian? And the baby you two are having together? What about* that *happy little family image?* Katie was torn. As she heard Danny give a brief explanation for the demise of his marriage--something about his wife being a whore and two men and a bar--her mind raced through the past year with Brian.

Nothing in the few letters he sent her in the beginning suggested that he would ever want to settle down with her and their baby. He had even gone so far as to suggest the baby wasn't his. Yet, here she was, still holding out hope that they'd get together when he came home from the Middle East.

"So, I've moved out, and I'm working for this lumber company here just south of Newton. We're doing okay, me and my boys. Lisa helps out with the boys when she can."

"That's good. Listen, Danny," Katie said, swallowing the lump in her throat, "I've got some news of my own." She paused a second, the courage in her building. Then the words tumbled from her. "I'm pregnant. Brian, my college boyfriend, he's the father. He's over in the Middle East right now, so we really haven't had a lot of time to process this together, but..." She really didn't know where else to go with her news. Or even if she should. Danny was just a friend to her now. Even though he'd been her first love, they were different people now, with different lives.

"Are you going to keep it?" The question from the other end of the line held no emotion.

"Uh, yes," Katie said, her voice pitching a little. She hadn't considered the alternatives. "Besides, I'm too far along now to end it and too much in love with my little jellybean to give her up."

"So, it's a girl."

"I don't know." Katie rubbed her belly and the baby rolled over. "I sort of hope it is. All I've known are girls. You know, I was raised by two strong women. And I have two sisters, so a girl would be comfortable."

"And what about what's his name?" Danny's voice came through the line clipped.

"Brian," Katie said. "Like I said, he's still on tour in the Middle East. I, uh, I haven't heard from him much. I guess he stays pretty busy in...Afghanistan." Katie tried to remember where the last letter had come from or what Brian had written about the town he was in. "I think that's where he's at. And the military keeps extending their time over there. I know he said something about a leave coming up soon, but some skirmish would happen and he chose to stay."

"Hmph. Sure he's not just trying to avoid you and his kid?"

"What kind of question is that?"

"I'm just sayin' is all. If he wanted to be here with you, he'd find a way, right?"

"Well, you don't know him or anything about our relationship." She felt her face redden but couldn't tell if it was from anger or embarrassment. Danny had a point, but she'd be damned if she proved him right by agreeing.

"Look, I didn't mean to get you riled up," he said. His voice was a little softer, which made Katie even more upset for some reason. "Especially in your...condition. I just thought, I don't know, that maybe we could talk. See where things went. But you've obviously got your life set now. I don't want to screw that up."

"Danny, I..." What could she say that would make things better between them. He was right. She had her life sort of the way she wanted it. Or maybe she was deluding herself. Either way, his timing sucked.

"It's okay," he mumbled. "Listen, I hope you have a good life, Katie girl. I'll talk to you later."

"Promise?" The question slipped from her lips and fell on a dead line. He'd hung up before he heard her.

Katie hung up the phone and set it on the nightstand in her room. As she straightened, the side ache that had been just an ever-present annoyance the last couple of weeks had her doubling over in pain. "Grammy! Shannon! Help." The tears welled in her eyes as she felt a trickle of liquid down her inner thigh and clamped her legs shut.

This is too soon, she thought. The baby wasn't due for at least another four weeks. The fear squeezed the breath out of her and she felt herself gasping for air. Then everything went black.

Five weeks later, Katie held Carlie in her arms as Holly and her grandma bustled around in the kitchen. Christmas morning was always a busy time for them with cooking, and presents, and extended family coming over later that day. Usually, it was Katie in there helping her grandma, but with the baby now, Holly graciously took over as Grammy's assistant.

The front door swung open, and Shannon stepped in, waving to the neighbor boy she'd gone to talk to. She plopped down on the sofa next to Katie and kissed Carlie's forehead.

"Will Hurst said this got delivered to them a few days ago." She handed Katie an envelope and took Carlie from her sister.

Katie glanced at the return address--*L. Tyner, Cypress Springs*--before opening it. She pulled out a Christmas card from Lisa, Danny's sister. Two pictures slid from the interior of the card. The first was of her and her husband, Mark. Katie smiled at the lovely picture of the high school sweethearts. The couple were embracing and held between them a red onesie that read 'a little Tyner elf arriving next year.' Katie's hand covered her mouth in surprise and joy for her friend.

"Lisa's pregnant," she told Shannon. Her little sister smiled but continued playing with her niece.

Katie shuffled to the second picture and her heart beat double-time. It was of Danny and his two boys. All three were dressed in red shirts and blue jeans. Katie was sure Lisa had a hand in staging the photo, but the sight of the little family took her breath away.

This should have been mine, she thought, as a tear welled in the corner of her eye. Shannon had risen from the couch and carried Carlie to the kitchen with her, so Katie was free to be with her thoughts privately. She swiped a finger under her eye and smiled sadly at what she'd lost.

CHAPTER 17
The Letter

THREE YEARS AGO

Danny

My life wasn't supposed to be this way, Danny thought. Or maybe it was inevitable, after the shitty childhood I had. Really, what did I expect when the people who were supposed to be my role models beat me for begging relatives for grocery money and school clothes. I didn't stand a chance.

Danny sat at his kitchen table and took a long swig from a cold Coors. In the sweltering haze of a late Friday afternoon, he sat there contemplating what had led up to this moment in his life. He *could* blame his parents for their lack of proper parenting. *But was it really their fault that I knocked a girl up at twenty? Did they force me to marry her and try to make it work? And they sure as hell didn't have anything to do with me finding my whoring wife fucking around on me in a threesome just for drug money.*

He set his beer down on the table and tossed the divorce papers in front of him. After months of useless counseling, prepping, going to court, and waiting for all the paperwork to finalize, thank god it was finally over. He finally had his boys, and Crystal was out of their life for good.

The custody trial and divorce took a toll on all of them. When small children were involved, the courts weighed all options regarding custody. It gutted him when the proceedings got ugly, with Crystal bringing up Danny's low paying job and him producing evidence of her drug abuse. But he knew it was best for the boys to be in the most stable home--his.

The divorce itself was easy, mutual, but custody of the boys turned into a real battle. Each side pled their case and produced character witnesses. Crystal's mom showed up to a couple of court dates to support her daughter, but even *her* character testimony wasn't enough to overcome Crystal's arrest record. Lisa, Mark, and Ronnie were all there for Danny. All three testified to his positive character and his devotion to the boys. There was no doubt in his mind that Trent and Clay were better off with him.

At one point, out of desperation or spite, Crystal threatened to have the men Danny beat up brought in to demonstrate his violent nature. However, when Danny reminded her of the circumstances of that altercation, Crystal dropped it.

The day the judge gave him sole custody of his children was the second happiest day of his life. After that, his life settled into a normalcy that eventually led to more fun and less struggle. He moved closer to his sister in Trinity so she could help him with the boys. He found a babysitter while he worked, a nice older lady that was friends with his aunt. The only thing missing was Katie, the one girl he could never forget, but that couldn't be helped. He was determined to make a life for his boys, and nothing would distract him from that.

A few months later, over New Year's that Danny met Karen at a party hosted by a guy he worked with. When the ball dropped, she was the closest one standing next to him and didn't hesitate to kiss him to ring in the new year. They moved in together right after, and their lives rolled along undisturbed by outside forces.

Now, as he sat here after work, having an evening beer, his thoughts circled around as they always did to how different his life could have been. Sure, he was comfortable with Karen, a good woman and a good mother figure to his boys and her own twelve-year-old daughter. And their life wasn't as volatile as the one he'd shared with Crystal, or his own childhood, for that matter. Everyone got along and Danny's life was okay by those standards. But was it enough?

He finished his drink and dropped checked the bottle in the trash. Folding the papers back up, he made a note to tuck them away with the other important papers he kept. A honk outside signaled Karen's arrival with the kids and Danny tucked away his unfettered longing for Katie--the one fire he couldn't douse.

One steamy June afternoon, Danny pulled up to his mailbox and withdrew all the letters. Flipping through them, he tossed them on the seat as he identified them. "Bill." Toss. "Bill." Toss. The third envelope was handwritten, and the return address was from Jacksonville. Danny pulled into the drive and put the truck in park. He tore open the letter and read the signature before anything else.

It was signed: Love, Katie

"Daddy, I've got to pee!" Trent cried from the back seat.

"Hold on, buddy." Danny folded the letter, tucked it in his shirt pocket, and pulled the car to the front of the house.

Once free from his car seat, Trent raced to the edge of the house, dropped his pants and relieved himself behind the hedges.

Danny shook his head, glad that he had boy children. If he'd had a girl, this might have ended in a messy catastrophe. He unlatched Clay and set the toddler down. The boy followed his brother up the steps to the front porch.

No one was home when the three of them entered the cool, dim living room. The boys took off down the hall to their bedroom. Seconds later Danny heard the crashing of toys followed by laughter and squeals of delight. He ambled to his own room and stripped from his work clothes. Sitting on the bed, he retrieved the letter from his shirt pocket.

Dear Danny,

I hope you're doing well and that the boys are all right. It's been a while since we've talked and so much has happened in my life since then. I have my daughter now, Carlie, though her daddy and I aren't together. That's another story for another time. Suffice to say that we didn't agree on what a healthy relationship looked like. So, we decided to go our separate ways.

His heart clenched at the thought of the one woman he never quit pining over having another man's baby, but he pushed out a breath of relief at the news that they weren't together. He shook his head, annoyed with the feelings of envy. What right did he have to be jealous? He had two children with Crystal. He was living with Karen now. He had no right to begrudge Katie those same things. He continued reading.

I teach now, also. Have been for about a year. A class full of second graders. Imagine trying to explain to them about why my tummy kept getting bigger! Every week,

*one of my little munchkins would comment
about me getting fat. Leave it to children to
speak honestly. I finally had to explain to
them about the baby growing in there. Of
course, that only led to more questions and
stories about their baby brothers or sisters.
That was definitely a nerve-wracking time
and a practice in patience and diplomacy.*

*So, I know you won't write me back, but
maybe you could give me a call sometime. I
miss talking to you, and I think about you all
the time. Some of my most favorite
memories involve you. Swimming in the
river. Watching the boat parade on the
Fourth of July. Climbing to the top of the
lookout tower my last night in Cypress
Springs.*

Danny paused here as the memory of that night caused a
pounding to ricochet in his stomach. That was the night he
and Katie almost made love. So many times, he'd replayed
that night and imagined how his life would be different now.
But he always came back to the same conclusion: they were
too young to commit to a long-term, long-distance
relationship. He flicked the paper to remove the glare before
continuing.

*Anyhow, I was thinking about you and
that I might come to Cypress Springs for the
Fourth of July to see the fireworks. Maybe
we could get together and catch up. I'd love
to see your boys. Lisa said they look just
like you! I can just imagine two little
towheaded, bronze boys with your blue
eyes and sharp attitude.*

He bristled slightly at the description of his personality,

but it was proof of how well she really knew him. His temper was fiery and, when he was in one of his moods, the words from his razor-edged tongue would slice a hole in anyone's self-esteem. He gave a wry smile and finished the letter.

I've already talked to Lisa, and she's willing to let me stay the night with her. If you're free and want to see me, let's meet at the ballfield where everyone picnics before the festival. I can't wait to see you, Danny. It's been so long. Hope to hear from you soon.
Love,

Katie

Danny read the letter a second time, then folded it before tucking it in his safety deposit box with all the other letters of hers he'd kept over the years.

Later on, Karen called and said she had picked up an evening shift and wouldn't be home until after midnight. Danny felt relieved and, after he got the boys to bed, he retrieved the letter from Katie. With everything that had happened in the last year, it was Katie's letters that had seen him through. Just the thought of her still caring, hoping that he was getting along okay, made some of the hardships in his life seem a little less difficult.

Now, he sat at his kitchen table, the radio playing softly from the living room, with a pen and paper in front of him. For the first time since he'd known her, Danny was going to write Katie back. And what he wouldn't give to see the look on her face when she pulled his letter from the mailbox.

But how would he even start a letter to her? Should he keep it short and light? Or maybe he should tell her that even after all this time he still loved her? In the end, he simply chose to answer her questions and share the same info she'd shared back with her. As the intro to Whitesnake's "Is This Love" flowed from the radio, he set pen to paper.

> *Dear Katie,*
>
> *I got your letter and that's great about your job as a teacher. I never saw you doing that. I guess I never really thought about you getting older, becoming an adult. But here we both are.*
>
> *And you've got a little girl. Wow. I bet she looks just like you, sweet and beautiful. Maybe you can bring her to the festival. I'd like to see her, and yeah, I'll be there. It's the biggest thing around here, which I'm sure you remember.*

He paused here, thinking about the time he'd helped her climb a tree just to see the boat parade better. Then later at his trailer, when they were alone, before his sister and the rest of the gang had shown up. The sweetness of her kisses, his hands on her body, the innocence in her eyes that stopped him. As the memories flooded back, so did the emotions. This was his one shot to share with her everything he was feeling right now, to write it down so it would never be forgotten.

> *And I miss talking to you too, seeing you, holding you. Damn, I miss everything about you. And I know I've done some stupid shit in my past, but the biggest mistake ever is letting you get away. I should have just said Fuck It when Crystal*

told me she was pregnant and moved to Jacksonville when you asked, but then, I wouldn't have my boys. And they are my life, but my life should have been with you too. Those boys could have been ours. Together. I just didn't think I would ever be good enough for you. Or enough. Look at you now. You've got a really good life. How can I ever compete with what you have? With your life there? I can hear you now. "You don't have to compete," but that's not how I feel. I do, with your life now, with our past, and the future we'll never have.

Well, if you do decide to come to Cypress Springs after all this, I'll be glad to see you and catch up. Maybe at the Fireworks Festival.
Danny

He couldn't sign it 'Love.' That just wasn't him, but he knew Katie would understand. He laid the pen down and reread the letter. There was so much more that he wanted to say, but just didn't have the balls to write. Maybe one day, if they were both free at the same time, he'd tell her the truth-- she was the only woman he'd ever loved, would ever love, and he was an idiot for letting her go.

He sighed and found an envelope to tuck his letter in. After addressing it and digging around in the bill box for a stamp, he folded the envelope in half and stuck it in the back pocket of his work jeans. He'd run by the post office on his way to work tomorrow and drop it off. For better or worse, he hoped that Katie realized the just how much he cared about her by the simple act of a hand-written letter--another piece of himself that he'd never given to another woman.

CHAPTER 18
Fireworks Festival

TWO YEARS AGO

Katie

When Katie wrote Danny that she might come to Cypress Springs for the Fourth of July, it had been a distant plan. One she hadn't really thought of following through on. She knew he had a girlfriend, if that was what one called an older live-in partner, and she didn't want to interfere with his life. But at Lisa's insistence, she'd asked her sister to keep Carlie for one night. She didn't tell Shannon or her Grammy where she was going, just that she might spend the night with a friend.

Now, she was in Newton, sitting in a Frosty's booth across from Lisa Carter, Danny's younger sister. Looking into the parking lot, memories of the summer six years ago came flooding back: the parade down the Cedar River, riding next to Danny in his Chevy Nova, and walking out of Frosty's to see Angel Michaelson wrapped around him. The last memory caused her to wonder what the devil she was doing here in Cypress Springs again.

"Does he know I'm going to be here?" Katie asked.

"No," Lisa replied. "I told him I wanted to see the boys

without having to go through his new woman." At the mention of the newest fill-in mom for Clay and Trent, they both rolled their eyes. "I guess he's trying to do the right thing and have a female presence in their lives, but he really could have picked a better one."

"She has to be better than Crystal," Katie said, not sure how Lisa felt about Danny's ex-wife. "I mean, what kind of woman walks out on her own children?"

"Well, if I'd had my druthers," Lisa stated, "you know I'd have Danny with you. They all three deserve better than what they've had."

Katie smiled at the compliment, knowing that it was Danny who had kept them apart all these years. *And if I'd had my way*, she thought, *those boys would have been mine, biologically and permanently.*

She saw him the minute he stepped into restaurant, and her body vibrated with the immediate attraction that always grabbed her whenever he was around. She cleared her throat and offered a half-hearted wave.

He carried a small boy in one arm and held the hand of another. Lisa had sent pictures of Clay, the toddler, and Trent, the four-year-old, but to see them in person nearly brought tears to Katie's eyes. Danny kept his sunglasses on. Katie couldn't tell from his face what his reaction to her presence was. His body language, though, was a whole other tale.

He paused just inside the door, and another patron spoke up behind him, forcing Danny to jump and step out of his way. He released the boy's hand, and Trent ran from his dad to his aunt.

"Aunt Sissa," the child cried.

"Trentasaurus," Lisa returned, scooping him up in a hug and pulling him onto her lap.

"Who's dat?" Trent asked, pointing to Katie.

"This is a friend of mine and your daddy's," Lisa explained. "Her name is Katie. Can you say, 'Hey, Katie'?"

"Hey, der, Katie," Trent said. He leapt from his aunt's lap to run to the counter and stare at the ice cream pictures.

"Well, you just gonna stand there scowlin' or are you gonna say hey?" Lisa stood and took the younger boy from her brother.

"Hey," Danny said, his response directed at both women.

"Sit down, you doof," Lisa said. "Katie didn't drive three hours to just stare at you standing there."

"Daddy, can I haf sum ice ceam?" Trent asked, pulling on his daddy's pant leg.

"I ceam," Clay mumbled in his small, baby voice.

"I'll get it for them," Lisa said. She jostled Clay on her hip, eliciting a giggle from the boy. She nodded at her empty seat. "You, sit. Talk."

Danny took his shades off, his eyes darting everywhere before landing on Katie. She glanced at her hands, then out the window, before finally looking up into those steel blue eyes that always had her on edge.

"Your boys are beautiful," Katie said, unsure of where to start. Her heart was racing at the sight of him. He still had dark blonde, shoulder-length hair, though most of the curl from his youth was gone. He wore a baseball cap that he tugged further down on his head. Katie guessed that it acted as a sort of shield, a replacement for the sunglasses.

His face softened at the compliment. "Yeah, well, no thanks to me."

"That's a lie," Katie answered. "Trent has your eyes, and that cleft you have in your chin." Without thinking, she lifted her hand and reached toward him. She caught herself and lowered it quickly to her lap. "But Clay," she continued, "he must look like..."

"Yeah," he interrupted. "He's Crystal all over. The dark hair, the dark eyes, the wild streak."

"He's only a baby. He can't be too wild." Katie looked over at the small boy Lisa was holding while trying to take the ice cream from the counter clerk. As if on cue, he shrieked loudly and arched his back at not being allowed to hold the cone.

"Don't you start," Lisa told him. "Or you won't get any." At that, the boy quieted.

"See," Danny said, as if it proved his point.

Katie was about to argue, but Danny continued, "Where's your baby?"

"Carlie's at home with my sisters and Grammy," she answered. "I didn't know how long I was staying, for just the day or if Lisa would let me stay the night with her, so I asked Holly to keep her."

"Oh," Danny answered. He picked up the saltshaker that held rice and shook it, the sound of the hard grains hitting the thin glass a faint tinkle, barely audible in the nearly empty dining area. He set the container back down, his fingers tapping on the table.

It was hard to believe he was sitting across from her. Katie had imagined this moment for years. The pair had talked a few times over the last three years, and she'd written to him, but she never thought she'd actually see him again. Yet, here she was, on a whim, back in the Newton Frosty's with Danny.

Lisa joined them. "Sure, you can stay with us," she said, apparently hearing the whole exchange. "Our spare room is tiny, but the bed's made. I'm sure Mark won't mind. You can go with us to the festival."

"They still put that on in Cypress Springs?" Katie asked.

Lisa stood Clay up on the bench between them, and Danny lifted Trent into the bench he sat on and put the boy's cup of ice cream in front of him.

"Oh, yeah," Lisa replied. "It's grown some over the years. And the boat parade--you remember that, right?" When Katie nodded, she continued, "It's gotten bigger also. We have so many new residents in Cypress Springs."

"It's because of that new planned community they built just south of there."

"Oh, I saw the signs on my way over." Katie grabbed a napkin and ran it along Clay's chin to catch the dripping ice cream. The child whined and tried to pull away, but maternal instinct kicked in a Katie captured his head against her side, wiped his mouth and released him before he could let out a single squeal. She spied the admiring smile that Danny hid quickly once her attention was turned back to him.

"You're pretty good at that," he said. He plucked a couple of napkins from the holder on the table and handed them to Trent. "Wipe your face, son."

The child did as he was told and put the wadded tissue in the cup in front of him.

"I've had some practice with Carlie," Katie replied. "Plus, I taught kindergarten last year. It seemed every time I turned around one of my students had a runny nose or had smeared his lunch all over his face. This year, though, I'm moving to third grade."

"You like it? Teaching I mean," Danny said. The indifference he'd entered the shop with had disappeared and a relaxed ease had settled on him.

"Yeah," Katie said, "I'm pretty sure it's what I was called to do. The kids are great, my principal is so understanding, and I have some amazing colleagues. I was pretty lucky to get the position at the same elementary school that Holly, Shannon, and I all went to."

Trent slid off the bench with the empty cup in his hand and ran toward the front of the restaurant. Seeing his brother gain freedom, Clay began to crawl across Lisa to get down. When the woman didn't let him by, he squealed and tossed his head back.

"I hate to interrupt this lovely little reunion," Lisa said, standing and propping the boy on her hip, "but these boys will be getting antsy in a few minutes. Mind if I take them with me tonight to the fireworks? It'd give you and Katie some time to talk." She looked from Danny to Katie and back again. "I mean, if you want to."

Katie's eyes met Danny's, and she shrugged, waiting for his response. When it took longer than she thought it should, she said, "Maybe we shouldn't--"

"No, Karen's working tonight," he said, sliding from the booth. "Sure, take the boys. I'll call you afterward to pick them up."

Katie released a breath she hadn't realized she was holding.

"Sounds good," Lisa said. "I'll get their car seat from your truck." She set Clay down next to Danny and ordered Trent back to the booth.

Katie helped Danny entertain the two boys until Lisa returned with his keys. The five of them exited the restaurant together, and Danny strapped his boys into Lisa's SUV.

"Alright," Danny said, reaching out to kiss Clay on the forehead. "You'll be good for Aunt Lisa?" he asked, though the boy couldn't answer him. "You, too, big boy. Mind Aunt Lisa and Uncle Mark." He hugged Trent before shutting the car door. As they pulled away, he turned to face Katie. From the look on his face, she feared she'd made a mistake in coming here. You couldn't repeat the past, could you?

"So, where to?" He said, twirling his keyring around his index finger.

"Huh?"

"You want to go somewhere to talk, or just back in there?" He pointed to Frosty's and Katie, dumbfounded, turned to look at the door.

"No, I, uh, I don't care. We can go wherever."

"You want to follow me. Or I can drive." Danny walked toward his truck, a few spots down from Katie's car.

Momentary apprehension swept over her. She shrugged it away. *This is Danny we're talking about*, she thought. "Hold on," she said, moving past his truck. "I'll get my wallet."

He pulled up in front of her, and she opened the passenger door. The bench seat spread between them and Katie's thoughts, like so many other times today, went back to six years ago. "You want to see some of the changes in Cypress Springs?" he pulled the truck out of the parking lot and pointed it toward the gulf coast.

"Sure," she said. As they drove west on SR 349, Katie's trepidation lessened. "When did you get rid of the Nova?" she asked, brushing crumbs on the floor. A glance from Danny had her folding her hands in her lap, blushing.

"Sorry about that," he said. Steering with one hand, he grabbed the couple of toys that lay between them and threw them behind him.

Katie peeked into the narrow back seat and saw it was strewn with clothes, and toys, and food wrappers, much like the back seat of her car with Carlie riding back there.

"I wrecked the Nova one night last year driving home from work." He took off his ball cap and shoved his hair out of his eye. "See that scar?" He tilted his head toward her. Not waiting for a response, he continued, "Took fifteen stitches to close it up. I'm still paying that doctor bill."

"Oh, man, that sucks," she said, reaching up to run her finger along the scar. It felt so natural, touching his face, the feeling of worry. It was like the time they'd been apart hadn't really happened. "I'm glad you're okay though."

"Yeah, the car was totaled, and insurance paid for this." He patted the steering wheel. "If I'd have been smart, I would have found a king cab instead of this crew cab and had more room for the boys' car seats. They're squished back there."

"There wasn't much room in the back seat of the Nova, if I remember correctly." As soon as the statement left her mouth, Katie bit her bottom lip and faced the window to hide her embarrassment. She thought she heard a soft laugh from Danny and ventured a look in his direction.

He smirked at her. "So, you remember what the back seat of my car was like?" He waggled his eyebrows and the anxious tension that had surrounded them during the short ride from Newton evaporated. Behind it, a comfortable familiarity settled in its place.

Katie smiled. "I remember it quite well. And quite fondly." She shifted in the seat to face him better. "In fact," she paused, her cheeks burning at the thought, "I almost lost my virginity in that back seat. It was your chivalry that saved me."

"As I remember it," he said, his smile widening, "you were the one who stopped us each time."

She nodded at the correction. If he'd only known how hard it was for her to say no back then, when all she wanted was to feel him on top of her, matching her rhythm to his. Six years ago, the time hadn't been right. She was young and inexperienced. He was barely an adult with too many responsibilities, and she didn't want to add to his burden. It seemed the time had never been right for them. Even now, as they rode in agreeable silence, she was acutely aware of a feminine presence. A delicate, plastic dolphin hung from rear view mirror emitting a mild floral scent.

"At any rate," she finally said, "it didn't happen. Nothing turned out like I expected." Catching his profile from the corner of her eye, she saw his lips draw into a thin line and suspected he shared her sentiment.

As they rode, she took in the scenery, so different from the last time she'd been there. "They're cutting down so many trees," she said as they passed a cleared area that was formerly wooded.

"Yeah, they've replanted, but housing developments are growing in quicker than the trees." He slowed as they came closer to the town limits. Turning left, he meandered along narrow, dirt roads that seemed familiar to her.

As they turned a corner, a small bridge with a driveway behind it veered off to the right and at the head of it stood a metal post reaching high into the sky. Atop it sat a martin house painted sunflower yellow.

"Isn't this..." she trailed off, peering down the drive. The lot was empty, but the blue dollhouse that she remembered

SUMMER RUSH

had once covered Danny's pump, sat in the far corner.

He pulled his truck into the drive. "Yep. Mr. Tillman sold the trailer once I moved to Newton. I think he's going to sell the lot too. So many out-of-towners are buying up the land here it's more of a vacation destination than the quiet little town I grew up in." He stopped the truck next to the pump house and cut the engine. It took no time for the cab to warm up though the sun had fallen behind the clump of trees to the southwest.

"So, tell me what you've been up to since your divorce," Katie said, unbuckling her seatbelt and shifting to face him.

"You know, same old same old." He found a station on the radio that played modern hits and turned the volume down low. "I work long hours at the dairy, get home in time to tuck my boys in, catch some zees, then start all over again in the morning." He hesitated to look at her for a long moment, then sighed and seized her attention with his piercing blue eyes. "What about you? Teaching's got to be a good job, helping little kids."

"It has its days, but most of them are good," she said, feeling the pride she had for the hard work she put in the classroom. "But nothing compares to being a mom."

As the darkness grew around them, the conversation turned to their children and the joys of parenting. They compared first words spoken and first steps taken, disciplining strategies and potty training.

"Boys are pretty easy," Danny said. "They just drop their drawers, aim and shoot."

"I can imagine." Katie laughed at the description. "Girls I imagine take a little more finessing. Carlie's not interested in potty training yet. We just got her off the bottle a few months ago. I can't imagine what it's going to be like when I take the binky away."

Danny's posture stiffened. "So, did he ever come around and decide to help out with her?"

"Who? Brian?" Katie asked, certain that she heard a hint

209

of jealousy in his voice. "No. He's gone career military and has very little to do with us." In the dark, she thought she saw his body relax. "My sisters and Grammy help me the most with Carlie."

"I'd really like to see her sometime." Danny slapped at his arm, turned over the engine, and rolled up the windows. "Damn mosquitoes."

"Remember how bad they used to be on Aunt Maggie's dock?" Katie smiled at the memory, her head tilting so that the light from the streetlamp fell across her cheek.

"I remember," Danny said, his voice husky. He shifted in the seat, moving a little closer, sliding a finger under her chin and lifting it so she faced him. "I remember spending hours out there with you driving me crazy in those tank tops and boxer shorts barely covering your ass." He slid nearer to her, and like a magnet, she inched toward him, closing the space between them. "I also remember"--his voice was barely a whisper--"the taste of your lips."

Without another word, he leaned in and claimed her mouth. One hand slipped around the back of her neck and pulled her face to his. The other hand found her waist to draw her against him. They met in the middle of the bench seat, the lyrics of Night Ranger's "When You Close Your Eyes" droning in the background.

Katie's heart raced with the emotion of having Danny there next to her, his arms around her, his mouth on hers. As the end of the song faded away, the first boom of the fireworks startled the couple and they parted.

Catching her breath, Katie's head cleared enough to remember that Lisa mentioned something about a woman. "I, uh, don't want to ruin a moment, if that's what we're having here, but don't you have a girlfriend?"

Danny scooted back a little further and stared intently at her. "Yeah, you could call her that, though she is eight years older than me."

Katie's mouth gaped open, but she caught it before Danny

saw her. "Uh...wow. How, um, where did y'all meet?" She slid further over to the passenger side and ran a hand over her hair. The fireworks blasted above them, but neither had the inclination to look.

"Do you really want to sit here and talk about the woman I live with?" He waited for her answer. When she didn't produce one, he continued, "Why did you come here, Katie?"

She felt the despair bubbling up in her chest and didn't trust herself to reply. Danny waited silently for her to say something. Finally, she responded, "I don't know. I guess I just wanted to see you. I mean, after the letter you sent, I just..." Her reply trailed off and she glanced up to view a gorgeous explosion of reds and oranges. Exactly how she was feeling at the moment.

"That letter was written in a moment of weakness," Danny said. His voice was barely audible, and Katie saw even in the darkness that his jaw was taut. "I shouldn't have sent it."

"I'm glad you did," she protested. "It was raw and vulnerable. Something I've only seen in you once before."

"Those things I wrote can never happen. My life is here and yours is back in Jacksonville."

"But they could! You just have to believe in it, in us." She straightened, the full force of her persuasion aimed at him. "Just move to Jacksonville. Say you want to be with me, and we'll make it happen."

"How? My job is here. I have help with my boys here."

"I can help you with—"

"No, we've talked about this. Our lives are just too different." He slid his seat forward and cranked the truck. "I'm glad I got to see you, but I don't think it's a good idea if you come back down here anymore. It's too much."

She turned to face the window, trying to hold back the tears that threatened. Same old Danny, always making the choice for her. Maybe he was right. Maybe they were too different. Maybe too much time had passed, but they'd never know because he wouldn't give them the chance.

"Fine," she said. She ran her finger under her eye as inconspicuously as possible. "Take me back to Frosty's so I can get my car. And you can go get your boys."

He followed the same winding path out as he did in, and fifteen minutes later they were in Newton.

Katie slid from the truck and unlocked her SUV. She thought about leaving without another word, but that would make it easy for him. She turned back to his truck and opened the door. "It didn't have to be this way. We could have made it work," she said. "For what it's worth, I still care." He didn't look at her. "Aren't you going to say anything?" She waited a moment more. "Then tell your sister that I don't need her spare room after all. I'm heading back home tonight." She saw his jaw twitch, and he turned toward her and nodded.

She got in her Explorer and, after he pulled from the parking lot, the floodgates opened. In that moment, she promised herself she'd never let him make her feel that way again. She was done.

CHAPTER 19
Back to School

TWO YEARS AGO

Danny

After spending the little time he did with Katie on the Fourth, Danny came to the conclusion that his life just wasn't that fulfilling anymore. Sure, he had his boys, and they were the main reason he got up every morning, but that was all there was to his existence. Just the sight of Katie ignited a fire in him that had burned out long ago. And when he thought about how he'd made her cry, *again*, and how he'd let her drive away without another word from him, he wanted to beat his *own* ass.

The latest live-in, Karen, grilled him all week about why the boys kept talking about ice cream and Daddy's friend, but what could he tell her? That he'd met up with an old flame? A woman he hadn't seen in years but was still in love with? No, Danny decided he'd have to bide his time until he could figure out his next move.

Katie was doing so well back in Jacksonville, he thought as he turned down the dirt road leading to the single-wide he shared with Karen, her daughter Miranda, and his boys.

Katie had a great teaching job, something she'd only ever mentioned in her letters, and a little girl that she obviously was crazy about. The baby's dad wasn't exactly father of the year material, but she'd said he was supporting her and the baby financially like he was supposed to. Yeah, her life was golden, and Danny had no right to shake that up.

Besides, his life, his work, was here in Trinity. He couldn't just pull up stakes and move his boys to a new city in the hopes that everything would work out. He didn't have Katie's optimism.

Still, he couldn't get her out of his mind. She'd matured a lot even in the four years since he'd last saw her after her high school graduation. And he'd heard that having a baby changes a woman's body, fills it out more. He'd seen those changes with Crystal's body when she had Clay and Trent, but Katie had gone from this thin, soft high school *child* to a fuller, stronger woman with curves he wanted to run his hands all over.

"Damn," he grunted, reaching to his crotch to adjust his jeans. He pulled the truck into the driveway and both boys came running out to greet him. Karen stood on the porch, arms crossed over her chest, a scowl on her usually pleasant face. Danny paused with his hand on the door handle. Trent stood on tiptoe to peek in through the window and Clay beat his little fists on the outside of the door. Slowly, he opened the door and was immediately jumped on by both of them.

"Daddy, daddy!" Clay cried as he threw his arms around his daddy's legs. Danny scooped him up and ruffled Trent's hair as he bounced beside his dad. "We get i'ceem?" he asked.

"That's all they've been talking about since last weekend," Karen called as the three of them approached the steps. "Your sister spoils them too much. They expect things we ain't got."

"Lisa does no such thing," Danny said, an exasperated sigh escaping from his lips. "And we can afford to get the boys ice cream every now and then." He set Clay down and walked in the house for a cold drink.

Karen followed him in and shut the door. Danny turned to face her. Her long, dark hair was up in a ponytail, pulled sharply away from her face, and giving her the look of a stern librarian. In the dimness of the trailer, he could still see the troubled look in her eyes. He sighed again.

"Seriously, I know money's tight, but we can do some nice things every once in a while." He peeled off his shirt and tossed it across the back of a chair, then took a seat. Popping the can tab, he took a long swig before glancing up at Karen. He could tell from her glare their conversation wasn't just about buying ice cream for the boys. "What?"

"Who else was there when you took the boys to Frosty's?" The creases in her forehead deepened. "Trent said it was some woman."

"Have you been grilling my boys now, too?" Danny rose from the seat, crushed the empty can between his palms, and hurled it toward the trashcan in the corner. It rattled against the wall, emphasizing the tension growing between the two. He'd been skirting the subject of seeing Katie all week, but he finally figured he owed Karen an explanation. "Fine. She was just a friend from a long time ago. Lisa called and said she was in town and wanted to see the boys."

"Then, why couldn't I come?"

"You were working." He leaned against the breakfast bar, facing her. "You said you didn't care if we went without you."

"If you'da asked, I would have tried to take the night off." She'd pivoted to follow his movement, but her expression hadn't changed. "I didn't know you'd be meeting some woman."

He didn't have a good reason why she couldn't have met Katie. Deep down, Danny knew that he wanted to keep Katie away from the mess his life had become. She was his ideal, his golden dream girl. The one he felt he didn't deserve. He also knew that Karen would read way more into the meeting than what it was supposed to be--two old friends catching up.

But was that all it really was? Did Karen have a reason to worry? No, not really. Sure, he'd kissed her, but Katie was from his past. Someone he didn't have anything in common with anymore. Karen was his now. He glanced around the tiny room at the secondhand furniture and lopsided pictures of the boys hanging on the wall. He always knew his life would be like this--stuck in a runty town doing menial work to make ends meet.

"Danny, answer me." Karen's voice brought him back to the present. "Why couldn't I meet her?"

He sighed, defeated. "Because I thought you'd feel weird meeting an old girlfriend of mine."

"I thought you said she was just a friend." The anger in her voice pitched as she settled her hands on her hips.

"Yeah, well, that's all she is now. Just an old friend." He picked up his shirt and made his way down the narrow hall to the bedroom they shared. Karen followed him and shut the door.

"Do I need to worry?" She sat on the edge of the bed while he rummaged through drawers for a change of clothes.

Finding an old pair of shorts and a tank top, Danny shoved the drawer shut. He turned to face her. "No, you have nothing to worry about. We're just old friends. She's got a life back in Jacksonville. And I'm...here." He realized, too late, that Karen would read more into that than he wanted her to.

"Here, with me. But you'd really rather be with her, is that it?" Her voice rose to a twangy pitch, and she drew a cigarette from the pack on the dresser. Lighting it, she waited for his answer.

"Yes, I'm here. With you and the boys." He discarded his jeans and pulled on the clean clothes. "If I didn't want to be here, do you think I would? Karen you've got to let this jealousy bit go." Shoving his renewed feelings for Katie deep down, he squatted in front of Karen and took her shaking hand. "I'm here, with you. This is my life. Katie is just a friend. Probably one I'll never see again."

She turned her head and blew a stream of smoke away from them. "Okay. But if she ever shows up again, don't leave me in the dark. I want to know. Otherwise, I'll think you're sneaking around behind my back again."

He dropped her hand and nodded. "All right." Standing, he grabbed his ball cap from the dresser. "I promised Ronnie I'd ride over and help him with the brakes on his car this evening. I'll be back in a couple of hours."

Karen crushed the cigarette in an ashtray on the dresser. "Don't be late for dinner," she called to his retreating back.

Twenty minutes later, Danny pulled his pickup in Ronnie's driveway on the outskirts of Newton. Like most everybody that had escaped the confines of tiny Cypress Springs, Ronnie had ended up in a double-wide mobile home that had seen better days. The side yard was overgrown with weeds and the trailer's skirting was cracked with large pieces missing in places.

Danny ambled around back and found his cousin underneath a '92 four-door Cavalier. His feet stuck out from under the bumper and Danny walked over to give his foot a nudge. "Bro, I'm here. What do ya need help with?"

Slowly, Ronnie wiggled his way from beneath the car. Standing, he brushed some of the dirt from his bare arms. "I've just about got the pads back on. Give me a few minutes and then I want to switch out some belts and change the air filter."

"So, what you're saying is you really didn't need me at

all." Danny leaned over the exposed engine, checking the fan belt and serpentine belt.

Ronnie grabbed a wrench and dropped back to the ground to wiggle under the car again. "Actually, I heard you had a visit from that little fox you dated a few years back. What's her name?"

"Katie," Danny said. Just the sound of her name made his stomach flip. He pressed against the car and rested on his elbows. "Who told you?"

"Your sister. I ran into her at the Piggly Wiggly and asked about you. I hadn't seen you in ages. I guess Karen keeps a tight rein on you."

Danny snorted. "She tries. She's on my ass now wanting to know why I took the boys to meet an old flame."

"You told her about Katie?" Ronnie crawled back out from beneath the car, swiping his hands down the front of his pants.

"Only after she pestered me for the last week. There's really nothing to tell."

"That's not what I heard." Ronnie waggled his eyebrows in Danny's direction and tossed the wrench into the box of tools at his feet. "Lisa said when she left with the boys, you two were still lost in your own world, reminiscing is my guess?"

Danny twisted away from his friend. The sun was setting behind the home across the street, and now he wished he'd never had come over. He didn't want to be sharing details of his and Katie's recent meeting with his cousin. Some things he liked to keep private.

"So? Any old sparks still flying or are you totally over her? Lisa said she was a college girl with a baby now. Bet that did a number on her body."

"Dude, shut up. You don't know how ignorant you sound."

"Then tell me. For the last six years I've been watching you go from one woman to the next trying to get over that girl. When are you going to admit it--you ain't over her. Not by a long shot."

Danny flicked away a piece of paper he'd been twisting. He turned to face Ronnie. "You're right. I ain't over her, but I can't be with her."

"Why not? When we were younger, you couldn't stand to be away from her. All I heard was 'Katie this' and 'Katie that'. Hell, if you weren't whining about not seeing her, you were planning on how you could get off work early to go over to Maggie's." Ronnie paused and Danny glanced up at him. He continued, "Now, she's come back into your life, and you have a chance to grab what you've always wanted. Ain't you even the least bit curious as to whether it'd work or not?"

"No, because I know it wouldn't. She's got a kid with another guy and her life's back all the way hell on the east coast." He knocked his closed fist on the car's side panel. "I've...made my life here with Karen and the boys. We're just too different now. Besides, what would a college grad like her want with some guy with two kids, who barely got his GED? Nah, it's better this way."

"What way? You breaking your back at the dairy to have a mediocre life that's barely worth living? Man, she came back here to see you. She's got to have some kind of feelings for you, driving across the state just to see you for what, one night?" Danny didn't correct him, and his cousin continued. "You could finally move out of Cypress Springs and be with the one woman that you've been Jonesing on for over a decade." Ronnie leaned over the engine and began pulling at a belt. "And that bullshit about you not being good enough for her? Dude, you're the best dad I know. The hardest working son of a bitch around. If anything, she doesn't deserve you."

Danny rolled his eyes, then punched Ronnie's arm good-naturedly. "Bro, shut it. You're making me feel weird with all this mushy touchy-feely talk." Then he grew solemn. "But seriously, what would I have to offer her? A dead-end job and two kids to feed. Don't get me wrong, I love my boys and wouldn't give them up for the world, but I won't have Katie supporting us."

"Hey, have you ever thought about going back to school?" Ronnie reached in his back pocket and pulled out a folded paper. "I found this on my windshield when I took Juliette to the clinic."

Danny took the paper from him and read about the state's new opportunity for single parents wanting to go to college. "I don't have the grades or the time to go back to school."

"You don't need grades. This is a vocational program, specially designed for working single parents. It says there you'd even get a stipend for daycare, whatever that is."

"It means they'd pay for someone to watch my kids some."

"See, you're smart enough to go back to school." Ronnie gave the belt he was holding one final tug and it shifted into place. "Where there's a will there's a way, man. If you want a better life for you and your boys, you've got to take the chance."

"Mind if I keep this?" Danny folded the paper back up and, with a nod from Ronnie, shoved it in his back pocket. If he had any hope of getting Katie back, he'd have to get his shit together first. Maybe this was the first step. If nothing else, he'd be able to get a better job that paid more than minimum wage. Now, to figure out what to do about Karen.

CHAPTER 20
Life Goes On

TWO YEARS AGO

Katie

A week after seeing Danny, Katie threw herself into preplanning for the new school year. Teaching third graders was going to be a blast. Getting her mind off the pain of yet another rejection by him was a welcome side effect of gearing up for the new school year.

She and her daughter were settled into their new rental house, just a short drive from her grandma's. Carlie was starting a new daycare. Katie's grandma had suggested it since Holly would be leaving in the fall for college and Shannon was still in high school. Though the older woman loved keeping the baby, she just wasn't as patient and energetic as the child required. Katie completely understood.

The preparation for her classroom filled her mind with new decorations for her word walls and all the new children she'd meet. These were last year's second graders, and some were ones she'd taught recently. It didn't bother her, though. She loved the school, the students, and her grade level team. She had truly lucked up with this placement.

The year started with little issue. Katie got into a routine, dropping Carlie off at daycare, working, picking Carlie up after work, and hurrying home to make dinner, do baths and bedtime routines, before crashing on the couch to grade papers while watching TV. All was going good in her life, until the phone call from Brian.

"What the hell, Katie?"

"Well, hello to you too." Katie rested the phone between her shoulder and jaw and settled Carlie into her highchair. Fitting the tray snuggly, she dumped a handful of Cheerios in front of the child and turned toward the fridge to find something for dinner.

"My CO is all over my ass about some letter the state sent him. That I owe them money for the birth of my child? What'd you tell them? Why are they sending me hospital bills?"

Katie sighed. After a long day at work, that ended with an angry parent conference during afternoon planning *and* a pointless faculty meeting, all she wanted to do was feed her baby, draw a bath, and have a glass of wine. "Because Carlie is *your* child, your responsibility, too, Brian. The hospital asked for the name of the father for the birth certificate, and I gave it to them."

"I told you: kids weren't in our future." She could imagine the thin veins bulging at his temples and his usually baby blue eyes darkening to a stormy cobalt. "How do I even know this one's mine, huh? It was at least four months after I left that you sent me that letter telling me you were pregnant. How do I know that you didn't find some other poor joker to knock you up and you're just telling me that it's mine? Huh?"

Katie slammed the chunk of frozen meat on the counter, then turned quickly to check on Carlie. She didn't want to frighten her baby. She ran her hand over the baby's head and hurried from the kitchen.

"Are you fucking kidding me?" Her voice low, she nearly

whispered the words through the line, though she felt the fire in every word. "Why would I lie about something like that? You've known me for nearly a decade. Name one time I haven't been honest with you?"

"Oh, okay. How about that time you went out of town to see your ex? Huh, how about that?"

"We aren't together! You've made it perfectly clear that you don't want a relationship with me, Brian. So, I have every right to meet old friends. But we're talking about taking care of your child! Carlie is your baby, whether you like it or not, and both I and the U.S. government expect you to honor your obligations to your child."

"Look, I gotta go." Katie heard him yell something unintelligible and imagined his hand covering the receiver. "There are other guys who want to call their families. But when I get home in two months, we're going to talk about this."

"You bet your ass we are." Katie felt the tears forming in her eyes but blinked them back. She cleared her throat and waited for him to say goodbye. Instead, she heard the click of a deadline and hung up her phone.

She peeked around the corner of the kitchen and saw Carlie engrossed in picking up the Cheerios and dropping them one at a time on the floor below. Katie sighed again. *This wasn't how it was supposed to be.* She wiped at the wayward tears that had escaped and ran her fingers through her hair.

"I will not shed anymore tears over that asshole," she stated before stepping into the kitchen to fix dinner. She poured Carlie a few more Cheerios on her tray with a reprimand to not drop them on the floor, then she swept up the few errant ones before turning to make dinner.

Maybe it was a good thing that Brian showed his true nature now, and not when he came home, and she would have to face him every day. At least knowing how he felt now would give her a chance to adjust her life to not having him be involved with her. Carlie was another story though. Katie wanted Brian to be a part of Carlie's life, unlike her own father who'd had very little to do with Katie or her sisters once he divorced her mother.

Maybe that's just the way it was, especially during their generation. The media talked all the time about the studies done on absentee fathers and the effects absenteeism has on the children. Or maybe she was making a generalization based on her one experience. Well, on her *two* experiences, if she counted Brian's reaction. Still, it sucked that moms were the ones who were left to be the sole providers of their children when dads didn't want to take responsibility.

As she made a quick dinner of spaghetti, her thoughts shifted from obsessing over her life as a single parent to the night's routine. After Carlie was fed, bathed, then put to bed, Katie settled down in front of the TV to grade papers. Alone with just the hum of the TV in the background, Katie allowed the full emotion of being alone envelope her. She set the stack of math papers aside and let the tears flow freely.

At least she now knew how Brian truly felt about them being a family. Accepting this would allow her to move on with her life, not that her life would change much. But at least she could meet friends when she wanted and go on dates if anyone ever asked her. Yes, she'd allow this grief tonight over the loss of an ideal family, but she vowed to not let it consume her. When Brian came home from this tour, she'd set him straight about what his role in Carlie's life would be, but that she, herself, would expect nothing from him in the way of a relationship.

Two weeks before Brian was supposed to come home, Katie got a phone call from his parents. Vivian and Bruce

Donahue had never gone out of their way to speak to her since the one time that she and Brian were dating the two couples had gone to dinner together. So, when Katie answered the phone and Vivian introduced herself, Katie was sure something was wrong.

"Are you sitting down?"

"Vivian, you're scaring me. You've called me out of the blue and now you want me to sit down. What's going on."

Katie heard the older woman sniffle through the line. "We just got a visit from the State Department. Brian was..." Vivian paused and Katie her a low wail behind a muffled receiver. Katie's stomach clenched and her whole body began to shake. A visit from the State Department could mean anything.

"Brian was what?" Katie asked, her voice thick and far away in her own ears.

"Brain was killed," Bruce said, obviously taking the phone from Vivian. "He died in a roadside bombing. Vivian and I just thought you should know since...since he'd last written us about possibly having a child. With you."

Katie dropped the phone. *Brian was killed. In a roadside bombing.* The words echoed in her head as she sank to the couch. Though he had made it clear he didn't want a relationship with her, Katie believed he'd want to get to know his daughter once he returned home from the Middle East. That was gone now.

She didn't know when the tears started as she stared at the floor, reminiscing about the good times she and Brian had had in college. The late-night study sessions that turned into make out sessions that led to her pregnancy. Homecoming week senior year and the Spring Formal in April before that year's graduation. Not that any of it mattered. He'd broken up with her right before he joined the military after graduation.

The buzzing of a dead phone line drew Katie from her thoughts. She picked up the receiver, listened to the buzz for a moment then returned the receiver to the cradle. A giggle from the baby monitor near the phone sounded so odd in the wake of the news. Katie rose from the couch and made her way to Carlie's room. Scooping up her smiling baby, she hugged the child close as the tears continued to trickle down her cheeks.

Two weeks later, Katie stood by Brian's graveside after a solemn service in a northside cemetery. Katie assumed it was a family plot. A double headstone was already in place with Vivian and Bruce's names on it. Their birthdays were engraved as well, but the death dates were obviously absent. Katie thought it was a bit morbid.

Nearly everyone who had attended the funeral had left. Brian's grandma, his parents, and his sister were all that remained behind. Katie turned to leave, but Bruce stepped in front of her.

"We'd, uh...we'd like you to come eat with us," the older man said. "We're going to Margiolli's. It's small, out of the way, and not too busy this time of day." He stared at her through the same sky-blue eyes that reminded her of Brian's, anticipation etched in his features.

"I have to get back," Katie said, a feeling of awkwardness overcoming her. Why would these people who hadn't spoken a dozen words to her in the last three years want her to come to dinner? "My Grammy is watching Carlie for me." When the child's name slipped out, Katie realized it. Their invitation had something to do with her daughter. She glanced at each family member, their faces a mixture of grief and expectancy.

"Well, that's what we want to talk to you about." Bruce shuffled, holding his hands out in front of him in placation.

Vivian laid a hand on Bruce's arm. "Honey, maybe now's not the right time."

"For what?" Katie asked. She wanted to hear it out loud. Though they had never been truly mean to her, Katie had always felt that she wasn't good enough for their family, coming from the 'dysfunctional' home that she did, being raised by her grandmother after her mother died. To have the couple admit that they needed her now, even in the morbid sense of holding onto a piece of their son's life through his child, was a small triumph for her.

"We want to talk to you about meeting...Carlie, your daughter," Vivian said. "Brian's daughter." The group stood there, staring at Katie, awaiting her answer.

Was it fair to keep them in suspense? Was it cruel to withhold Carlie from them? It was a little ironic that now that Katie had something they wanted, she was worthy of their attention. She studied the ground, thinking over the possibilities. She could allow them to see Carlie, be part of her life in a sense that Brain couldn't or didn't want to, or she could be vindictive and cut them out. They didn't want her. They wanted Carlie.

It was Barbie, Brian's sister, who stepped forward. "Look, Katie," she said, gently touching Katie's hand. "We've all lost Brian. And we don't know the exact nature of the relationship you had with him, whether it was serious or casual." Her shoulders sagged as she appeared to choose her words carefully. "He didn't share much with us after he went overseas. Heck, I hadn't seen him myself in over a year, and Mom and Dad said his calls were quick. And it sounded like the military and his deployment changed him." She stopped again. Her shoulder length blonde hair blew gently in the cool, fall breeze.

"At any rate, I'm not making excuses for him. We just want to meet Carlie and get to know her." Barbie offered a soft smile. "I'm sure she has plenty of people who love her, but wouldn't it be nice if we could add to that?"

"What's that saying," Bruce piped up. "It takes a village to raise a child."

Vivian finally spoke up, her words measured. "Let us be a part of that village, Katie. Yes, we want to meet Carlie, be a part of her life, because she's Brian's daughter, but dear, you can never have enough help with a small child. We just want to offer an olive branch and hopefully build back some kind of trust that we apparently lost years ago. For that, we're truly sorry."

Katie bit her bottom lip. It all sounded sincere, but she couldn't forget some of the truly ugly things that the Donahues were rumored to have said about her when she told Brian she was pregnant. To just forget that pain, let bygones be and all that, was something she'd have to think about.

"Today's not a good time," Katie finally said. "Give me your number and I'll call you to set up a lunch date one Saturday in a couple of weeks."

Vivian opened her mouth in what Katie thought might be a protest, but Barbie held up a hand. "That sounds fair, doesn't it Mom? Dad?"

"Yes," Bruce replied. "Today is too emotional. We need some time to adjust." He handed Katie the funeral program with their phone number scribbled at the bottom. "Give us a call when you decide."

Vivian stood beside her husband, her hands clutched against her chest, a tissue twisted in her fingers. She looked as if she wanted to say something but held her tongue.

"Okay, then." Katie tucked the program in her purse and turned toward her car. Walking back to her Explorer, conflicting thoughts waged a war between her mind and her heart. She wanted Carlie to know Brian's family, now that the child had lost her father, but Katie still held hard feelings about the insults the Donahues had placed on her.

She slid in the driver's seat and snatched a glance at the family that remained. They huddled together in a family hug, each of them shaking in what Katie presumed to be sobbing. Her heart softened a little, and she knew she'd be calling Brian's parents soon.

CHAPTER 21
Resting

PRESENT DAY

Katie

"That was Glenn Stoker," Maggie said when she returned from taking the phone call. "He's bringing over a shrimp net for me to mend."

"Wow, still doing that, huh?"

"It's a living," Maggie said, reclaiming her rocker.

"Do you think you'd have time to run me back to the hotel? I should be getting back there. It's been a couple of hours. I'm sure Danny has returned by now." She ran a hand across her forehead to wipe away the dripping sweat. "Probably wondering where I'm at."

"Glenn said he was heading right over," Maggie replied. "As soon as he gets here, I'll run you back. Besides, we haven't finished our visit. You haven't told me anything about your wedding or how he proposed or how the kids are getting along."

Katie smiled at the memory of Danny's proposal. It was sweet and simple, but definitely romantic and memorable. A wave of nausea threatened to bring up her lunch, and Katie swallowed hard. She tugged at the front of her shirt trying to capture a bit of air and stood up. "Whew, it's hot. Let me get a glass of water and then I'll tell you all about it."

Returning to the porch to resettle on the swing, Katie rubbed the frosted glass across her forehead and took a bite of a cracker she'd found in Maggie's cabinet. The older woman raised an eyebrow in question and Katie shrugged. "This heat is making me nauseas." She took another sip of water and set the glass on the table beside her.

"So, what led to y'all getting hitched?" Maggie propped her feet on the stool in front of her, spritzing herself with a water sprayer.

"Well, like I said, we kept in touch," Katie said. "We talked a lot on the phone, but I didn't really think anything would come of it. I guess I was waiting for Brian to come home from Iraq and finally tell me he wanted for us to be a family. I should have known that wasn't going to happen. He'd abandoned us even before Carlie was born."

"I'm sorry, honey." Maggie offered a sympathetic smile.

"And I had my kids at school," Katie continued. "I couldn't abandon them if he'd asked me to pack up and move." She looked at her aunt for confirmation. Maggie nodded, and Katie continued, "Then news came that Brian was killed in a roadside bombing while on patrol and that ended that fantasy. So, I threw myself into teaching and caring for Carlie. Danny's calls were just pleasant distractions from my daily life. Ones that allowed me to reminisce about happier times." She paused here to eat another cracker.

"Then, the last time he called me, we had this argument," she said, her voice softening at the memory. "I told him I couldn't keep doing this, hoping that he'd be with me and get my heart broken time and time again."

"Sounds reasonable."

"He said this time was different, but I didn't believe him. And I didn't hear from him for another month." She glanced up at her aunt, happiness lifting her spirits. "Not until he showed up at my door telling me he'd moved to Jacksonville and was renting a little house on Hecksher Drive."

"What?!" Maggie's surprise made Katie smile wider.

"Yep. Out of the blue. No phone call. Nothing. I just opened the door and there he was." Katie pushed at the floor with her toe, sending the swing into motion again. Her thoughts drifted back to that night, and she blushed. Their reunion had been ten years in the making. A decade of yearning, dreams, promises and pain, but that night had made up for all of it.

"So, what happened next?" Her aunt's question drew her from her reverie. "Did he make amends?"

"And then some." She couldn't tell her aunt of the passionate night they'd spent together, but she did explain the past three months. "We've always known we were meant to be together, so there was no question that we'd blend our families. Shortly after our reunion we got the children together to play and see how they got along. They're young, six, five and four, so of course there are little squabbles, but they act like they've known each other their whole lives. We moved Danny and the boys into my house a little over a month ago and planned the wedding in a matter of weeks."

"So, how is it again you're sitting here with me on your honeymoon instead of being with your husband?"

"That stupid disagreement." Katie rose from the swing and immediately sat back down. She covered her face with her hands. "Whoa, I got a little dizzy there. This heat is nothing to play with."

"Maybe we should go back inside?" Maggie crossed the porch to her and helped Katie in the house. "Why don't you lay there on the couch with the fan on you. I'll get you a cool washcloth for your head." The older woman shuffled from the room and Katie was left alone.

Her thoughts drifted back to six months ago, when Danny showed up at her door declaring his love for her. She smiled at the memory, closing her eyes to get lost again in that feeling of all-encompassing love.

In a matter of moments, she was asleep.

NO ONE BUT YOU

CHAPTER 22
Alone Again

ONE YEAR AGO

Danny

Choosing to go back to school was easier said than done. Danny had to work out daycare, which, though paid for by the stipend, meant a new activity in his routine. The boys didn't mind it. They made new friends to play with in the evenings. But after a long day at the dairy, Danny was exhausted while sitting in class. The instructor was proficient and the information interesting. Danny was just tired.

The classes were three nights a week. When Karen first heard about Danny going back to school, she complained about having to watch the boys. Once Danny explained about the evening daycare and getting another job that made more money, she was all for it. Until the end of the second week.

They sat together at the kitchen table, Danny slumped over the plate of food in front of him and Karen across from him, a cigarette dangling from between her fingers.

"How many more week of this do you have?" She took a long puff and blew the smoke above her head. Danny felt the trailer shake and knew her leg was bouncing, a sign that she was agitated. And he really didn't feel like dealing with her insecurities tonight.

"It's a four-month program, Karen." He scooped another spoonful of rice into his mouth and chewed slowly, controlling his temper. He'd be damned if he let another woman derail him from his dream of a better life for him and his boys. He swallowed the food and took a sip of tea. "This is the end of week two. So, fourteen more weeks."

"Shit." She took another drag and leaned forward. The clock on the wall, an old-fashioned one Karen brought to the home when she moved in, chimed on the half-hour. They both glanced up.

Ten-thirty, Danny thought and sighed. He hurriedly shoveled in the rest of his meal. *Four A.M. comes early, and I still need a shower.* He rose and rinsed his plate at the sink.

"You think you'll be able to keep this pace up?" Karen stood, partially blocking his way out of the tiny kitchen. "I mean, you barely have time for the boys, much less me and this place." She waved a hand indicating the single-wide. "Is it worth it? Losing four months of your life just to find another back-breaking job? I mean, we're doing all right, with you are the dairy and me at the home health center, aren't we?"

Danny ran his hands over the top of his head, entwining his fingers at the nape of his neck. He rose up to his full height and stretched, feeling the joints along the length of his back pop. "I won't be losing four months. I'll be gaining a skill, a real skill, that will help me earn more to take care of my...family." He was about to say, "my boys," but he didn't want to exclude her and catch hell for it. "Besides, this isn't enough. I don't want to do *all right.* I want better for my boys...and you." He'd caught himself, but it was too late.

"And myself. I want better than the way I was raised. And you should want that too, for yourself and Miranda."

"I do," she said, stepping toward him and wrapping her arms around his waist. "I just don't want to lose you." She stood on tiptoe and kissed him. "Ever since you started this *journey* to a better life, you've been gone so much I barely see you." She released him and leaned against the kitchen's arched entryway. "With our opposite work schedules, it's bad enough. Now, on my nights off, you come in from classes so late, you just eat, shower, and go to bed." She ducked her head and dug her toe under the small rug, then looked back up at him. "I miss you. I miss time together. Alone time."

She lowered her eyes and looked up at him through thick, artificial lashes. Her gaze traveled down his whole body, lingering at his crotch long enough for it to register with him—she missed the sex.

He felt a tiny twinge in his pants, but his exhaustion overruled his desire. At least that's what he told himself. The truth was, he'd stopped feeling passionate about Karen a while back. Sure, she was a good lay, very attentive in the sack, but the rest of the time he felt like she was mothering him, trying to run his life, telling him how to raise his boys.

He'd put off her sexual advances long enough that she was starting to suspect what he already knew. Did he really want to sleep with her just to pacify her insecurities? Hell, he'd done it before, with his past relationships. What made Karen any different? Besides, it was easier to give in than to fight, especially this late at night. A quickie after his shower would satisfy her need for intimacy and would make for an easy drift off to sleep for him.

"Let me grab a quick shower and I'll meet you in bed, okay?" To hurry things along, he tugged his shirt over his head and unbuttoned his jeans.

Karen's lips stretched into a sultry smile, and she grabbed him for a deep, tongue-filled kiss as he tried to maneuver around her. "Don't be long or I'm joining you." She turned from him and sauntered down the hall.

Danny sighed. He was exhausted. His brain was achy from learning and his body tight from work and, though he hated to admit it, from Karen's sexual advances. He wasn't really feeling the mojo tonight, but to keep peace in his relationship, he'd play along. At least for a while longer.

Playing along lasted just two more weeks. It wasn't a big blow-up, like he'd expected. One day, Karen just decided that she had enough, or rather, wasn't getting enough of him--his time, his attention--and she needed more.

They had all planned to go to the river to fish and relax on a beautiful spring day. Danny and Karen would bring all three kids, since it was her weekend with her daughter, and pack a picnic lunch. A real attempt at family time instead of hurrying off to work or making repairs around the house. Something the couple had tried only a couple of times.

Maybe that's the problem, Danny thought, as he rolled on his side. *We haven't really tried to do family things.* He glanced at the box fan that was propped in the open window. Pieces of duct tape held the front cover against the fan box, and he was reminded of yet another minor repair that needed to be done. The fan was turned off, a sign that Karen had been up for a while. It was her signal for him that it was time to wake up. In the Florida humidity of late April, the room became stuffy without the air circulation.

Danny kicked off the sheets and rolled onto his back. The ceiling of the single wide trailer was dotted with taupe-colored circles where rain had seeped through. He sighed as he added roof repair to the list. *With everything that needs to be done around here, who has time for fishing or relaxing?*

He rubbed a hand up his chest and his mind drifted to the future, where he was making more money as a welder. He'd be able to afford a better home for his family.

He imagined coming in from work and being greeted by the boys running up and hugging his legs like they did every evening. He'd sweep Clay up onto his hip and tousle Trent's hair as the boy yammered on about school or his friends or what he watched on TV that afternoon. But when he imagined the woman that would be there waiting for him, it was always Katie. And that made him feel guilty.

It wasn't like he was using Karen. They were both adults, and each came into this relationship with their own baggage. He just didn't realize she'd expect so much from him emotionally. Sure, he cared about her, but in the beginning, it was a physical attraction that brought them together. Now, that attraction had been replaced with complacency. They were just used to each other. The desire he'd felt early on had faded, and he didn't know how or if he should tell her.

He let out a long, low grumble and swung his feet from the bed. As he stood and stretched, a gnawing sense of unease rubbed at his subconscious. This wasn't the life he'd wanted. He pulled on his joggers and lumbered from the room, completing his usual morning routine without the usual haste.

As he cleared the hallway and entered the small living room, he noticed suitcases and a couple of boxes lined up in front of the entertainment center. A peak inside the top one revealed Karen and Miranda's personal bathroom items. How had he missed those not being scattered on the counter just a few minutes before?

Karen sat at the kitchen table, a coffee mug in front of her. She didn't look up when he moved to the coffee maker to pour himself a cup. A fog of tension permeated the room, and the early morning silence of the home added to it.

"I guess I'll be Mr. Obvious and ask," he said waving a hand toward the bags and boxes. "What's going on?" He set his mug on the table and slid into a dining chair. "It looks like you're packed for a trip. Where you going?"

"Gainesville," Karen said. She lifted her gaze to meet his. She gripped her cup with both hands, and Danny noticed the tightness of her fingers.

"What for?" In his heart, he already knew. Karen had family, a sister, in Gainesville. And this much packing was for something other than a quick weekend trip.

"I'm moving there." Karen glanced out the window to the small front porch, and Danny followed her gaze. He hadn't noticed Miranda sitting in the camp chair out there, but the teen glanced back toward the couple. Catching Danny's eye, she dropped her gaze and ducked a little lower in the chair.

"Again. What for?" Though he knew he should be more upset than he was, Danny couldn't make himself care any more. He had a limited number of fucks to give and most of them were already assigned to bigger, more pressing issues. Besides, he wanted to hear her say it. He wanted Karen to be the one to end it.

"My sister has lined me up a job at Centiva making more money."

"But you could drive from here to Gainesville for that." Was he really trying to convince her to stay, or just putting on a good front? Even he couldn't tell.

"And drive nearly an hour one way?" She let out an exasperated huff. "That'll waste too much gas."

"So, what? You're just leaving us?"

"Come on Danny. You knew this was just temporary." She rose from the seat and set her cup in the sink. She didn't return to her chair, so Danny swiveled to face her. "As much as I wanted us to be a family, you're still trapped in the past with that girl."

It was his turn to avert his gaze. Katie was his kryptonite, his one weakness. And Karen was right. He was just surprised that he hadn't hidden it better. "I thought..."

"What? That I couldn't tell?" She crossed her arms in

front of her chest. "Ever since the Fourth of July you've been different. Distant. And now this new vo-tech class? You sure as hell aren't changing for me."

A wave of guilt washed over him, and he wanted to rise, to pull her to him and tell her she was wrong. But he didn't because the truth was, she wasn't wrong. He wasn't doing all this for her. This was for him, and his boys. So that they could have a better life, regardless of what woman was in it.

"Bet you didn't think I'd call you on it, did you?" Her words weren't hateful, just honest. And sometimes honesty hurt worse than hate. After a long pause, Karen moved to the living room. "So, we'll be staying with Donna for a while until I've saved up enough to get my own place."

He rose from his seat. "Need any help?"

"You aren't even going to try to stop me? Ask me to stay?" She set down the bag she held.

He blew out a long breath, the muscles in his arms tightening. He could be a nice guy and ask her to stay, promise to work harder to make it work. Or he could let her go, and they would both be free to find their own happiness. His lack of response was enough of a response.

"Never mind." She picked up the bag again and trudged through the door. "Miranda, go get your bags and tell Danny bye."

The girl tiptoed in, careful not to make too much noise, and picked up a box. "Bye, Danny. Tell the boys I said bye."

"Sure thing, kid." He stroked her hair, then she turned from the room to carry the box to her mom's car. His heart felt heavier at what this break-up would mean to the kids, but he reasoned that they'd be better off in a single-parent home than an unhappy one.

Danny lugged two of the largest suitcases out to the car and loaded them in the trunk.

"I'll be back next weekend for the rest of my things." Karen stood by her driver door, appearing to be waiting for something. When Danny didn't move, she walked to him and kissed his cheek. "I hope it's worth it."

"I hope you enjoy your life in Gainesville." He pulled her to him for a quick hug, then released her just as quickly to return to the porch. He watched as she drove out of the yard and out of his life as easily as she had come in.

And he was alone again.

CHAPTER 23
The Last Phone Call

SIX MONTHS AGO

Katie

Katie jumped from the recliner in a hurry to grab the phone from its cradle. Hannah was asleep on the sofa and Katie didn't want the ringing to wake her. They had been watching a Barney video when Hannah drifted off, and now Katie watched reruns of *Party of Five*.

"Hello?" she nearly whispered into the receiver so as to not wake Hannah.

"Hey," the male voice on the other end returned. The voice sounded vaguely familiar, like a hazy, buried memory trying to resurface.

"Who is this?" Katie questioned. She hated phone games, especially with all of the freaks out there now who tried to take advantage of unsuspecting women.

"Who is *this*?" the voice mimicked, a hint of teasing and mischief tickling through the phone line.

"Look, I don't have time for games. Tell me who this is or I'm hanging up," Katie threatened. Her blood pressure rising with the exasperation she was feeling at the stupidity of the game the caller wanted to play.

"Well, now, if you hang up, you'll never find out who this is will you, Katie-did," the voice said. A light switched on in Katie's head. Only one person other than her Grammy ever called Katie by her childhood nick name, Katie-did. And she remembered vividly the day she'd explained her nickname to the beautiful blond boy from her past.

"Danny?" Katie barely breathed. "Is that you?" The question nearly stuck in her throat like a swallowed ice cube, freezing yet suffocating.

"Who else would it be?" he responded.

Katie thought of the last time they'd seen each other at the Fourth of July festival. They'd said their goodbyes, for what she thought was the last time. Yet here he was calling her again. And here she was, feeling the same mix of trepidation and love. Yes, she still loved him after everything he'd put her through. Maybe it was the hope that they'd eventually find their way back to each other that kept her accepting his calls and wishing that he'd finally day she was the only one for him. She took in a ragged breath and tried to steady her nerves.

"Hey, did I lose you?" His voice, a little lighter than she remembered, brought her out of her reverie.

"Oh, no. I'm still here." Katie found her voice. "I just can't believe it's you. How did you get my number? What's been going on? How's Lisa and the boys?" The questions shot out of her rapid fire, and she paused to catch her breath.

"Ease up, darlin'," Danny said, a chuckle drifting through the phone line. "You got time to talk?"

"Sorry, I'm just so surprised to hear from you," Katie said breathlessly. "I mean, after the way we left things..." Her voice trailed off and she wondered if he was also thinking about their last meeting. "Yeah, I can talk." So she didn't wake Carlie, she walked to her bedroom. It gave her a minute to her emotions in check. This was his effect on her--all logic went out the window where he was concerned.

"Okay," she said, shutting the bedroom door. "So, what have you been up to? It's been a while!"

"Just working," Danny answered. "I've been working for a construction company now for a couple of years. Remember?"

"Yeah, I remember you saying something about it. How's that going?" She stretched out on her stretched out on her bed, savoring the sound of his voice, but having trouble conjuring a mental image of him.

"I travel a lot. Lisa and my aunt Linda keep the boys for me when I travel out of town."

"Yeah? Like where to? Just in Florida or out of state?" It was still hard for her to believe she and Danny were making small talk after everything they'd been through. Memories flashed rapid-fire through her mind of the many times over the years that they'd talked and seen each other: Katie's high school graduation when he told her he was getting married and going to be a father; the times she'd visited Lisa and saw Danny and his family in passing, not really talking to him; the summer she'd moved to Tallahassee and begged Danny to move there to be with her when his wife had left him. His refusal had devastated Katie; she had expected him to jump on the chance to be with her, but she'd realized that they weren't the same young kids who'd fallen in love that summer of '85.

Though it had ended too quickly, and she left Cypress Springs with her heart broken, the burning belief that they were soul mates and meant to be together had supported her through the many hardships and heartaches of high school, college, and beyond. Now, the sound of Danny's voice on the other end of the phone line brought her to the present with descriptions of some of his more recent trips for his work. He told Katie of jobs all around the state, specifically the year he had to move to Miami after Hurricane Andrew to help rebuild.

"So, what about you? How's your baby? Carlie, right?"

His voice softened at the mention of her child and Katie's heart clenched.

"Yeah, she's my life," Katie answered. "She's just turned two and is as sweet as can be."

"Does she look like you?" Danny asked.

"Mostly, yeah. But she has Brian's ears, poor baby," Katie said.

"And how's that going?" Danny's voice shifted, tightened, at the mention of Carlie's dad, and Katie imagined his eyes darkening with jealousy.

"Lisa didn't tell you that part?" Katie sighed. "He was killed in Iraq right after being deployed."

"Oh, baby, I'm sorry." The clipped tightness was gone, and his voice was soft and loving life she remembered those nights spent on her aunt's dock.

"Yeah, well, it ended for us even before Carlie was born. Then he left for Iraq, but it's still sad for Carlie. She'll never know her daddy."

"But she's got you to tell her about him, and I know you won't believe me, but I'll be there for her if you'll let me."

Did she just hear him right? After all these years, did he finally want to be with her? Katie's breath caught in her chest at the suggestion.

"Yeah, sure." She didn't hide the sarcasm in her reply.

"Seriously, I've thought about nothing but you since last July," he explained. "I should have just packed up then and left this runty county with its bassackward ways, but I was so stupid."

"Why didn't you call me since then?"

"I wanted to protect you."

"From what?"

"From me. I'm not the most...*forthcoming,* when it comes to sharing my emotions. I thought if I got with you, I'd just find some way to fuck it up."

"Didn't you think I was capable of making my own choices? You took that away from me."

"With good reason. I didn't want to hurt you. Again." He offered the same excuse he had for years, and Katie was finally starting to realize it was his crutch. His way of trying to avoid failure and heartache. From what she knew, he *didn't* have the best luck with relationships. Maybe he was trying to keep from breaking her heart, *again*.

Katie's own emotions were a jumble of joy and hope and heartache and disappointment. She'd always thought they were meant to be together, but too many times life had interceded and put them on different paths. Almost like it was warning them. Of what, she couldn't figure out. And now there was Carlie to think of. And his boys, though with everything she knew from Lisa about his life, they were probably used to the changes.

Eventually, she found her voice again. "But you did hurt me. Every time you made up an excuse not to be with me, you hurt me. And if this time I say yes and you don't come through, I don't know if I'll survive it. I've already lost you more times than I can count."

"Baby, that won't happen again. I promise."

"How can I be so sure? You're a master of cut-and-run."

"Katie, baby, that's not fair," Danny pleaded. "You don't know what my life's been like. Everything I've had to deal with. But now, I've got my shit together. And I want to make it right with you."

"It's too little, too late. I've begged you to be with me, to move to Tallahassee, or Jacksonville. What if you decide, by the time we get off the phone, that you don't want to move. Or you don't want two more to take care of. What if" –she stifled a building sob— "I'm not enough for you?" The silence dominated the line. "I can't risk that. I've got Carlie to think of."

"But this time I mean it, Katie. You are the only woman I have ever truly, madly loved, and the only love I've ever regretted not following through on. I won't change my mind. Not this time."

"My heart can't risk it, Danny." Katie heard a whine from the living room. "I've got to go. Carlie's crying."

"Fine," Danny said, his voice tight. "Woman, you're in my blood. I love you, always have and always will. But I won't be calling again. It hurts me, too."

Tears welled up in her eyes and caught in her throat. "I understand. Have a good life." The line was silent. Katie thought Danny had hung up.

"Danny? You still there?"

"Yeah."

"I love you, too." And she hung up. The tears fell freely then, but only for a moment. She heard Carlie cry out again in the other room and rose to go comfort her child.

CHAPTER 24
Rebuilding

PRESENT DAY

Danny

Danny set the receiver back into the cradle. The anger in his chest threatened to explode. His boys were asleep in their bedroom, and he fell onto the couch, disgusted with the way he'd let his life get so out of control in the past. He'd let his temper and insecurities drive away the one woman he wanted to spend the rest of his life with. Katie wouldn't even talk to him anymore. And who could blame her? She'd had enough of his bull and called him on it. Precious Katie, the girl who'd claimed his heart a decade ago was now the woman who haunted his dreams.

And he'd let her get away one too many times. Sure, his life was pretty good now. He had his boys and a good paying job thanks to the New Horizons program he'd enrolled in last year. He even had a place of his own. No more shacking up with women just to have help with the boys and a warm place to rest his dick. And his boys were happy, not worrying if he was going to leave them like their mom or other women in his life had. Sure, he worked a lot, but Trent and Clay knew their daddy would come home every night.

No, I can't let her slip away again, he thought.

As he lay there watching another rerun of *Hawaii Five-0,* a ridiculous idea sprouted in the dank, murky depths of his self-pity. He'd win her back! Somehow, he'd prove to her that he wanted forever with her, that no other woman would ever be enough for him. The plot expanded and with it, hope. He sprang from the couch, excited with the new plan and anxious for the morning to come so he could put it into motion.

The next morning, he called in to work, requesting a couple of personal days. Next, he phoned his sister before driving over with the boys.

After outlining his plan, he looked over at her but couldn't get a clear read on her thoughts. "So, go ahead and say it, I'm bat-shit crazy, right?"

Lisa tilted her head and stared at him. She jumped at a squeal from the back of the house. Finally, she replied, "I'll give you this--you definitely understand the meaning of go big or go home."

"But do you think it'll work?"

"I guess. I mean, as long as you can really convince her you're serious. That this isn't like all the other times before."

"It's not. There's no way I'm letting her go this time." He rose from the dinette chair and went to find his boys. After giving them hugs and reminding them to be good, he thanked his sister again and was gone. He had four days to completely flip his life upside down. With the five grand from his savings box, he jumped in his truck and hit the highway pointed toward Jacksonville, excitement and fear warring inside him. *If this doesn't work,* he thought as he sped out of Newton, *then I'm fucked.*

Four weeks later, Danny and his boys had settled into their new routine in Jacksonville. He'd lucked up and found a small two-bedroom fixer-upper on the river to rent for super cheap. He'd also secured a job at Blount Island using his welding skills on the cargo ships docked there. One of his coworkers had lined him up with a relative who had an in-home childcare business to watch his boys. He'd seen all these easy adjustments as signs that he was on the right path. Now, he just had to contact Katie.

Many times, over the last few weeks, he'd imagined what their reunion would be like, but he could never get past the image of the last time he physically saw her. As he was leaving the Frosty's parking lot nearly two years ago, he'd glanced back in his rear-view mirror and saw her seated in her car, her head bent, her body shaking. He assumed she was crying. It took everything in him to not turn around and go to her then. But he'd reasoned with himself that it was best for them to try to move on with their lives. Boy, was he a fool!

Now, he waited for Clint's daughter to arrive to watch the boys. He'd arranged ahead of time for sixteen-year-old Gracie to spend the evening with the boys. He'd stocked the fridge with everything he thought a teen girl would want for snacks and had bathed the boys already. All she had to do was keep them from tearing up the house and put them to bed at eight-thirty, then she could watch all the cable T.V. she wanted.

She arrived at six, a bag flung over her shoulder. "My daddy said he didn't have a problem with me getting home late if you needed me to stay past eleven." The tall, athletic girl dropped her bag by the couch and bee-lined it to the kitchen for a soda. "But I do have a ball game tomorrow at noon, so I may be zonked out on the couch when you get in. If it's too late."

"Not a problem," Danny said grabbing his wallet and pulling out two twenty-dollar bills. "I don't think I'll be out past eleven, but you know where the extra blankets are, right?"

The girl had kept the boys a few times already when Danny and her parents had gone out when he first moved to Jacksonville. She was responsible and the boys liked her, though sometimes she could be too direct. She took the offered money and popped the tab on the soda before plopping down on the couch. "Wake me when you get in." With that, she flipped on the T.V. and quickly forgot about her employer.

Danny closed and locked the door behind him. The short ride from his home to Katie's neighborhood gave him little time to think about what he would say or do once he saw her. Though he'd been in Jacksonville for over a month, he could never quite figure out how he would approach Katie, but he'd put it off long enough. Every day that went by and he wasn't with her, he could feel himself getting a little more disheartened.

Now, the closer he got to Katie the sweatier his palms got. He followed the neighborhood roads to the address he'd memorized and mapped. It was imprinted in his mind, though he'd only visited once--graduation. As he pulled into Katie's family home, he thought it best to leave that lousy memory in the past.

He exited his car and trudged up the steps to knock on the door. A moment later a young woman, not more than seventeen, peeked through the window before opening the door a crack and sticking her head out.

"Hey," Danny said, reaching up and removing his ball cap, "I don't know if you remember me, I've only met you once before."

"Sure, I do," the girl said, "You're that guy who came by the day of Katie's graduation party. Danny, right?"

"Yeah." The tightness in his jaw lessened and he smiled at the girl. "Are you Holly or Shannon?"

"Shannon." She stepped onto the front porch and waved

at the neighbor across the street. "I'd invite you in but no one's home right now."

"I understand," he said, glancing behind him as the neighbor stopped her watering and watched them intently. Danny gave a nod and turned back to Shannon. "Actually, I'm here to see Katie. Know when she'll be back?"

"She doesn't live here anymore," the girl said.

Danny's body, along with his hope, deflated. *I drove all this way and she doesn't even live here anymore. How stupid can I be?*

"She moved a couple of miles away. To her own place."

With that, his spirits lifted. Then it wasn't a lost cause. He still had a chance. "Would you mind giving me her address? I'd really like to see her, and her little girl, Kayla?"

"Carlie." Shannon stared at him for a long moment, then a smile stretched across her stern face. "I guess so. I'll bet she's gonna flip when she sees you. Wait here." The girl disappeared inside and returned a moment later with an address scribbled on a piece of paper.

"Thanks," Danny said, he smiled back at the girl. "You don't know what this means to me."

"Sure thing." Shannon waited until Danny cleared the porch and started his truck before she went inside.

As he backed out of the driveway a new concern gripped him. What if Katie wasn't alone?

He followed the map to the modest ranch home a couple of miles from Deringer Road and parked on the street in front of it. For the fourth time that day, he checked his nerves. He removed his cap and dropped it in the seat beside him. Hopping out of the truck, he glanced down at his shirt and ran a hand over his stomach. *Good, no stains.* He took a deep breath, circled the truck, and made his way up the walk.

Before he could ring the bell, the front door flew open and there stood the woman who'd claimed his heart a decade ago. Still looking like the very breath of summer. Her hair was darker, her body a little fuller, but those big, beautiful brown eyes that looked on him with love twinkled with surprise.

"Danny?!" she said, her voice soft and breathless. "What-
-" She didn't finish her statement but propelled herself into
his arms.

He pulled her against him, the feel of her skin beneath his
hands, her breath on his neck. He inhaled long and deep, the
smell of her hair filling him with nostalgia from years ago.
This is the kind of reunion he'd dreamed of. One where they
wouldn't have to exchange words, where everything would
be perfectly understood.

After a moment, Katie released him and stepped back.
"What are you doing here? The last time we spoke you said-
-"

"I know what I said," He interrupted her. "But I also know
how stupid that was. I love you Katie and I can't lose you
again." He waited patiently as she took her time, deciding
whether to let him in or not. Finally, she stepped back and
waved him in. He gave himself a mental high five and
hustled over the threshold.

The room he entered was small and neat. The foyer
opened into a living room decorated in country charm, blue
with white accents. A sofa, a couple of chairs and side tables,
and an armoire housing a TV filled the space. Images of a
little girl with Katie's dark hair and sweet smile hung on the
walls around the room. To his left a hall stretched into
relative darkness. In front of him, a squared threshold
separated the eat-in kitchen from the living area.

He turned at the sound of the door closing and saw her
standing in the entryway, arms crossed over her chest. He
took in the sight of her--barefoot, hair in a messy bun, no
make-up, in pajama pants and a t-shirt--and his heart
swelled. This was the woman he had loved for nearly a
decade. He knew that now, knew it in a place that couldn't
be disregarded anymore. He'd tried to forget her, tried to
move on with his life, but she was always there. Even when
she wasn't. Now, he just had to convince her that this time

would be different. Hopefully, she'd give him the chance without kicking him out on his ass first.

"Where are the boys?" Katie's question brought his attention back to the moment. She dropped her defensive stance and pointed for him to sit. "Do you want something to drink?"

"Uh, yeah, sure," he said, sitting on the sofa. "Whatever you got."

She disappeared into the kitchen and returned a moment later with two glasses.

He took the offered drink and set it on the side table near him. "The boys are staying with a sitter for the evening."

"A sitter? For the evening?" She repeated his response, a perplexed look on her face. "You're going to drive all the way back to Newton tonight? It' nearly seven already."

"Actually," he said, waiting for her to get comfortable in her chair. "I don't live in Newton anymore. I rented a house on the river. Off Hecksher Drive here in town."

She nearly choked on her drink when he said that and had to set the glass on the table. She ran a hand over her chin, wiping away the dribble of tea. "You live *here*? In *Jacksonville*? Since when?"

He leaned forward, resting his elbows on his knees. "Since about a little more than a month ago. After our last phone conversation, I, uh, had to see you, face to face. I wanted to, uh, tell you..." He stumbled over the words, not used to baring his soul. At least, not since he was a teen, on a dock, in the dark, with this very girl.

His heart pounded, and he ran his sweaty palms over his denim-covered thighs. He glanced at Katie, her feet drawn under her waiting for him to go on. If he hurt her again, he wouldn't be able to live with himself.

Dropping to his knees in front of her, he took her hands in his. "I made a massive mistake, letting you go." Once he opened his mouth, everything he was feeling tumbled out. "I had too many chances to be with you, and I fucked them all

257

up. Each time, I came up with an excuse for why it couldn't work out. But no more. I'm here now, in Jacksonville, and I want to be with you."

She pulled her hands from his and set her feet on the floor. "Wha--what? Are you crazy? You can't just show up after months of us not even *speaking* to each other and drop news like this on me."

"Why not?" He settled himself back on the couch and a fiery sensation bloomed in his chest. The urge to bolt washed over him, but he held firm. If he wanted any kind of shot with her, he'd have to prove that he was steadfast. That she could finally rely on him.

"Because you just can't." She pushed herself up from the chair, pacing to the front door and back. "There may be too much pain in our past to overcome, did you ever think about that?"

"Actually, I did. That's why I'm here." He'd matched her move and stood in front of her. "I know I hurt you, but I swear to god it won't happen again. I love you. And I want to be with you." He stepped closer to her, pausing to see if she would pull away, and when she didn't, he settled his hands on her hips. The scent of flowers wafted from her and sparked stirrings in him that he hadn't felt in years. "I'll do anything, *anything*, to get you back," he murmured.

She bit her bottom lip and shifted her gaze. "What makes you think I'm available now?"

Danny felt the words like a punch to his gut. She was right. Why did he think he could just waltz in here and tell her he was ready and expect her to drop everything to be with him? He'd uprooted his life and moved his boys to a new city all in the hopes of winning back the one woman he could never let go of. Now, if she didn't want to get back together, would he run again? *Nah*, he had a good job and friends to help him here. He'd stick it out and make the best of it. But still, would any of it be worth it if he didn't have Katie?

"Are you?" He pushed the words through a forced calm.

"Seeing anybody?"

She dropped her chin, exhaling sharply, nearly touching his chest with her forehead. "No," she whispered.

He let out a breath he didn't realize he was holding and guided his arms around her waist, drawing her into his embrace. After a moment he heard a sniffle. Tucking a finger under her chin, he titled her head up to meet his gaze. "Baby, are you crying?" It was a stupid question. He saw the tears collecting on her lashes, threatening to spill down her cheeks. He lifted his hand to her cup her face and rubbed his thumb along her high cheekbone. "Please don't," he whispered, pressing his lips to the salty rivulet under her eye.

"It's just that" --she drew in a ragged breath-- "I never thought this day would come. That you'd be in my house telling me that I'm the one you want."

"You've always been the one, Katie-did. I was just too stubborn to accept that my life could be anything more than what it once was--a poor bastard whose luck always ran out quicker than his grit." He pressed her head to his shoulder, wrapping her protectively in his arms. "I should have believed in myself, in us, as much as you did. You knew all along what we had; I just didn't trust it enough."

She broke his hold and backed away. "How do I know you won't get spooked and run again? I've seen it too many times before, Danny. And not just with you, but with other men. Like Carlie's dad. I have a daughter to think about now. I can't be getting my hopes up that I'll finally have the happy little family I've always dreamed of all for it to come crashing down again when you get scared. Or angry."

"I promise, it won't be like that. I've changed. I've learned from my mistakes. For god's sake, I moved my kids here to Jacksonville to be closer to you, Katie. That's gotta count for something." He tucked his hands in his pockets, afraid if he didn't, he'd reach for her again and scare her away. He knew had to give her time to think things through on her own.

The moments they stood there in silence seemed like an

eternity, but he wanted her to trust that he wasn't going anywhere nor that he would rush her. Finally, she blinked hard and cleared her throat.

"Okay, let's say you are here to win me back, or whatever. What's the plan? Dinner, dating? Having our kids get together for play dates?" She busied herself with returning the glasses to the kitchen, and he followed.

"We could go that route," he said, watching from behind as she rinsed each glass and set it in the dish drainer. "But I think we know each other well enough already. We've been talking for *years*. Still, having the kids get together could be fun. See how they get along with each other." He stepped closer to her and brushed a hand over her shoulder. "See how we get along with each other."

She tilted her head to connect with his hand, and he found her turning to face him. Before he could move, she lunged at him throwing her arms around his neck and kissing him passionately.

Oh, yeah, he thought as he returned her kiss, *we are definitely going to get along*.

CHAPTER 25
The Wedding

PRESENT DAY

Katie

Katie's lips pressed hard against Danny's, parting for his roving tongue. She felt herself lifted off her feet and situated against him, her legs locking around his waist. His hands shifted under her bottom for leverage as he turned toward the living room.

"No," she murmured between kisses. "Down the hall."

Danny drew back, looking at her through hooded eyes.

Katie tilted her head, indicating the hallway. "Second door on the right," she said and captured his mouth in hers again.

The couple fell onto the queen-sized bed, their bodies still intertwined and mouths melding into each other's. The pressure of Danny's body above her sent a wave of heat washing over her. How long had she waited for this? To be in his arms, the swelter of their emotions suffocating any doubt that this wasn't right.

Danny lifted off her long enough to tug off his shirt and chuck it to the floor. His hard, bronzed chest towered over

261

her in the dim light of dusk peeking through the drawn window shades.

She allowed her hands to glide up his chest as he wrestled with kicking off his shoes. Packed muscle rippled under her fingertips as she traced each ridge that ran across his stomach. Her fingers dropped to the button of his jeans and popped it open in one deft move.

He arched an eyebrow. "In a hurry?"

"I've waited ten years. What do you think?" She drew her shirt over her head, exposing bare breasts.

"I think we have a lot of catching up to do." And he wasted no time in shucking his clothes.

They met, naked, in the middle of the bed. His body was just as she remembered it--lean contours bronzed by a lifetime of working in the sun. The hair that covered his chest was thicker and darker than when he was eighteen, but pressed against her bare breasts, it elicited the same electric sensation as it did when they last found themselves in similar situations over the years.

Now, though, she would have what she'd always longed for, what had always been hers. Him. She laid back on the bed and pulled him down with her. His body covered her, and she felt his swollen, insistent need prodding the inside of her thigh. Her hands glided down his back to finally rest on his buttocks, giving a little squeeze that pulled a groan from him.

He kissed her, taking her tongue in his mouth to mold and caress with his own. His hands played along her curves, and she was thankful that he couldn't see her extra weight and the thin, white stretch marks of childbirth. She sucked in a breath when her attention was arrested by his fingers between her legs. The feeling intensified as he dropped his head to enclose her nipple in his mouth.

With his tongue playing havoc on her breast and his exploring fingers driving her to a sexual frenzy, it was all she could do to think about his pleasure. She reached between their bodies and encircled his shaft in her fist. She thought of the many times in their youth when they'd stopped just short of reaching this very position. Nothing from then prepared her for the overwhelming awe she felt now at having him there with her.

Her hand slid up and down his erection, causing him to shudder with each apex. She ran her thumb over his tip, and he groaned, the vibration reverberating throughout her chest.

His mouth moved from one breast to the other, and a new set of sensations smothered her. His fingers, slacking in their duties until this point, found the entrance they'd been seeking. In moments, she was matching her rhythm to his as he drove her toward fulfillment with his touch.

Before reaching her climax, she stopped him. "No," she whispered, her breath escaping in gasps. "Come here for that." She slid her hands under his arms and tugged on him, spreading her legs further apart.

He shifted to meet her mouth with his again. Their bodies aligned and he pressed his shaft into her.

The sensation of him inside her set her body ablaze with desire. As he rocked into her, she met his rhythm and lost herself to the overwhelming emotion of the moment. A moment she'd waited ten long years to happen. She was going to savor every second of it.

Three months later, Katie fidgeted in front of the full-length mirror in her sister's bedroom. Her hair wasn't curling right, and she was considering this her sign.

"God, if you're listening to me, please speak louder if this is your sign," she whispered. Actually, the tears were pooled in her chestnut eyes, but she blinked them back. Jana Blake, her best friend and fellow teacher, had threatened to never speak to her again if Katie ruined her make up. Jana had just gone to the kitchen to get them something to drink.

"What kind of sign are you looking for?" Jana asked as she entered the small bedroom. The walls were still covered in little girl wallpaper, white with tiny pink roses on vines running up to the ceiling. Jana set the two half-size tumblers full of punch on the edge of the dresser. The carbonation bubbled to the top and made a fizzing sound that drew Katie's attention to the cup.

"It's Seagram's," Jana said, noticing the dazed and confused look on Katie's face. Katie raised one eyebrow quizzically, thinking that she should wait to get drunk until after the *I dos,* and everything that had to do with the wedding went off without a hitch. "I thought we could both use a little something to loosen us up," Jana commented, practically reading Katie's mind. "It's only eight fluid ounces. I checked the cup package. I don't think you can get inebriated on one cup of wine cooler."

Carefully, Katie picked up the drink so as not to spill it on her ivory slip. She'd had the good sense to not put on her wedding dress until *after* everything was done: make-up, hair, nails, and drinks. She took a long, slow sip.

"So, what sign?" Jana asked again. "You're not getting cold feet, are you?"

"Well," Katie began, then stopped. It wasn't actually cold feet. She had waited an awful long time to be with the man she loved. They'd been through some stupid shit in their young lives. "I don't think it's cold feet. I just want to be absolutely sure that this is what is supposed to happen. I mean, what if we get married today and two weeks from now Danny stresses out and decides that a wife and another child are too much for him?"

She started to shake and set the cup back down on the dresser. Her sight was becoming blurry again from the tears. She sat on the edge of the bed and reached for her old tee shirt to dab them with. Jana came to her and knelt down in front of her, taking one hand in hers and patting Katie's slip-covered leg with the other hand.

"Oh, hon, don't cry! Your make up will run," Jana said.

Katie sniffed back a runny nose, and looked wide-eyed at Jana, her lower lip trembling, then the two women burst into laughter. They fell back on the bed laughing hard and loud.

"*My make-up will run.* Good one, Jana," Katie said through the giggles. Her sides were hurting from the laughter. She sat back up on the bed and looked at Jana who was still lying down. "I guess there could be worse things happening in my life right now than marrying the love of my life, huh?"

"Yeah, sweety, there could be," Jana said seriously now. "But you've got to make sure that marrying Danny is what you really want. You don't have to do this if you don't want to." Jana stared at her friend, and Katie suspected the other woman was waiting for her to offer any inkling of doubt that might still be lingering.

"No, I love him, and I've waited so long to be with him, to marry him, so I guess it's fate," Katie said. She got up from the bed and walked to the mirror to check her face. Amazingly, the only thing wrong with her make-up was black smudges under her eyes from the running mascara. Jana came up behind her with lotion in one hand and a Q-tip in the other.

"We'll fix you back up into your beautiful self, then you can walk down that isle and into the arms of your destiny," Jana told her. Her friend always had a way of listening without being judgmental. And she always said exactly what a person wanted to hear. Katie appreciated that about her friend.

It reminded her a lot of her mother, a thought that caused Katie to sigh deeply. She missed her mom, especially today, a day of celebration. It was so unfair that her mom had died so young.

Katie caught herself slipping back into a place where the

tears were waiting, but she pulled herself back. She had to move forward, not dwell on the past. Not today, anyhow. She took a seat on the vanity's stool again and waited for Jana's instruction.

Jana dabbed a little bit of lotion onto the end of the Q-tip. "Look up," she said. She aimed for Katie's under-eye. Katie blinked and looked up toward the ceiling fan circling overhead. It was warm for April, even with the air conditioner and ceiling fans running.

The lotion felt cool on Katie's flushed face, if only for a brief second. Jana turned Katie to face the mirror and began working again on her hair. Katie wanted her dark auburn tresses pulled up into a French twist with loose tendrils framing her face and neck. A picture of the style was taped to the mirror for reference.

Jana glanced over her shoulder at the clock on Shannon's nightstand. "Uh oh, we've got to hurry. We don't have much time before the ceremony starts." She gingerly touched the curling iron to see how hot it was.

A knock at the door made both women turn. Shannon, Katie's youngest sister, entered wearing her bride's maid dress. The lavender dress, an off-rack prom dress, accentuated her dark blond hair and brown eyes.

"Oh, Katie," she said, her voice low and full of emotion, "you look beautiful." The gentle teen, the youngest of the three sisters, stood in the doorway as Katie and Jana finished the final touches on Katie's hair. "Grammy said it's time to start. The kids are getting restless."

Katie and Jana glanced at each other, a look of worry passing between them. Jana took her friend's hands and touched her head to Katie's. "Breathe. It'll all be over in thirty minutes, and it'll be so, *so* worth it."

Katie let out a long breath, closed her eyes, and whispered a short prayer of gratitude. "I'm ready then," she said, lifting her head and smiling at the two women. "Holly, tell Miss Libby to get the kids ready and let's get this party started."

The three women laughed, scooped up their respective flower bouquets, and exited the room.

As they stepped out of the house and onto the screened back porch, Katie's gaze swept across the small back yard. A couple of dozen people sat in the folding chairs Libby Montgomery, a friend of a friend of Danny's and voluntary coordinator of the tiny backyard ceremony, had borrowed from the neighborhood community center. And though the decorations were lovely, the only thing Katie was searching for was her soon-to-be husband.

She spied Danny standing near the floral-wrapped archway, also borrowed, squatting in front of the children. Her heart swelled with the patience she saw in his demeanor as he sat each child in a seat. She imagined the gentle reprimand he was giving for them to stay seated.

He stood as Libby approached him, then took his place in front of the notary who would marry them. Katie saw him glance toward the porch where she stood. She knew he couldn't see her that well, as the screen on the porch was so dark, but she smiled in his direction anyway.

Libby hurried up the steps and through the screen door. "Ready, dear?" The woman clasped her hands beneath her chin. "You look breathtaking. Danny is so lucky to have you."

"I think we're both lucky," Katie said. She took a couple of deep, calming breaths as Jana adjusted her veil and Libby nodded to a young man near a music console. A moment later, music drifted across the back yard and Libby opened the screen door.

As she stepped from the porch and onto the stone path, Katie felt a rush of love and hope swell in her. She waited for her cue from Libby, and when the older woman touched her arm, Katie began her short journey to her future self as Mrs. Daniel Carter.

Later, with the festivities over and the guests gone, the new family of five settled into their first week together with little conflict. All of the kids seemed to get along, much in part to the time Danny and Katie had spent getting them together before the wedding. They had let the children decide their relationships with each other with little interference from them, and the conflicts that had arisen were negotiated as fairly as the parents saw fit.

Now, Katie and Danny were packing for their short honeymoon after the intimate, backyard wedding. And it wasn't the children who were in conflict.

"I just don't see why you have to let those people keep our daughter. Miss Lena and Shannon or Holly are perfectly capable of keeping all three."

"Yes, for a few hours, but Grammy is near seventy. And my sisters have their own lives, with school and work. They can't just drop what they're doing to cater to us." Katie tossed a shirt onto the bed and her stomach gurgled. She released a quiet burp and rubbed her upset tummy. "Excuse me," she whispered, then spoke up louder. "Besides, it's their weekend. I couldn't very well keep her from them on their weekend."

Danny rolled up the shorts he held and shoved them into the small suitcase. Katie winced at the display of anger. She hated it when his temper flared. He'd never been violent with her or the children, but she knew all too well the depths of his emotion. If she'd thought about it, she would have planned to let Brian's parents keep Carlie on a different weekend. They were attentive, loving grandparents, regardless of how their son had ended his relationship with her. Katie just didn't see the point in upsetting the relationship she'd taken the time to build with them, as tenuous as it was after Brian's death in Iraq.

Another sound of something being thrown into the overnight bag made Katie jump. She blinked back tears. But her own anger got the better of her and she turned to face her husband of one week. "And *those people* are her grandparents, too. Like it or not, they're a part of Carlie's life. A part I'm not willing to cut off right now. They are good to her, and she deserves to know her father's parents."

A finger of ice ran down her spine as Danny's eyes narrowed. The blood vessel in his neck thickened and he breathed in deeply, causing his nostrils to flare. Katie blinked, and for a split second, thought about giving in, but Carlie was *her* child, at least for now. And as such, Katie had every right to judge and decide who could keep her daughter.

"Fine. That's how you want to play it now." He slammed down the lid to his suitcase and snatched the zipper closed. "I'll wait here while you meet them to drop her off, then we'll leave for Cypress Springs." He left her at the foot of the bed, speechless, with tears welling in her eyes.

Two hours later, they stopped for lunch, a silent affair except for the ordering, and were back on the road an hour later. As the houses of Lake City gave way to pastures with livestock then thick woods on the two-lane highway, Katie wondered for the dozenth time if she'd made a mistake. And just how the two of them would ever get past their pain to make the most of their lives now.

CHAPTER 26
Danny Gets Advice

PRESENT DAY

Danny

He was so angry with himself. How could he let his temper best him like this? Leaving Katie there at the hotel while he took a ride to cool off seemed like a good idea at the time. Thinking back on it, the devastated look on her face nearly killed him and he should have turned around to go talk to her. He promised her when they got back together that he'd never do this. Yet here he was back to the same old MO when things got tough. He slapped his palm on the steering wheel, determined to get his emotions in check before returning to his wife.

The ride to his sister's house in Trinity took Danny about twenty minutes, giving him enough time to think about the events of the day. Katie had insisted on dropping Carlie off at the Donahues' house before they left for Cypress Springs. When Katie returned for them to leave on their weekend getaway, Danny could tell from the way Katie slung stuff around that she was upset.

They had ridden in near silence all the way to the gulf

coast. Danny's ego wouldn't entertain the idea that his new stepdaughter needed anything from her other grandparents. He could take care of his own children--all three of them— without anyone's help.

Now, as he stewed over the morning's events, he hoped his sister would be home so he could vent to her. She understood him. She'd seen everything he'd been through with their parents and his ex-wife. And she knew about his temper. Yeah, Lisa would know what to say.

He pulled into her driveway and noticed that both vehicles were gone. He'd told her that he and Katie were coming over to the gulf coast for the weekend, but they hadn't made plans to stop by or anything. He cut the engine, got out, and went to the back door. A note was taped to the glass.

Danny,

If you come by and nobody's home, we're probably at Aunt Linda's for a cook-out. Y'all come on over.
Lisa

He snatched the note from the door and crumpled it up. How could he show up to his family barbecue by himself? He'd never hear the end of it. Still, he needed to talk to somebody. His brother Jimmy was out of the question. The two of them had drifted apart after Jimmy left home the month he'd turned eighteen. Ronnie was an option, but that meant driving all the way to Archer, and he didn't want to be out that long. Plus, Ronnie wasn't really that good at offering constructive advice. Danny shook his head. The last time he'd talked to Ronnie about anything serious, Ronnie's advice was to get shit-faced and worry about it tomorrow.

As he debated about whether to go to the cook-out, a

spark of hope lit his eyes. Uncle Rex might be able to help him. He'd been in a similar predicament with his son, Tommy. If anybody understood what he was going through, it would be his uncle. He hopped in the rental car and turned left out of the driveway toward his aunt's house. Hopefully, Lisa hadn't shared the news of his nuptials yet. That was something he wanted to do himself.

Danny pulled into his aunt's yard a little after lunch and the aroma of barbecue caused his stomach to rumble. He hadn't eaten since he and Katie had left Jacksonville that morning. Katie. The thought of his new bride in her simple ivory dress walking from the back steps of her grandma's house to meet him at the altar the previous Saturday made his heart swell. The feeling didn't last long though. The pain in her eyes just an hour earlier turned his soft heart into iron. He knew he should go back and make amends, but pride got the better of him.

He slammed the door of the rental car and followed the aroma and laughter to the back yard. Behind the privacy fence his whole family, minus his parents, were gathered in groups, chatting and laughing over some secret story Danny couldn't make out. He clamped the gate shut behind him and searched for his Uncle Rex and Aunt Linda. Spying them near the black barrel of the smoker, he continued his trek through the crowd, stopping a couple of times to hug one relative or another.

"Danny boy!" Uncle Rex called when he saw Danny. "What are you doing here? I thought you lived in Jacksonville now." He extended his hand and Danny took it, giving it a vigorous shake before being pulled into the older man's half-embrace.

"I do," Danny replied. "I'm just down for the weekend. On a little vacation."

"Oh, yeah," his aunt Linda said, holding a plate for his uncle to stack hamburgers on. The two always worked as a fluid pair. It was something Danny both admired and envied about them. And he longed to have that same connection with a woman. With Katie. "Where are the boys?"

"At home."

"So, you came here all by yourself?" Lisa Tyner, Danny's sister, joined them from a group of cousins and eyed her brother.

Danny shot her a look, knowing that Lisa knew about his wedding and about Katie.

"Not exactly," he said, avoiding her piercing stare. "That's what I came here to talk to Uncle Rex about, but you guys mind if I get a burger first? I'm starving."

His aunt, who always made sure he and his siblings had enough, shoved a plate at him. "Of course, honey. Get what you want. I'll go pour you some tea."

His uncle turned his attention back to the grill, leaving Danny there with his sister.

"Where's Katie?" she asked, glancing around the yard. "Y'all did just get married, didn't you? I'd expect that you wouldn't leave your new wife home by herself so soon after the wedding."

"Can you please let me tell everybody about that?" Danny's eyes darted around the group, and he smiled and nodded at a cousin he hadn't seen in years. "I need to talk to Uncle Rex without fielding a million questions about why my wife isn't with me."

"Why isn't she here?"

"Not. Now." Danny slapped his burger on his bun and grabbed a handful of chips.

"Here you go, honey." Linda handed Danny a glass filled with iced tea and looked from one sibling to the other. "What's going on with you two?"

"Danny was just telling be about his recent wed--"

"Welding job," he interrupted her and shot her his hardest *shut-the-hell-up* look. "Yeah, it was a real bit--beast." He took the offered drink and downed half of it, never taking his eyes off his sister.

She smirked and tossed a chip in her mouth. Clucking her tongue, she turned from him at the sound of her husband Mark calling her.

"So, this welding job," Linda said, "where is it? Down south again."

Danny sighed. There was no way he could stand there and blatantly lie to the woman who had practically raised him. "No, Aunt Linda. It's in Jacksonville." He set his plate with a half-eaten burger on the table. "Look, could I talk to Uncle Rex for a few minutes? Alone?"

"Sure, honey." She patted his shoulder and took the spatula from her husband. "Tommy," she called, and a man a few years older than Danny popped his head up from a crowd seated at a picnic table. "Come over here and man the grill for your father for a few minutes."

Tommy didn't hesitate and rose from the table to hurry to his mother's side.

Rex guided Danny inside, and a cool blast from the air conditioner caused the hairs on his arms to stand on end. They found a pair of recliners in the living room, each sitting expectantly.

"So, what's on your mind, boy?" Rex leaned forward, resting his elbows on his knees and clasping his hands in front of him. He stared at Danny through thick readers.

"I have a question for you, and I need you not to tell Aunt Linda about it until I'm ready," he said. His aunt and uncle had been married for nearly thirty years. He was sure that his request would probably run into some resistance from Rex, but he wanted things to be done on his terms. He waited as his uncle contemplated the request.

After a moment, Rex nodded. "I guess I can do that, but you know how persuasive your aunt is. Best if you ask your question, then make up your mind to tell Linda what she's gonna find out sooner or later."

Danny shrugged one shoulder in acknowledgment and said, "I know Tommy has a different dad than Pam and Jeff.

How did you deal with his other family when you and Aunt Linda started dating?"

"Oh, wow. That *is* a question there." Rex scrubbed a hand over the stubble on his chin. "Why do you ask, son?"

"This is what you can't tell Aunt Linda," Danny said, searching his uncle's eyes for understanding. When he realized he wasn't going to get a promise of secrecy, he took his chances and spilled the news of his recent wedding. "I got married last weekend in a quick backyard ceremony to this amazing woman--you've probably heard me mention her before--Katie. She has a little girl from a previous relationship."

"Oh, and you don't know how to handle this second family's influence. It interferes with your family," Rex said.

"Sort of," Danny replied. "I mean, I know Katie has a past and that it'll be a part of our lives, but I just don't know how to deal with it. The guy died about a year ago, but his parents still want to see Carlie--that's Katie's daughter." Danny smiled at the thought of the three-year-old carbon copy of Katie. "I get that they're the girl's grandparents, but I feel like Katie is giving them way too much freedom with visitation. She let them keep Carlie this weekend while we came on our honeymoon."

"You're on your honeymoon?" Rex's eyes popped, and Danny felt his cheeks redden from shame. "Where's your bride? You didn't bring her?"

"We, uh, got into a fight," Danny admitted, "and I was so pissed that I, uh...I left her at the motel."

"You *left* her? On your *honeymoon*?" Rex sat back in his chair, his mouth pressed into a thin line. "Boy, I thought you'd left that ugly dog of anger in your youth. You can't let it control you like this."

"I know, I just..." He trailed off, clenching his fists and shaking them, grunting.

"You have to talk to her. That's the only way you two can work anything out. Running away from your problems doesn't solve anything."

"It's worked before," he said, thinking of the times he left other bad relationships. Sure, it was tough being a single parent, but at least he was the final say in his household. But Katie was a different story. He'd seen how his running had hurt her, and he'd rather rip out his own fingernails than watch her cry one more time over him. Yet, here he sat after driving away from her, knowing full good and well she had been crying when he left. *What a dick I am*, he thought.

"Do you love her?" Rex's question caught him off guard. "I mean, you married her, so I suppose you do."

"More than anything." He meant it. The last three months they'd been together were like the summer they'd met. He hadn't smiled so much in his whole life like he had this spring. And it was because of her. Katie brought out the best in him. It was his own stupid pride that got in his way. He made asinine decisions because of it.

"Well, then, it doesn't matter what I tell you. I could explain how I invited Pete and his new wife to Tommy's birthday parties because it was the right thing to do. Tommy's wellbeing was what was most important, not my stubborn pride."

Danny blanched at the thought of Vivian and Bruce Donahue at his house watching his baby girl blow out birthday candles on the cake he bought. Still, if his uncle was right, and he probably was, Carlie's best interest had to be top priority, not his own.

"So, you've got to decide what's more important: your pride or those girls?" Rex rose from his seat and glanced through the kitchen window. "And another thing, you better be ready for your aunt Linda to ream you out over leaving that girl at the hotel on your honeymoon."

Danny dropped his head in shame. "I know. I'm an idiot."

Rex turned to go back outside, then stopped. "I tell you what. I'll hold off your aunt while you go get your wife. You can bring her back here and introduce her to us proper."

277

"Thanks Uncle Rex." Danny's heart felt lighter as he shook his uncle's hand and exited the house unseen. He had a lot of groveling to do if he was going to win back Katie's trust. He just hoped he hadn't totally destroyed her this time.

CHAPTER 27
In The End

PRESENT DAY

Katie

When she woke from her nap, Katie found herself alone in her aunt's front room with a damp cloth on her forehead. She removed it and set it on the coffee table before gingerly sitting up. Her stomach bubbled, but her head was clear, and she stood to hunt for more crackers and her aunt.

At the table she found the same sleeve of Saltines from earlier and a letter from Maggie. She'd ridden with a neighbor Katie didn't know to the dock to gather some more crab traps. *You were sleeping so soundly I didn't have the heart to wake you. I'll be back soon and run you to the hotel.* A giant M closed out the letter, and Katie dropped it on the table.

The clock read three-forty-five and Katie took her crackers and a glass of water to the dock. Clouds blew by in the hazy sky as storm heads grew on the horizon, typical for June in Florida. There was the scent of freshly fallen rain on the breeze and narrow puddles dotted various boards on the length of the walkway leading to the dock.

Reaching the dock, Katie took a seat on one of the covered benches and stretched her bare legs in front of her. The warmth of the sun, peeking intermittently between puffy clouds made her skin prickle as the gulf breeze tousled her hair.

Sitting there on the dock brought back a flood of memories. Ten years ago, she had arrived here at her aunt's house to spend the summer, a punishment by her grammy. But that summer had changed her life. She'd fallen in love that summer of '85 with the man she was now married to. They had been through so much in the last decade that, now, Katie refused to accept that she'd made a mistake in marrying him. They were destined to be together. She believed it with every fiber of her being. For it to end even before it had a chance to begin was unacceptable.

Tears began to roll unchecked down Katie's cheeks. She absentmindedly rubbed her abdomen. The crackers and water she'd found inside Maggie's house did little to calm her upset stomach. She'd spent that afternoon, the first day of her honeymoon, visiting with her aunt, spilling her story to the older woman. Per usual, Maggie hadn't offered advice but let Katie vent and left her to come to her own conclusions.

Now, as she waited for her aunt to come back and take her to the motel, she wondered if Danny was back yet and worried about her. She hadn't left a note. Surely, he would think of coming to look for her at her aunt's house. Without warning an inkling of fear crept over Katie. *What if he leaves me?*

He'd promised her he wouldn't, but it was his habit--to cut and run when things got too tough, too intense for him. It'd happened many times over the years. But they were married now. He wouldn't just leave her in Cypress Springs to find her own way home, would he?

Katie wiped at the tears with the fresh tissue she pulled from her pocket. She debated about not waiting for her aunt and walking back to the hotel. It was only a couple of miles away, and maybe the walk would do Katie some good. Help her work through some of the worries she had her life, her marriage, and their new family situation.

She took one last look down the canal, imagining the first time she and Danny sat out on this dock and declared their feelings for each other. A melancholy sigh escaped her lips as she stood to return to the house, but her reverie was broken by a loud yell from a passing car. The car screeched to a halt in the middle of the road, did a three-point turn, and turned onto the side road that led to Maggie's house.

Katie spun around to face the house, realizing the car she had just seen was the rental car she and Danny had ridden in that morning. Before she could take three steps, Danny emerged from the side yard and hurried down the dock to meet her. A jumble of emotions bubbled up inside her at the sight of Danny standing before her. Sadness won out.

"Man, it's been a while since we've been out here, huh?" He took her hand and led her to sit on the covered bench. "You remember the first time we came out here? It took everything in me not to lay you back and have my way with you then."

Katie kept her gaze on their joined hands. If she dared look at him now, she knew her emotional dam would crack. When she didn't respond, he squeezed her hand.

"Baby, I am so sorry," he said, raising her hand to his mouth.

His lips brushed her knuckles, leaving a warm trail that made the hairs on her arms stand on end. She didn't want to make it too easy for him. He'd left her, for god's sake! But she had never been able to stay angry with him for long. as his long strides took him to her side.

"I meant to be back sooner," he continued, "but, well, it doesn't matter. I'm such an asshole. I never should have left you, ever." The implied meaning of his statement wasn't lost on her. She knew they'd both wasted so many years trying to find what they were looking for in other people only to find it in each other in the end.

"I got worried." She paused, looking up into his eyes. "That you wouldn't come back for me." She read the pain and self-loathing in his face. She was tempted to soften her words, but she wanted him to understand the full effect of his actions. "You forget how well I know you. How I know you get freaked out, especially when your feelings seem like they're too much to handle. Or you think things are going too well that something's going to come along and mess it all up."

She stood and he followed. He tried to pull her to him, to draw her into his arms, but she kept her distance. He wouldn't deter her from telling him just how much his actions affected her.

"But I love you, dammit." She punched him lightly in the chest. "I'm not letting you go. I've waited ten long years to be with you. I've sat by while you tried first one thing then another to feel complete and I know, *I know*, that neither of us will feel whole without the other. You *are* my destiny. The man I'm supposed to spend the rest of my life with, and I won't let you run again. If you get scared, I'll be there. I'll hold you. I'll love you. But I will not let you run. I won't lose you again."

Her tears came in great heaves, and seconds later, she ran to the edge of the yard to vomit in the marsh grass. Her stomach wouldn't unknot itself, and this added stress didn't help. She'd have to tell him about her sickness eventually.

"I won't leave you," Danny said definitively. "Besides, we're married now." He held their still-linked hands at eye level, wiggling his ring finger. "It'd be a damn shame to have to send back those matching bath sets my aunt Linda sent us." The joke lifted the mood a little. They each wrapped an arm around each other's waist and ambled to the shade of the back porch.

"It's been a long time since we were here," Danny said, returning to his original conversation. "We were just kids back then. So much has happened, and my biggest regret is that I let you go. I mean, I had to back then because, well you know. But I knew then that I loved you, and I wanted you in my life." He draped his arm across her shoulders and gave her a little squeeze. "I was such an idiot for letting you get away then. I promise you, Katie-did, I will never let anything keep me from you again. That's a promise."

"That's good," Katie said, breathing deeply to try to calm the queasiness. She popped a cracker in her mouth and chewed.

"Baby, you're white as a bedsheet," he said, his voice laced with concern. "How long have you been sick?"

"About a week, but today's been pretty bad. I guess with all the wedding excitement, then our argument, I haven't really been feeling too hot."

"Can I do something?"

"No, it'll pass."

"Is it the flu or a virus? Maybe food poisoning?"

"No, I don't think so." Katie smiled softly. "You have to promise me, swear, that you'll never leave me. I couldn't handle you leaving again, especially now."

Waving his ring-bearing hand at her again, he said, "I told you, I ain't going anywhere now."

"Well, that's a good thing." She shifted to face him, readying herself for his reaction to the news she was about to share.

"Katie, what is it that you're not telling me? Is it serious?" Danny's eyebrows furrowed above his storm cloud blue eyes.

Katie couldn't help herself. For everything he'd put her through that day, she wanted a little payback. He'd always been the one who played tricks; now it was her turn.

"You're right," she said, struggling to keep a straight face. "It is serious. Very serious."

"Whatever it is, baby, we'll face it together. I swear, I'm here for you. Just tell me." He gripped her upper arms, staring intently into her eyes. The fear she saw there wasn't worth keeping him in suspense any longer.

"Danny," she began, her voice even, then let out a huff of air. "I can't do this."

"Can't do what?"

"Tease you like this." She watched his fear shift to confusion. "You thought our life was hectic with littles at home? Wait until New Year's."

"What? What are you saying?" As the meaning of her words became apparent to him, Danny's jaw dropped. "Are you saying..." His gaze swept from her face to her abdomen.

"I'm saying we're gonna have a baby." Yet again, her eyes rimmed with unshed tears. This time, they were tears of joy at the shear happiness on her husband's face. "I'm pregnant."

He pulled her to him in a strong embrace, and the love they held for each other multiplied and washed over them. He leaned back and looked down into her eyes. "I'm a prideful, selfish son of a bitch that has a lot of making up to do to you, but I swear on everything I love in this world, that I will work hard to be the man you need me to be. I love you so much, Katie-did."

She rested her head on his shoulder, letting his words sink in. She knew there would be struggles ahead, problems to work through, arguments to test their relationship. But there would also be love, so much love, in the family that they were building together. She rubbed her stomach absentmindedly and listened to the water lap at the dock beyond them. She felt the rise and fall of her husband's breath under her cheek and knew her world was complete.

EPILOGUE
SIX MONTHS LATER

Welcome, baby girl

NOVA
Destiny Carter

January
21

7
pounds
4
ounces
20
inches

We love you! Mommy, Daddy, Trent, Clay, & Carlie

ABOUT THE AUTHOR

Tracie Roberts is a native Floridian who laughs loudest at her own jokes, ODs quite frequently on 80s nostalgia, and eavesdrops on perfect strangers to glean story ideas. She has been writing for nearly a decade but has been telling stories since she was old enough to realize she could make people believe her lies. She's a creative storyteller who writes all shades of romance—sweet to steamy, contemporary to paranormal—all with happy endings across multiple pen names, including Macie Collins and Kacie Kent.

Find out more about Tracie (or Macie or Kacie—we're all one in the same) at tracieroberts.com or connect with her on Facebook (/tracie.robert13) or Tiktok (@tracieroberts13).

PARANORMAL ROMANCE BOOKS BY TRACIE ROBERTS

The Destined Series:

He was her fantasy. She was his destiny.

A summer romance ignites an epic love that defies the laws of man and magic.

Spirit

Everyone has a past. A past that guides their destiny...

Before they were Derek and Tara, the soul mates who finally find each other, they were Derek–a carefree mechanic with a manipulative girlfriend who won't take no for an answer. And Tara, a newly-inducted witch with a broken heart preparing for her college graduation.

Derek and Tara lived very separate lives before ECHO. In SPIRIT, see how past choices and disappointments made their connection that much more magical.

Echo

He's the one she's been dreaming of... but is he the one she's destined to be with?

Tara McAllister has her life figured out: graduate from college, get a job teaching at her old high school, and find a boyfriend that won't care that she's a practicing witch. Everything is falling into place...until the visions begin. Tara's practice has given her a gift--she sees the future. And for her, it includes a gorgeous man that she's never met but definitely knows. She can *feel* it. Now all she has to do is find him.

Derek Williams just wants to get by. He goes to school, works to help support his family, and enjoys the occasional party with his friends—as long as his gift doesn't create a problem. Derek is an empath, born to feel what others feel and able to change their emotions with a touch. His inherited gift comes with an added benefit—the ability to find his soul mate, the one person he's meant to be with. And he's found her; he just has to convince her of their connection.

As their relationship heats up and their abilities grow stronger, Tara and Derek must overcome family objections, former flames, and a secret that could ruin them both—*if* their love is to survive.

Whisper

A clandestine romance—sparked by heredity, fueled by choice...

Tara McAllister and Derek Williams have chosen to continue their relationship, despite the age difference...and the legalities. They strive to overcome the obstacles they faced last summer only to be confronted by new attacks from past enemies and the whispers about their suspected attraction.

It's only when they embrace their ancestral bond that Tara and Derek finally understand that they can endure anything. Together.

Blur

Joined by an ancient magic, their love was predestined. Now, that fragile bond is in danger of being shattered.

Tara McAllister has come to terms with her soul mate being underage *and* a student in her class. She knows that it's illegal, but legalities are inconsequential where the heart's concerned. The soul deep connection that drew them together over the summer has strengthened. Just as she feels comfortable enough to dream about a future with her élan, a tragic accident threatens to rip her happiness from her grasp.

Derek Williams chose to pursue the one woman who made his whole existence worthwhile, despite the fact that she was older *and* his English teacher. Once he convinces her that they are meant to be with each other, he finally feels at peace planning their future together. Then one night and one misstep jeopardize everything they've built and fought for.

Tara and Derek's love story—the story that explores the balance between what's right and what matters—continues in BLUR, Book 2 in The Destined Series.

Bound

Bound by destiny, broken by tragedy, two lovers realize that what they thought was the end may only be the beginning.

Haunted by tragedy, Tara McAllister doesn't know if she'd ever be whole again. But with a baby who depends on her, a family who supports her, and a job that provides for her, she finds a way to move on with her life. But when Drew Thomas—handsome, talented, and sexy as hell—takes a position as head chef at Harmony House, Tara is distracted and tempted to give love another chance.

As the two spend time together, working side by side at the inn, their attraction heats up. But Drew has secrets of his own that could destroy their relationship before it even starts. Then Tara's daughter contracts a mysterious illness, and the two must work together using family heritage and ancient magic to save her baby's life.

Caught between obsession and addiction, past and present, the pair are forced to travel a dangerous path—one that could lead to destruction or redemption.

SWEET ROMANCE BOOKS BY MACIE COLLINS

The Lantana Beach Series:

In Lantana Beach, the only thing stronger than a rip current is the love of a southern woman. ***These men don't stand a chance.***

Lifesaver

Jamie Scott fled to Hodges, Florida., a suburb of Lantana beach, to escape an abusive husband. With hard work and generosity, she rebuilt her life in the adopted community that supported her during her darkest moments. Permitting herself no time for love, Jamie volunteers. With a victims' advocacy group, discovering a purpose beyond her solitary, complacent life. Her comfortable routine in place, Jamie finally feels safe until she is faced with a situation eerily similar to one she thought she left in the past.

As a sheriff's deputy, Cooper Ross has seen both the worst and the best of humanity. His bachelor lifestyle grants him the opportunity to serve his community without the burden of a family. Even if he wanted to, his. Work doesn't allow time for dating, much less love. Then a chance encounter with his reclusive, though alluring, neighbor forces him to reevaluate his ideas on love, and human nature .

In the face of suspicion and danger, Jamie and Cooper must each overcome their own misguided notions of love and duty if they are to find what they didn't know they were looking for—each other.

Skimming the Surface

When shop owner Savannah Montgomery goes for her morning beach run, she never imagines that it will lead to pulling a distressed swimmer from the floor to surf. She uses her lifeguard training to rescue one of the most attractive men Savannah has ever seen, but she swore off love after her cheating husband tried to take everything in the divorce. Besides, these days she's hustling to get and keep what's hers, all while working to block the destruction of local marshland by a greedy developer. Who has time for romance?

Sports talent scout Tyson Carafello hopes to make enough money signing young athletic stars to lucrative contracts with the end goal of saving his parents' home from foreclosure. When he takes a relaxing walk along Lantana Beach's shore during one of his scouting trips, he doesn't realize the ocean's danger and is quickly swept away by the volatile waves. His savior—a beautiful, feisty brunette—leaves in such a hurry that he doesn't have time to thank her period. Now, he's on a second mission—to find the angel who saved his life. But in his search, a new danger is exposed. One that will test his character and, ultimately, the budding relationship he hopes to build with his southern Siren. Will he be able to protect all that's at stake?

As the couple's feelings for each other grow, a Tempest of a different kind is brewing. Trapped by an advancing storm and deadly henchmen, both Savannah and Ty must overcome their insecurities and winds left by past betrayals to learn to trust one another with their hearts., and their lives.

Rescuing Christmas

All Holly Nichols wants is to do this winter break is hole up in her historic home and try to make it through another Christmas. Since losing her husband two years ago to a drunk driver, Holly has fought her way out of an all-consuming darkness to find some remnants of joy as an elementary teacher. With the encouragement of family and friends, her daily life has moved forward, but she's sworn off love. As her holiday break begins, so do the numerous issues of her turn-of-the-century home. At the suggestion of a friend, Holly hires David Reed, a single dad new to Lantana Beach to do the repair work. With his gentle manner and rugged good looks, David easily breaks through Holly's emotional fortress, and she finds herself looking forward to the time spent with him. But is she ready to love again?

David Reed is trying to make the most of a precarious situation. Ever since fleeing a monstrous gulf coast hurricane and landing in Lantana Beach, his daily life has been a tightrope walk between patience and panic. His one priority is making sure that his young daughters are insulated from just how desperate their situation is. Fortunately, David has new friends who help him begin to build a foundation in the small coastal community. And there's the attractive young widow in need of his handyman skills. Can he repair her broken heart along with her quaint Victorian home?

As these two troubled souls find themselves working side-by-side at Lantana Beach's holiday festival and trying to make the holiday special for David's children, will they find in each other the reason for the season and a way to rescue Christmas?